DARK QUEEN WAITING

Paul Doherty

CRÈME de la CRIME

This first world edition published 2019
in Great Britain and 2020 in the USA by
Crème de la Crime an imprint of
SEVERN HOUSE PUBLISHERS LTD of
Eardley House, 4 Uxbridge Street, London W8 7SY.
Trade paperback edition first published
in Great Britain and the USA 2020 by
SEVERN HOUSE PUBLISHERS LTD.

British Library Cataloguing in Publication Data
A CIP catalogue record for this title is available from the British Library.

ISBN-13: 978-1-78029-127-7 (cased)
ISBN-13: 978-1-78029-656-2 (trade paper)
ISBN-13: 978-1-4483-0354-0 (e-book)

All Severn House titles are printed on acid-free paper.

Severn House Publishers support the Forest Stewardship Council™ [FSC™],
the leading international forest certification organisation.
All our titles that are printed on FSC certified paper carry the FSC logo.

Typeset by Palimpsest Book Production Ltd.,
Falkirk, Stirlingshire, Scotland.
Printed and bound in Great Britain by
TJ International, Padstow, Cornwall.

DARK QUEEN WAITING

To my very good friend Linda Gerrish.
Many thanks for all your support and help

HISTORICAL NOTE

B y October 1471 the House of York was supreme. Edward IV seized the reins of power and held them tightly. The Yorkist cause was triumphant in both London and the kingdom beyond. However, tensions still remained. Bitter rivalries surfaced as other dark forces emerged. Edward of York could trumpet his success claiming the House of Lancaster was vanquished but that was not the full truth. Edward's own court was divided by deep factions which could in a matter of days spill into bloody, prolonged conflict, especially the rivalry between Edward's two brothers Richard Duke of Gloucester and George Duke of Clarence.

Nor was the Lancastrian cause totally annihilated, its leading claimant Henry Tudor had successfully escaped from England to be given safe shelter by Duke Francis of Brittany. From there young Henry and his uncle Jasper Tudor could watch events unfold both at home and abroad. More importantly, the Tudor exiles knew that they had the total and utter support of Margaret Beaufort, Countess of Richmond, mother of the young Prince Henry. Margaret played a dangerous game. She smiled and bowed to her Yorkist masters but, with the assistance of her two henchmen Reginald Bray and Christopher Urswicke, Margaret plotted to bring the House of York crashing down so her own son could be crowned as the rightful King at Westminster . . .

HISTORICAL CHARACTERS

House of York

Richard Duke of York and his wife Cecily, Duchess of York, 'the Rose of Raby'.

Parents of:

Edward (later King Edward IV),

George of Clarence,

Richard Duke of Gloucester (later King Richard III).

House of Lancaster

Henry VI,

Henry's wife Margaret of Anjou and their son Prince Edward.

House of Tudor

Edmund Tudor, first husband of Margaret Beaufort, Countess of Richmond, and half-brother to Henry VI of England. Edmund's father Owain had married Katherine of Valois, French princess and widow of King Henry V, father of Henry VI.

Jasper Tudor, Edmund's brother, kinsman to Henry Tudor (later Henry VII).

House of Margaret Beaufort

Margaret Countess of Richmond, married first to Edmund Tudor, then Sir Henry Stafford and finally Lord Thomas Stanley.

Reginald Bray, Margaret's principal steward and controller of her household.

Christopher Urswicke, Margaret Beaufort's personal clerk and leading henchman.

The verses quoted before each part are from the poem 'Dies Irae' (The Day of Death), written by the Franciscan Thomas di Celano.

PROLOGUE

'Oh Day of Wrath, Oh Day of Mourning!'

'**A** City of Robbers, a den of thieves, the manor of murder and the haunt of lost souls.' Such was the judgement of the Chronicler of St Paul's who maintained the Annals of the City. A truly scathing description of London in the late October of the year of our Lord 1471. A keen observer of the foibles of his fellow citizens, especially the Lords of the Earth, the Chronicler had reviewed and stridently proclaimed his chilling conclusions. Certainly this was the season of murder and sudden death, as the great ones clashed at the ferocious battles of Barnet and Tewkesbury in the early summer of that same year. The city had also suffered the bloody violence of the age: the clash of sword against shield whilst the bray of war trumpets rang along London's streets. Parts of the city had been burnt to the ground as the gorgeously embroidered standards and banners of both York and Lancaster fought their way through the columns of smoke which hung like clouds over the narrow, stinking streets. It truly was a fight to the death. King Edward, York's own champion, had passed the order 'to spare the little ones of the earth and kill the leaders' amongst their enemy. In the end, however, Death was the only victor. Corpses cluttered the alleyways. The remains of the dead littered the city streets, as common as leaves driven by the wind. Cadavers rotted in lay stalls, sewers, ditches, cellars, and all the other stinking, dark holes of the city.

The different guilds tried to do their best. Men and women who belonged to fraternities such as 'The Souls of the Dead', 'The Guild of the Hanged' and 'The Hope of the Faithful' tried to provide decent burial. Great pits were dug in graveyards and along the great common beyond the city walls. Nevertheless, Death reigned supreme. Unburied corpses, bloated and ruptured, were stacked like slabs of unwanted meat in many city churchyards. Funeral pyres burned day and night, their fearful flames illuminating the sky, their black smoke curling along the arrow-thin runnels. The cadavers of the great ones, those lords defeated and killed by the power of York, were treated with a little more respect. However, this was only because Edward the King, along with his two brothers George of Clarence and Richard of Gloucester wanted to proclaim to all, both at home and abroad, that their enemies were truly dead. Accordingly, the corpses of the old Lancastrian King Henry VI, together with those of his principal commanders, were exposed in different churches for the good citizens to view. St Paul's was commonly used for this macabre ceremony and the citizens turned up to queue, as they would for a mummers' play or a Christmas masque. The corpse of King Henry was abruptly removed when it began to bleed, drenching the inside of his coffin and forcing the world to wonder what had truly happened to the old King during his sojourn in the Tower. Had he suffered an accident or been murdered at the dead of night? The Chronicler of St Paul's dared not comment on that except to write, 'that only God knew the truth so it was best to leave it at that'.

Peace came at last though fraught with fresh dangers. The soldiers who fought for York and Lancaster were freed from their indentures. After the great Yorkist victories, there would be no more alarums in this shire or that. Some former soldiers took themselves off out of the city, tramping the winding lanes and coffin paths to seek employment or return to half-forgotten trades. Many former soldiers, however, stayed in London, and looked for mischief to replenish both purse and belly.

Foremost amongst these was Otto Zeigler, a giant of a man with a fearsome reputation as a soldier in the service of York: a mercenary with a special hatred for the Welsh and the House of Tudor in particular. According to common report, Zeigler was the by-blow of a Breton woman and a Flemish merchant. Skilled in language, Zeigler was even more proficient in the use of arms and, since his youth, had donned the mailed jacket of the profes-sional mercenary. Once the struggle between York and Lancaster subsided, rumour and gossip seeped like a mist into the city about the atrocities perpetrated in the shires after the great Yorkist triumphs. The cruel executions and hideous punishments inflicted became common knowledge, and people whispered that Zeigler had carried out the most gruesome tortures on those he captured. Zeigler also acquired a most fearsome reputation as a dagger man, a born street fighter, a reputation he cleverly exploited after he'd been dismissed from the royal array. Zeigler became a riffler, a member of one of those fearsome gangs which prowled the nightmare of London's underworld. These street warriors were truly feared and, in some cases, protected and favoured by the city merchants, who used the rifflers for their own secret purposes. Zeigler soon won their attention as he fought his way through the ranks to become a captain of the Sangliers – the Wild Boars, a pack of cutthroats and murderers who sported the livery of a scarlet neckband. Zeigler, dressed in the garb of a Franciscan friar, a mark of respect to a priest who'd treated him kindly, the only soul who ever had, was often seen in the city swaggering through the markets to receive the bows and curtseys of those who should have known better.

Nevertheless, despite all his arrogance, Zeigler sensed the dangers. If he was leader of the pack, then he had to ensure that when they hunted they caught their prey. Accordingly, Zeigler, his fat-shaven face glistening with sweat which also laced his bald, dome-like head, was delighted to hear reports of a treasure trove, a truly juicy plum, ripe for the plucking. Apparently there was a warehouse near Baynard's Castle crammed with luxurious goods imported from the Baltic by the prosperous Philpot family of merchants. These included costly furs, precious woods, skilfully woven tapestries as well as chests full of vessels and other ornaments fashioned out of gold and silver and studded with the most precious stones.

Zeigler's appetite was whetted. The warehouse was undoubtedly secure, standing as it did in the garden of Philpot's riverside mansion; a strong, one-storey, red-brick building with reinforced doors and shutters. Usually this warehouse stood empty. However, according to the reports Zeigler had received, Edmund Philpot had decided to store his treasure there before moving it in a well-guarded convoy to the Great Wardrobe, a truly formidable and fortified arca or strong room close to the Guildhall. Edmund Philpot was being cautious: the treasures he owned had been brought from a cog berthed at Queenhithe only a short distance from his mansion. However the journey to the Great Wardrobe was long, tortuous and fraught with all kinds of danger, so Philpot was waiting to muster a strong enough guard from the Guildhall.

Zeigler paid well for such information; what he learned seemed to be the truth. Sir Edmund had tried to keep the garden warehouse a secret. The merchant certainly did not wish to attract attention to what he had arranged, paying only two of his bailiffs to guard his treasure trove both day and night. Zeigler made his decision. He and his henchman Joachim chose a dozen of their cohort, secured a war barge and prepared to seize what Zeigler called 'a prize for the taking'.

On the eve of the feast of St Erconwald's, long after the vesper bell had tolled and the great candles and lanterns been lit in the soaring steeples of the city churches, Zeigler led his coven down to a deserted Dowgate quayside and boarded the waiting war barge. Zeigler had chosen well. Six of his coven had worked on the river; these now acted as oarsmen and the barge was soon untied and made to depart. Zeigler, standing in the prow, stared into the freezing cold mist now spreading across the river, blinding the view and deadening all sound.

'We are truly blessed with a night like this,' Zeigler whispered to his henchman Joachim. 'We will slip like ghosts along the river.' Zeigler, pleased with himself, gazed around. The Thames was deathly quiet. The nearby quayside empty, nothing but the constant horde of hump-backed rats foraging for food whilst trying to avoid the feral cats which hunted them. The mist shifted and Zeigler glimpsed 'Death's Own Gibbet', as the river people called it, a monstrous, six-branched gallows used by the city sheriffs to hang river pirates and other such malefactors. Thankfully, it was now empty of its rotting fruits. Nevertheless, the stark, soaring, sinister column was a chilling sight.

Once again, Zeigler reflected on the information he'd been given. Apparently one of Philpot's own clerks had stumbled into a tavern, much the worse for drink, and sat muttering about the busy day he'd spent organising an inventory for Sir Edmund's chancery. Deep in his cups, unaware of the true identity of Joachim who sat drinking close by, the clerk had referred to the garden warehouse and all it contained. At first Zeigler couldn't believe his ears; nevertheless he led a pack of wolves and they had to be fed. He and Joachim could always hold their own but, if they successfully plundered that warehouse, they'd be rich and free of all danger.

Zeigler scratched the side of his head, wiping away the spray as the tillerman whispered instructions and the barge surged forward, battling the strong pull of the river. Zeigler tapped the pommel of his sword, there would be no turning back. Fortune had cast her dice and they were committed. Zeigler half closed his eyes as he quietly cursed the House of York who'd employed him as a captain of mercenaries in their struggle but, once they were done, had dismissed the likes of Zeigler to fend for themselves. Times were hard. Winter had arrived. Last summer's harvest had not been good. Food was scarce, prices were rising. During his service as a mercenary, Zeigler could help himself to what he wanted. Now he had been turned out, it was different.

After London had been pillaged and looted, Edward of York had moved to crush all opposition and impose his own peace. The scaffolds and gibbets were busy and Zeigler's concern for himself had only deepened. He needed treasure, gold and silver coin to buy sustenance for himself and the pack he led. There were already grumblings amongst the Sangliers and Joachim had warned that they would not be the first riffler leaders to be assassinated. Zeigler had to establish himself as a successful freebooter. Philpot's warehouse and the treasure it contained would undoubtedly make him a prince amongst thieves. He recognised the risks but the dangers of doing nothing were even greater.

'We are almost there,' Grimwood, the sharp-eyed lookout, whispered hoarsely. 'Turn the barge in.'

The oarsmen, on the direction of the tillerman, did so. The river mist shifted and the barge slid gently along the jetty. Ropes were fastened tight. Zeigler and his gang put on their visors and pulled deep hoods over their heads. They grasped weapons, silently disembarked and made their way forward towards the lanternhorn glowing on the post of the water-gate leading into the garden of Philpot's mansion. Zeigler and his coven were grateful for the cloying mist which closed in about them, though they were wary of slipping as a fall into the freezing-cold river would be fatal.

They reached the gate. Zeigler pressed against it and could not believe his good fortune. The gate had not been barred, bolted or locked from within. A costly mistake! They pushed the gate open onto the pebble-crammed path which wound by flower, herb and spice plots all tinged white by the constant frosts. Lights glowed from the rear of the stately mansion. The rifflers edged forward; the soles of their boots had been wrapped in soft leather cloths to deaden all sound. Nevertheless, they moved cautiously. Zeigler lifted a hand. The rifflers paused, staring through the dark at the two guards sitting in a roughly built bothy before the warehouse: both men were warming their hands before a weak fire.

'Now,' Zeigler ordered.

Two of his coven, seasoned crossbow archers, lifted their arbalests and released the catch. The bolts sped out; one struck a guard, smashing into his skull. The other caught the second high in the shoulder. The latter staggered to his feet, his ragged clothing flapping under the cutting breeze: a grotesque sight illuminated by the flames leaping up from the makeshift fire. A second bolt was loosed, catching him full in his bearded face, and the guard fell back.

'Quick, quick!' Zeigler urged his men towards the door of the warehouse. The riffler chieftain realised it was unbarred and glimpsed the beam lying on the ground pushed deep into the shadows. Zeigler froze, mouth gaping. Something was very wrong! A spurt of fear made him stare back the way they'd come. He cursed his own recklessness. He'd been too greedy, too quick! The garden gate had been left open, the bar to the warehouse door was off its clasp. As for the guards, that second one – with his unkempt hair and beard, garbed in motley rags – was no bailiff, the other was no better. They were not household retainers but beggars. Zeigler took a step forward, his coven were opening the warehouse door, thronging together, eager to seize the piles of promised plunder.

'On your guard!' Zeigler shouted.

He hastened towards his comrades. The door swung open, his men faltered, staring into the dark but it was too late. An arrow storm whipped through the air followed by a clatter of weapons as the mailed men-at-arms sheltering deep in the warehouse, soldiers wearing the Guildhall livery, seemed to emerge as if from nowhere. The riffler leader drew his sword to meet hobelars all harnessed for battle; these swiftly ringed him, blades at the ready. One of them carried a sconce torch lit from the makeshift hearth. Zeigler turned like an animal at bay even as his heart sank: his coven were either being cut down or fleeing for their lives. He was now trapped by a circle of armed men. Zeigler's fear deepened. He knew he was immediately recognisable in his earth-brown Franciscan robe, yet he had not been harmed; no arrow, no swift blade thrust, so why? He decided to test his opponents. He darted forward but the hobelars, swords still extended, simply retreated.

'Well, well, well.' A cheery voice hailed from the darkness. 'Good morrow, Master Zeigler, we are ill-met by moonlight. Yes?' The circle of hobelars parted to allow Sir Thomas Urswicke, Recorder of London and great Lord of the Guildhall, to come sauntering through. Sir Thomas hitched the costly, fur-edged robe more firmly about his shoulders to provide greater warmth as well as to enhance the gleam of his elegant Milanese breastplate. The Recorder pulled back his hood and loosened the delicately linked coif which framed his smooth, smiling face. 'Put down your weapons, Master Zeigler.' The riffler did so. Sir Thomas snapped his fingers for silence then cocked his head as he listened to the moans and groans of those rifflers brought down by arrow or sword. 'In heaven's name,' he shouted, 'cut their throats and stop their moaning. As for him,' the Recorder pointed to Zeigler, 'bind him fast and follow me.'

The Recorder led his cohort across the garden and through a wicket gate guarded by a company of Tower archers. They went along the side of the elegant mansion and onto the broad cobbled expanse which stretched along the thoroughfare and its row of the stateliest mansions in the city. Zeigler, surrounded by hobelars and Tower archers, realised it was futile to resist; his hands were bound tightly with a lead fastened around his neck as if he was a dog. The mailed procession moved swiftly as they entered the demon-filled darkness of what became the city after dark. On either side of the column, soldiers carried fiercely burning cresset torches, these illuminated the hideous spectres of the night, more dire and dreadful than any poem or fresco describing the horrors of Hell. Beggars, faces and hands mutilated and bruised, lurked in the shadows whining for alms. A cohort of lepers, dressed in dingy white robes, had been released from the lazar house: these could only beg for help during the hours of darkness, though they would be lucky to receive even a pittance. The lepers passed like a tribe of chattering ghosts going deeper into the blackness around them. The shadow-dwellers, the men and women of London's Hades also prowled; they stayed out of the light searching for anything or anyone they could profit from. Such denizens of the night disappeared like snow under the sun at the approach of the armoured cohort.

Cursing and spitting, struggling violently against the harsh rope around his neck, Zeigler, sweat-soaked and exhausted, realised they were now approaching the heart of the city, the great open expanse of Cheapside. The stalls, of course, had been cleared and were nothing more than row upon row of long, high tables beneath which the poor now sheltered. Great bonfires had been lit to burn the rubbish from that day's trading, as well as to afford some solace and comfort to the homeless and dispossessed who gathered around to seek warmth and cook their putrid meat over the flames. The constantly darting tongues of fire also illuminated the brooding mass of Newgate prison. The great concourse before it was now the hunting ground for a horde of vermin which scurried across to forage amongst the stinking, steaming midden heaps piled either side of the prison's iron-barred gates. Zeigler thought they would enter Newgate but the Recorder's cohort abruptly turned left in the direction of the Fleet and, Zeigler quietly moaned, the grim gibbet yard overlooking Tyburn stream. They proceeded up past the Inns of Court and onto the execution ground, a truly macabre place with its row of four-branched gallows. From some of these the cadavers of the hanged, bound tightly in tarred ropes, shifted eerily in the blustery night breeze.

Sir Thomas Urswicke had definitely prepared well: bonfires roared around one of the gallows, empty and desolate, except for the ladder leaning against the main gibbet post and the black-masked hangman waiting patiently beside it. The cohort stopped before the steps leading up to the execution platform. Zeigler began to panic. Seasoned felon, he recognised what was about to happen; it would be futile to protest. He had been caught red-handed committing the most serious felonies so he could be hanged out of hand. Sir Thomas strolled out of the darkness, his hooded face smiling, as if he deeply relished what was about to happen. He ordered Zeigler to be tied more securely, feet as well as hands, he then dismissed the guards out of earshot. Once they had withdrawn, Sir Thomas stepped closer.

'You can hang, sir,' the Recorder hissed, 'and I could arrange that now.' Zeigler remained tight-lipped. 'You once fought for York,' the Recorder continued, 'a captain of mercenaries. You have a Breton mother and a Flemish father. For God knows what reason, you were brought up in Wales. Something happened there, I am not too sure what, and I don't really care. One thing I have learnt, you hate the Welsh.'

'What you say is true,' Zeigler rasped. 'But why do you mention it now, Sir Thomas?'

'You recognised me immediately.' Sir Thomas seized the end of the rope tied around Zeigler's neck and pulled hard so the knot dug deep into the prisoner's flesh. 'You recognised me, sir?' he repeated.

'Of course I did. Your face is well-known, Sir Thomas, as is your loyalty to the House of York.' The Recorder once again pulled at the rope and Zeigler gasped in pain. 'Good, good,' Sir Thomas whispered, 'you know my name and now you know my nature. So, Master Zeigler, you too fought for York at Tewkesbury, you were with Hastings' phalanx. Your task was to seek out a coven of traitors, Welshmen under the command of their leader Gareth Morgan, now popularly known as Pembroke. Yes?'

'I recall that bastard and the tribe of traitorous turds he commanded.'

'Quite, quite. They called themselves the Red Dragon Battle Group because they fought under the treasonous standard of Jasper Tudor who failed to join that fight. You do remember?'

'As I said, of course.'

'Now the Red Dragon Battle Group were to seek out our noble King Edward, together with his two brothers, and kill them. They were following the pattern of the great conflict at Evesham over two hundred years earlier when the household knights of Prince Edward, son of King Henry III, vowed to search out and kill the Crown's most insidious rebel, Simon de Montfort, Earl of Leicester. They were successful, Pembroke was not.'

'We wreaked great damage on them. They broke, they fled. I

nearly captured Morgan, or Pembroke as he now calls himself.
I threw him into a bear pit after Townton: if I had caught him
at Tewkesbury I would have impaled him.'

'I know what you did, Otto Zeigler, and I know who you
are. Now listen carefully. You will be lodged in Newgate and,
when I decide, you will be visited. We shall reach an agreement.
Either that,' Sir Thomas shrugged, 'or you will strangle on that
gibbet.'

'How do I know that? You tricked me once, did you not, my
Lord? That clerk who claimed to be from Sir Edmund Philpot
was your creature, and not as deep in his cups as he pretended
to be? You left that gate open, the door unbarred whilst those
guards were beggars from the street?'

'Yes, yes.' Sir Thomas took a step forward. 'So, Master Zeigler,
when you enter my employ, I sincerely hope, for your sake, that
your wits are sharper than in this present situation.'

Zeigler stared at the ever-smiling Sir Thomas. The riffler felt
a deep sense of relief even as he abruptly realised that he could
not die here. Just before the battle of Tewkesbury he had visited
a witch outside Ludlow: she had told him that he would only
die if he entered a wooden cage floating on water, and he had
no intention of doing that.

'You have a henchman Joachim?' Sir Thomas continued. 'He
also dresses in a brown robe. We allowed him to escape tonight.
I shall arrange for Joachim to be our intermediary, and he will
be faithful, yes?' Sir Thomas's smile widened. 'If not to you,
certainly to me otherwise I will hang him out of hand. Now
Joachim will bring my messages.' He sighed noisily. 'And, at
the appointed time, your fortune Master Zeigler will take a turn
for the better. But, let me whet your appetite. Pembroke is back
in the city! Oh yes,' Sir Thomas smiled at Zeigler's abrupt change
of expression, 'the man you threw into a bear pit is back and,
listen to this, he is not alone. So,' the Recorder rubbed his hands,
he then pulled his gauntlets out of his warbelt and put them on,
'we have talked enough. Master Zeigler, your Newgate chamber
awaits you.' Sir Thomas patted Zeigler on the cheek. 'I am going
to place great trust in you, yes Otto? I have a very special task
for you to complete. First, in this kingdom, and then beyond the
seas in Brittany. You are fluent in the Breton tongue I understand.

What if, my friend,' the Recorder took a step closer, 'what if I also gave you the opportunity to strike at Pembroke?'

'I would seize it.'

'And the traitor Henry Tudor in exile abroad?'

'I would be equally eager.'

'Good, good. My task, Master Zeigler, could make you and yours very wealthy, rich beyond your wildest dreams. If you fail or you don't keep troth, if your wits are not sharper than they were this evening, well, as we take you back to Newgate you will pass the common gibbet: those of your company whom we cut down tonight are to be hanged there naked as they were born, throats all cut. A warning to other rifflers not to break the law.' Sir Thomas's smile widened. 'But, as we both recognise, my friend, it's also a reminder and a threat to you about the cost of failure.'

'When will all this happen?'

'When I decide, Master Zeigler. And now your chamber at Newgate awaits whilst I have other urgent business to attend to . . .'

The great two-masted war cog *The Glory of Lancaster*, was battling the waves off the small inlet at Walton-on-the-Naze Essex. Some dark-winged demon of the abyss had flown up to stir the seas and create a heavy swell which threatened to drive the cog and all it carried onto the ever hungry rocks. John de Vere, thirteenth Earl of Oxford, master and owner of the cog, stood leaning against the taffrail of his battered vessel. He watched the ship's bum-boat being lowered down the cog's side, clattering and banging as his ship pitched and rolled, plunged and shuddered on the fast-running sea. De Vere scratched his unshaven chin, half listening to members of his crew as they lowered the boat, desperate to keep it in place, safe and secure for the four men who would follow it down. De Vere peered through the dark; his watchmen had glimpsed the message sent from a shuttered lanternhorn somewhere along that lonely sea-swept beach. Yet, this was England, his country, his home. De Vere swallowed hard at a stab of profound homesickness. He had attached his star, his personal escutcheon, the five-pointed silver mullet of Oxford to the House of Lancaster and, because of that, he and all his own had been forced into exile. York was triumphant. Edward IV, as he styled himself, was King, supported by a cohort of loyal and ruthless henchmen, such as Hastings, Norfolk and others of that ilk, not to mention Edward's two dark shadows, Richard of Gloucester and George of Clarence. Oxford steadied himself against the rolling pitch of the tide and watched the bum-boat on its slow descent, inch by inch to the waiting sea. He glanced at the four men waiting to go down the rope ladder once the boat was ready.

'God have mercy on you!' Oxford called out. 'I call upon the Holy Trinity with faith in the Threeness and trust in the Oneness of the world's great maker. May he have great pity on you for our enemies certainly will not.'

Oxford wiped his salt-caked lips on the back of his arm sleeve. What he'd just said was the truth. In the life-and-death struggle between York and Lancaster no mercy was shown, no quarter given. Edward and his henchmen had inflicted grievous damage on Oxford and all his kin and he would return blow for blow, but not just yet. England was now a Yorkist fief. The power of Lancaster had been utterly shattered at those two devastating battles of Barnet and Tewksbury earlier in the year.

'Bloody defeat and total annihilation,' Oxford whispered to himself. Two great disasters in which the House of Lancaster had been truly culled, its great lords either killed in the battle slaughter or executed on makeshift scaffolds soon afterwards. Horrible, cruel deaths; hanged, drawn, quartered and disembowelled. The tattered heads of Oxford's friends and family now decorated the gateways of many English cities, be it Bristol, York or Canterbury. De Vere thanked God every day that he had been spared. He also prayed that Lancaster's one and only hope, Henry Tudor, son of the redoubtable Margaret Beaufort, Countess of Richmond, would survive. Prince Henry was now safely in Brittany whilst his mother Margaret sheltered deep in the shadows, smiling and bowing to her Yorkist masters whilst playing the most dangerous secret game, to sustain and strengthen the fortunes of her depleted house and exiled son.

Oxford closed his eyes as he recalled the diminutive Margaret, small of body but with the courage and the stamina many warriors would envy. Margaret was a mistress of deception. She would smile and smile again at her enemies whilst devising her own day of destruction, a time when the Yorkist strongholds would fall, the board be cleared and a new reign begin. The countess plotted for the return of her son with an army which would be welcomed, but that was for the future. In the meantime, the likes of Oxford could only wait and watch as they were doing now, yet it was so hard! Edward of York was wearing his enemies down with the humdrum passing of the days which showed little hope for their cause. Oxford acknowledged this was true of himself. He was growing tired of this wolfshead's life, lurking in crumbling taverns, sleeping on mattresses with nothing in them but chopped straw crammed with fleas, the stumps of twigs piercing the ragged coverlet. A bed of pain with stinking, thread-bare blankets affording the only protection against the winter damp and cold. Once again Oxford peered through the dark which was now beginning to thin, the rising sun's light tingeing the sky behind him. He would land these men and then go back to sea. In the meantime . . .

The exiled earl stared longingly at the coastline; beyond that dark ridge stretched fertile fields. His fields! His orchards which, when spring came, would bend their branches to the ground, their fruit so heavy, full and luscious. Around such orchards stretched meadows which housed wild deer, fleet hares, fat cattle and heavy-bellied swine; the source of much good food and revelry. But not now. This was a dark hour. He and other Lancastrians had no choice but to shelter in foreign parts beyond the Narrow Seas. They were reduced to begging for help and favour from this great lord or that powerful duke. They dealt with princes who could not be trusted and would soon play the Judas if the price was right. Oxford and his ilk lived in constant fear of being betrayed, arrested, bundled into some filthy prison before being bound hand and foot and delivered to an English cog despatched by Edward of York.

Oxford shook his head, wiping the spray from his face. He glanced over the side. The bum-boat was now down and its oarsmen would see their four passengers safely ashore. Oxford crossed himself and murmured a prayer to St Anne, his patron saint. What was happening now was the other side of the coin he'd been dealt. Sheltering in foreign parts could only be for so long, it was not just a matter of waiting. Pressing business demanded their attention. Oxford and other Lancastrians needed to fan the flames of rebellion and dissent across England, and so it came to this, sailing one of his precious war cogs off the English coast. He heard a voice hailing from across the water. Oxford raised a hand in salute at the fast disappearing boat, its rowers forcing it forward against the stiff-running tide.

On the moorland overlooking the beach two others watched the sea and both whispered a prayer of thanksgiving as they glimpsed the faint outlines of the approaching bum-boat. The two watchers, garbed completely in black, had hidden themselves cleverly in a thick clump of gorse using their gauntleted hands to pull across the bracken and sharp twigs, over and around their place of concealment. Christopher Urswicke, clerk of the privy chamber in the household of Margaret Beaufort, Countess of Richmond, had chosen the place. Now he crouched, hood pulled across his gleaming auburn hair, his fair-skinned face, which one court lady had likened to a cherub, daubed black. Urswicke's companion and comrade Reginald Bray, steward of the same countess, needed no such disguise. 'Black of hair, black of soul and black of face.' As Bray had once described himself.

Bray was a street fighter, a man who found it hard to keep still, and now the steward just wished he shared some of his companion's calm composure. Indeed, Bray was deeply agitated and had been so since they first arrived. They had been despatched to greet the four men in the approaching bum-boat, here on this desolate wind-swept beach well away from the busy ports of Harwich and Orwell. The Essex coastline was a place of darkness and the stretch of beach below them was a truly lonely haunt. Nevertheless Bray, who had fought as a secret assassin in France, believed his own apprehension was justified. Despite the darkness, the rolling crash of the sea and the occasional shriek of some bird, Bray just felt that they were not alone. Some danger threatened. Some terror was closing fast. He had sniffed the sea-salted breeze. He was sure he caught other smells: horseflesh, leather, dung and the waft of unwashed bodies. Bray prided himself on his keen sense of smell and his sharp eyes. They were not alone! He had hoarsely whispered his suspicions to Urswicke but the young clerk just shook his head. In reply Bray had quoted his own experience. He was thirty-five years old to Urswicke's twenty-six. He had, as he reminded his companion, fought on land and sea across Europe. He had served on the carracks of the knights hospitallers. He was a skilled seaman as well as a soldier, a dagger man and a spy. In reply Urswicke had just given that lovely smile, patted his companion on the arm and said they must wait and see.

They now crouched, staring into the darkness. The bum-boat had breasted the waves, the rowers resting on their oars as the boat entered the shallows, its keel crunching through the pebbled sand. Urswicke stared out at sea. He could make out the faint outlines of Oxford's cog waiting for its boat to return. Urswicke abruptly tensed. A thin mist rolled across the water yet he was sure he had glimpsed, just for a few heartbeats, flickering lights to the right and left of Oxford's cog. Was that an illusion? A deceit of the eyes? A trick of the mind, or were those lights from Yorkist warships closing in on Oxford's cog? Had they been standing off the coast waiting for this moment? Urswicke glanced down at the shoreline. The bum-boat was now beached, its passengers climbing out, all four of them staggering across the sand whilst the rowers pushed their boat back into the water. Urswicke sensed that they too were alarmed by those lights out at sea which now glowed more constantly. The men left on shore also paused. The light of a full moon in a cloud-free sky bathed the beach clearly enough for Urswicke to see what was happening. There was danger out at sea but the four men who had just landed were now looking to their left. Bray cursed, clutching Urswicke's arm with one hand as he pointed up the beach with the other.

'Horsemen, Christopher!' he hissed.

Urswicke, heart in mouth, stared into the darkness on his right. At first he hoped, he prayed that it was all an illusion. The mist cleared. Urswicke heard the rumble of iron-shod hooves and the clink of steel. Then he glimpsed them. A cohort of fast-moving horsemen pounding along the beach. Even as Urswicke stared, the cavalcade broke up, fanning out on each flank.

'Stay.' Bray pressed his arm. 'Stay, Christopher, there is nothing we can do.'

Urswicke watched despairingly as the four men fled, desperate to leave the open beach and lose themselves in the gorse land overlooking the coast. The horsemen closed, garbed in battle harness, weapons gleaming; they spread out in an arc, a cohort of death's dark messengers. Some of the riders carried crossbows, these turned into the waves, loosing bolt after bolt at the sailors manning the bum-boat. All four were struck, collapsing into the water, their boat twirling pathetically, a plaything of the tide. Urswicke stared out at sea: those lights now glowed stronger. Urswicke realised that Oxford's cog would be desperate to break free of the closing trap and lose itself before daylight. Onshore, meanwhile, the horsemen had caught up and surrounded the four men. Urswicke and Bray could only watch and weep at the cruelty shown. Some of the riders had dismounted, punching and kicking their prisoners. Men and horses swirled. Abruptly two of the prisoners broke free, fleeing swift as hares with crossbow bolts whirling above them. They reached the sand hills, scrambling up to hide themselves in the sea of sharp gorse. So easy for them on foot, whilst the horsemen who had set off in pursuit found it almost impossible to spur their mounts up the shifting, sand-strewn slide. The three who managed to, had to turn back from the forest of thick, sharp bramble.

The pursuers returned to the beach and joined the circle of horsemen surrounding the remaining two prisoners. The view was clear enough. Urswicke could only stare in horror at the collapse of their plan and, more importantly, that of his mistress, the diminutive, manipulative Margaret Beaufort. The melee below was a disaster for them. Four of her most valued agents had been trapped, two taken and the others fleeing for their lives. These men were strong links, clasps in a secret chain which bound the countess to her beloved son, Henry, as well his protector and Margaret's close kinsman, Jasper Tudor, now sheltering in the Breton court. Urswicke, distracted and agitated, half rose, staring down at the beach watching the two prisoners being roped. One rider broke free from the rest, urging his mount closer to the two prisoners. Urswicke, Bray clutching his arm and begging him to be careful, moaned as the lead rider pushed back his cowl and pulled down the bottom half of his woollen coif.

'Father!' Christopher hissed. 'My father Sir Thomas Urswicke, Recorder of London!'

'And at this moment our most mortal enemy,' Bray whispered hoarsely. 'For the love of God and his angels, Christopher, compose yourself or we,' he pointed to the beach, 'will be as trapped as they are. Please!'

Urswicke crouched and watched what was happening below. Sir Thomas was now shouting at the prisoners but the wind carried his words away. Urswicke glanced up, the salt-laden sea breeze was strengthening, dark clouds sweeping in. A flock of gulls appeared, white slivers of white circling above the bum-boat now at the mercy of the surging tide, its rowers floating nearby, legs and arms splayed out, all caught and killed by the arrow storm from the riders on the beach. Out at sea the lights had disappeared. Urswicke could only pray that Oxford's cog had given the enemy the slip, using his vessel's speed to go deeper into the northern seas and lose itself in the rolling banks of fog which constantly hung over those freezing waters. Oxford had escaped, but two of the men he had sent ashore were doomed. Sir Thomas Urswicke, standing high in the stir-rups, was now gesturing further down the coastline. Bray followed his direction.

'The gallows, Christopher,' Bray declared, 'they are going to hang their prisoners out of hand.'

Urswicke turned and glimpsed the outline of a soaring three-branched gibbet, built on a rocky outcrop just below the summit of the sand hills. The two prisoners were dragged towards this. Some of the horsemen dismounted, pushing and shoving their captives towards the scaffold. The prisoners fiercely resisted, kicking and screaming. Sir Thomas Urswicke replied with a litany of curses but the prisoners just yelled back. Christopher's father dismounted, drew his sword and, without a moment's hesitation, drove its two-edged blade into one prisoner's chest and then the other. Both men collapsed, their spraying blood greedily swal-lowed by the sand. The grim pageant then continued. The corpses were inspected, their belts, pouches and other items removed before being dragged to the foot of the gibbet. Two of the Recorder's retainers climbed up using the step spikes driven into the main post of the gallows. Ropes were fastened and the two bloodied corpses hoisted to dangle by their necks. Urswicke groaned and sank deeper into the protective gorse.

'We will wait,' Bray whispered. 'We will wait, then we will be gone.'

Jacob Cromart, mailed clerk in the service of the Countess Margaret and Jasper Tudor, squatted in the sanctuary enclave behind the high altar of the ancient church of St Michael, which stood within arrow-shot of the Thames. Cromart closed his eyes, trying to ignore the disquiet in his belly. He sat, legs stretched out, his back against the cold stone wall as he listened to the different eerie sounds of that truly ancient place. St Michael's was a simple, stark building, standing in its own stretch of land surrounded by an overgrown, weed-choked cemetery – God's Acre, though it looked as if neither God nor man cared a whit about it. St Michael's certainly held no mystery: it consisted of a nave with two transepts added on. The floor was mildewed paving stones, which stretched up to the roughly hewn rood screen carved decades ago, its wood and paint slowly crumbling. The narrow door through the rood screen led into the sanctuary which contained the high altar with a pyx chain hanging beside it. Behind the altar stretched the apse which housed the sanctuary enclave. Cromart had fled here, a place of safety in London where he could invoke some protection. Cromart now knew every inch of the church. He had arrived two days previously, grasping the horn of the high altar as he gasped out his desire for sanctuary.

The parish priest, Parson Austin Richards, had come bustling down to read the petition of acceptance. Once he had finished gabbling through the words as he stood next to the high altar, the priest turned on Cromart and delivered a short, sharp homily on what sanctuary entailed. Cromart was now protected by the church against summary arrest by any royal official or law officer in the kingdom. Violation of that right would incur the most serious sanctions the church could impose: excommunication by bell, book and candle, which decreed that the violator of sanctuary was cursed for life and damned for eternity. He or she would burn in hell and suffer the full consequences of his heinous sin against Holy Mother Church. In return, Cromart could stay in the church for up to forty days. He must carry no weapons or take any sustenance from anyone except the parish priest, who would serve him a simple meal three times a day. The parson would also provide water and a napkin to wash and, when Cromart left, some clothing, sturdy boots and a penny. The sanctuary man could use the jake's hole which stood outside the sacristy door in a makeshift garderobe built into an enclave of the church above a sewer. Parson Austin declared that he didn't care why Cromart was in sanctuary or what would happen to him in the future. St Michael's was an ancient church which enjoyed the right of sanctuary and that was enough.

Cromart crossed himself, his belly now truly agitated. He scrambled to his feet and wondered about the cause. Earlier in the day he had eaten nothing except what the good parson had brought and he had shared the bread, water and wine with the other sanctuary man, a city pick-lock, hotly pursued by Guildhall bailiffs. Ratstail, as the felon called himself, certainly showed no sign of any belly upset as he lay sprawled in the sanctuary enclave with a bundle for a pillow and his ragged cloak wrapped tightly around him. Ratstail now slept like a babe, impervious to the world or to the misty, clammy dampness of St Michael's. Cromart, rubbing his belly, inspected the hour cradle, crossed the sanctuary and entered the sacristy. It was almost time. He opened the door leading out to the jake's hole, undid his points and squatted down in relief above the reeking sewer. The pain subsided. Cromart drew himself up, made sure he was comfortable and walked back into the sacristy. He heard a sound behind him and turned as a shape emerged from the murk.

'Ratstail?' he demanded. 'Or is it . . .'

The dark figure swept towards him. Cromart saw the crossbow levelled. He stopped gaping as the hand-held arbalest was pushed closer towards him. Cromart heard the click of the cord and gagged as the barbed bolt smashed into the left side of his chest . . .

Parson Austin Richards rolled over in his cotbed and then pulled himself up. He thought he had been dreaming of a clanging bell echoing through the darkness. It was no dream! No trick of the mind! Someone was ringing the church bell, sounding the tocsin at some danger pressing close. But what could that be? Parson Austin sat on the edge of the bed and groaned. He realised something like this might happen ever since he became involved, once again, with Master Pembroke. 'The past never leaves you alone,' he murmured, 'it simply reaches out to catch you when you least expect it.'

Parson Austin closed his eyes. He momentarily recalled those hurling days when he served as a chaplain in the Yorkist array; those were sterling times and he had been rewarded with this small yet fairly wealthy parish close to the Thames. St Michael's was well-endowed with legacies from merchants who plied their trade in the nearby quaysides. Life had been sweet and serene, but now this! Groaning and moaning, the parson pushed back the coverlets, slipped his feet into sturdy sandals, wrapped a hooded cloak about him and went down out of the priest house. The night was very cold, the breeze sharp and cutting. Yet it was one of those strange English autumn days with clear skies but hard morning frosts. Parson Austin crossed himself as he stumbled up the corpse path to the main door of the church. The bell was still tolling, its metal tongue a constant peal warning of impending danger, then it abruptly stopped. Parson Austin dug into the pocket of his robe, drew out the cumbersome keyring and thrust the longest into the lock, turning it fully. He paused, drew a deep breath and pushed the door open. He expected to see some light, some indication of who might be pulling at the belfry ropes but there was none. The bell now being quiet. An eerie silence reigned. Parson Austin stared into the darkness of his church. The only break in the blackness was the flickering sanctuary lamp burning beside the pyx hanging on its chain. He could glimpse this through the open door of the rood screen. Parson Austin stared around. All the candles and tapers before the different statues and shrines had long fluttered out leaving nothing but a deep stillness broken only by the squeak and scrabbling of vermin.

'Is there anyone here?' he called out, his voice echoing along the nave. The priest tried to curb his growing fear. He turned to the left and hurried across to the door leading into the bell tower. He pushed this open and went into the musty stairwell. Again, no light. No sign of who had been there to pull so strenuously on the belfry ropes. Parson Austin walked further in, stumbling over different items stored there. He crouched down, his hand going out until he felt the huge lanternhorn with a tinder kept in the tray next to it. Quietly cursing the cold and his own chilling fear, Parson Austin struck the tinder until he had a flame to light the thick, squat tallow candle fixed in the centre of the lanternhorn. He sighed with relief as the flame burned greedily on the oily wick. He fastened the shutter and, lifting the lantern-horn, made his way up the stairwell which housed the long bell ropes. There was no one there. The ropes dangled with no sign of who had pulled at them so vigorously.

Parson Austin, now truly alarmed, left the bell tower. He locked the main door and walked up the nave holding the lanternhorn before him. The dancing light illuminated the garish paintings on the pillars which divided the nave from the narrow, shadow-filled transepts. Pictures and images which he usually ignored now caught his eye. Frightful scenes depicted in garish paint by long dead artists who had laid out a nightmare landscape thronged with bellowing, venomous demons, fiery-haired devils, great-jawed lions, plunging hawks, roaring dragons, all the denizens of Hell, that place of everlasting fire.

Parson Austin paused, closed his eyes, blessed himself and continued on. He walked through the open door of the rood screen and into the sanctuary. He heard a moan, a stifled cry, and edged around the altar into the apse which housed the sanctuary enclave. Ratstail the pick-lock cowered against the wall, his unshaven, unwashed face lit by the single candle he held on its pewter spigot.

'In God's name!' the priest exclaimed.

Ratstail, his face all wet with tears, simply pointed across to the sacristy. Parson Austin walked across into the room which reeked of incense and charcoal. He lifted the lantern and glimpsed what looked like a bundle of clothing strewn on the floor. At the same time, he abruptly recalled that Cromart was not to be seen. The priest, now drenched with sweat, resisted the urge to flee. He walked forward, lifted the lantern again and breathed a prayer. Cromart lay sprawled in a thick puddle of his own blood. Parson Austin crouched down, placing the lantern beside him as he fought to control the fear seething within him. He muttered prayer after prayer, gabbling the words, begging for divine help. He sketched a blessing in the direction of the corpse, clambered to his feet and staggered back out across the sanctuary. Hobbling and stumbling, he hastened down the nave, desperate to reach the bell tower and ring his own tocsin, a plea for help against the abomination his church now housed.

PART ONE

'See What Fear Man's Bosom Rendeth'

Guido Vavasour crouched before the meagre fire he had
lit in the gloomy, dank cellar of The Hanging Tree, a
derelict tavern standing on the corner of Dung Alleyway,
a narrow runnel which wound down to Queenhithe quayside.
Vavasour warmed his mittened fingers over the flames and
wondered what to do next. It was so strange to be back in London.
Now a different city. King Edward had stamped his seal on every
aspect of civic life. Men-at-arms and archers wearing the different
Yorkist insignia swaggered through the streets. The gallows and
gibbets were decorated with those who tried to protest. Street
warriors, hired by the great ones, also made their presence felt.
Guido hailed from Pembrokeshire. He always found the streets
and alleyways of London a truly sinister world, yet this was
where the countess kept a sharp eye on all proceedings. He
wondered how she would execute the plan she had devised to
get as many of the Red Dragon Battle Group safely out of the
kingdom to join her son in Brittany. Guido had landed at Walton
for that purpose. He and Pembroke were to give the countess
every assistance whilst the other two . . .

Guido just shook his head. He was still shocked, even terrified,
at what had happened. He was desperate to contact his brother
Robert hiding somewhere deep in the crowded slums of
Whitefriars. Guido, however, realised it would be very foolish
to show himself on the streets. York's searchers swarmed everywhere; the street swallows, the informants, the spies, the Judas
men, and all the myriad of what Guido described as 'the secret
people', sharp of eye and keen of wit. Many of them were King's
approvers who searched for any face, description or name of
anyone the Yorkist lords at the Guildhall wished to take up and
question. During the sea voyage from Brittany, Pembroke, the
Lord Jasper's constant and faithful courier, had warned his

comrades how London had changed. He had advised them to
keep a keen eye on Sir Thomas Urswicke in particular, as he
nourished a special hatred for the countess and the entire House
of Tudor. On board *The Glory of Lancaster*, Guido openly
wondered how the countess could possibly cherish Christopher
Urswicke, Sir Thomas's only son, who also happened to be
Margaret's principal chancery clerk. Suspicions about Christopher
Urswicke's true allegiance was a constant bone of contention
amongst the countess's retainers. Pembroke agreed that the young
clerk might well be a traitor but, as yet, the countess's confidence
in Christopher could not be shaken.

Guido sipped from the battered wineskin he had filched from
an ale shop earlier in the day. So much suspicion, so many
betrayals! The Yorkist lords seemed to have everything in their
favour. For a while Guido dozed, recalling merry childhood days
with his brother Robert on their father's manor deep in the
Pembrokeshire countryside. Guido half smiled and shook himself
awake. He must remember he was deep in mortal peril. He
recalled that bum-boat crunching on the sand in Walton cove.
They thought they were safe hurrying towards the sand hills when
the devil's own horsemen appeared, Sir Thomas Urswicke and
his comitatus, thundering out of the night to surround them. How
had that trap been sprung so easily? Who had given the Recorder
the time, the date and the location? Of course, there were spies
and watchers in the Breton harbour of La Rochelle, and the same
was true of Dordrecht in Hainault. *The Glory of Lancaster* had
berthed in both ports. The cog was well-known and could be
watched and followed, especially when it slipped through the
straits of Dover to turn north, as close as it could, to the English
coast. So many mysteries! Danger on land, danger at sea.
Pembroke had assured him that De Vere's cog could give the slip
to any enemy ship. 'Thank God for Pembroke,' Vavasour whispered, and 'thank God for his grotesque mask.' Pembroke had
assured him that this had undoubtedly frightened the horses of
those who'd confronted them: it had created a gap in the enemy
ranks through which they had fled.

Vavasour sipped at his wine. Pembroke had been a great
comfort and strength, yet such camaraderie did not disguise the
fact that a traitor lurked deep in Countess Margaret's household.

Perhaps it was Christopher Urswicke or even a brother-in-arms, a member of the Red Dragon Battle Group? Guido wondered what had happened to Pembroke after they had separated? Sooner or later, he vowed, he must make contact with both Robert and Pembroke their leader. He closed his eyes and prayed for the other two who had been captured when they came ashore. Did one of them carry what York was undoubtedly hunting? The Dragon Cipher, which contained such vital information about the support Tudor enjoyed in Wales? Yet where was that cipher? He and others believed it was secretly held by one of Countess Margaret's retainers. But who? Guido returned to the nagging question of who the traitor might be. Fleeing through that sea of gorse on the sand hills overlooking Walton cove, Vavasour had realised, as if in some vision, that he was fleeing from a traitor desperately plotting his death.

'But who is this?' Vavasour pleaded with the darkness. 'In God's name, what do I do now?'

Vavasour took another gulp of wine and stiffened as he heard a sound from above. The Hanging Tree was derelict and desolate, perhaps a beggar had broken in? Vavasour drew his dagger and carefully made his way up the cellar steps. He pushed the trap-door open, he was halfway through it when shapes emerged from the murk. Vavasour smelt sweat, leather and the gust of ale fumes. He glanced to his right then screamed at the blow to his head which sent him falling into a warm, welcoming darkness.

Vavasour woke shrieking with pain. He struggled hard but the cords which bound his ankles and wrists to the four corners of the rack held firm. Vavasour stared up into the darkness. Nothing but cracked, mildewed stones dripping with water. He glanced to his right and left, braziers glowed and sloping figures passed like ghosts through the fitful pools and puddles of torchlight. Vavasour breathed in and caught the iron tang of flames, steel and blood. He peered down at his own sweat-soaked body, stripped of all clothing except for his loincloth. He abruptly jerked, screaming at the pain which shot like tongues of flames from his arms and legs.

'Pity please!' Vavasour gasped. The figures, however, standing at the far end of the rack, continued to turn the levers which tightened the iron-hard cords in jerky movements.

'Enough, enough for the moment.' A shadowy figure walked up to the top of the rack and smiled down at the prisoner. 'I am Sir Thomas Urswicke,' he tapped Vavasour gently on the face. 'I am the Recorder of London and you, sir,' he jabbed a finger hard against the prisoner's belly, 'and you, sir, are Guido Vavasour, an attainted traitor who has entered this kingdom without leave or licence. You are a former adherent of the Red Dragon Battle Group. You attempted to perpetrate the most horrible treasons at Tewkesbury. Now you have returned to curdle more mischief. So, what is your specific purpose here?' Sir Thomas leaned down. 'You, sir, are now lodged in the dungeons beneath the great keep in the Tower of London. Rest assured, you will certainly die here or in a place close by. You are on the rack commonly called the "Scavenger's Daughter". Those two gentlemen at the far end of the rack are the scavengers. They will pull and draw you until your arms and legs pop out of their sockets like peas from a pod. You are going to die, Master Vavasour. All you have to decide is how. Before that, you are going to be questioned. If you coop-erate, all to the good. If you do not, then my good friends here are going to be very busy. So, why did you return to this kingdom?' Vavasour shook his head. 'You will tell me all,' the Recorder whispered, 'because you have all been betrayed.' Vavasour, racked by pain and anger, glared up at his tormentor. 'You have been betrayed,' the Recorder repeated.

'By whom? Your son who nestles so close to the countess?' Vavasour spat back. 'Like father, like son! It's true, the apple never falls far from the tree. We know him to be a traitor.'

The Recorder lifted a hand, the scavengers standing at the foot of the rack turned the wheels until Vavasour screamed for mercy.

'Very good, very good.' The Recorder, who had walked away, came back as the torture cords were loosened. 'So Guido, we will begin again. Why did you come to England?'

'Two of us were to help the sanctuary men escape. The other two were needed as messengers by the countess.'

'Ah yes, you mean to her allies in Wales? And the Dragon Cipher. Oh yes, we know all about that. Do you have it?'

'No.'

Again the Recorder lifted a hand and watched as Vavasour

was stretched until his bones cracked and he could hardly breathe. The Recorder leaned down.

'The Dragon Cipher?'

'In God's name I do not have it. It exists but we do not know who carries it.'

'But it exists?'

'It exists. The countess has made reference to it.'

'And the court of Duke Francis in Brittany? Oh yes, we do need some help here.' The Recorder called over to a clerk sitting on a wall bench deep in the shadows. The clerk, his white face peaked, constantly dabbing at his ever-dripping nose, scurried over to stand beside Sir Thomas. 'This is Osbert.' The Recorder patted the clerk's bony shoulder. 'A truly skilled scrivener. I want you, amongst other things, to describe for him where young Henry Tudor lodges at the Breton court. Which buildings? Which churches? The number of armed retainers? Of course Guido, you may lie, but what we know should match with what you tell us. Oh, by the way, before you speak to Osbert, where is your brother Robert?'

'I don't know. I have just returned to the city myself. I was searching for him when you took me up. Who told you where I was?'

'Never mind that. Where is Pembroke the traitor who came ashore with you at Walton?'

'I don't know, we separated. I was about to search for both of them when you came. Who betrayed me?'

'Oh my son can guess as well as anyone.'

'And our landing at Walton?'

'Again, the same source. So, where is your brother? Where is Pembroke? I want to see both hang.'

'I don't know. I truly don't.' Vavasour gasped. 'Ask your son!' he jibed.

Sir Thomas stared down at the prisoner then walked away, summoning the torture-chamber clerk and the two scavengers to follow him. Once away from the prisoner, he beckoned them close. 'You have my list of questions, Master Osbert?'

'Yes Sir Thomas.'

'And how long will this take?' He turned to the scavengers. 'We can expect the usual lies but how long do you think it will take?'

'My Lord,' one of them replied, 'I have never met anyone who lasted longer than an hour. The prisoner is soft, a mailed clerk. You will have the truth, whatever that is, within the hour.'

'Good, good,' the Recorder whispered. 'I have posed some of these questions already. Find out about the cipher and the where-abouts of Pembroke, that must be asked as a matter of logic. We would also love to meet his brother Robert and, indeed, any of his coven not yet in sanctuary, still hiding from the law. Well, you have my instructions, follow them.'

Osbert said they would and led the scavengers away. Sir Thomas crossed to an enclave where a servant had laid out viands, bread, some thick, creamy cheese and a jug of the best Bordeaux drawn from a cask in the royal cellars. Sir Thomas sat down and sipped gratefully at the wine, quietly revelling at his own success. Across that murky, miserable chamber the scavengers had now become busy as they pushed at levers and turned the small wheels which created a chilling, eerie sound as the ropes tightened and creaked. The Recorder listened to this dire hymn of torture, a pattern which kept repeating itself. The rack would shudder, almost as if it was protesting at what it was doing. Vavasour would scream then this would die away, lapsing into a sombre silence broken only by Osbert's constant questions and Vavasour's gasping replies. Sir Thomas continued to sit with his back to the rack, tasting his wine and savouring the rich cheese. At last the racking and the questioning ended. Osbert came scurrying over and took the stool Sir Thomas kicked towards him with the toe of his boot.

'You have finished?'

'Yes, my Lord. The scavengers maintain Vavasour is broken. He has told us what he knows but,' the scrivener, cradling his chancery satchel, wiped his dripping nose on the back of his hand, 'he has, indeed, told us very little. Undoubtedly there is a Dragon Cipher but he does not know where it is. He has confessed to entering the realm to assist the sanctuary men in leaving this kingdom. Apparently, once he had spoken to Pembroke and his brother Robert, he would join them in seeking sanctuary in some London church.'

'And so join his comrades' departure from these shores? All to the good.' The Recorder whispered almost as if he was talking to himself. 'And whom has he met since his return?'

'Nobody! But on one matter,' Osbert replied, 'he is very sure, that your son Sir Thomas is the traitor in the countess's household. Yet I find this difficult to believe. Surely you would know that anyway?' Osbert stared at the Recorder who just gazed bleakly back. 'Sir Thomas, why does he confess that?'

'To prove, perhaps, that we do not completely have the upper hand. Secondly, if my dearest Christopher is suspected as a traitor amongst the Tudors, his life is truly in danger. A threat which, despite our differences, I would take very seriously.' Sir Thomas tried to control his temper. 'Vavasour is baiting me. How dare he threaten . . .'

'My Lord, I thought as much myself. So I asked about your son's standing amongst those who serve the countess. He replied that many respect your son as a very able, skilled clerk. Of course . . .' Osbert coughed and cleared his throat. 'Of course he would be, with a father such as yourself, Sir Thomas.'

'Flattery is like perfume, Osbert. You smell it but you don't drink it. Continue.'

'Well, others are more cautious about your son because of his parentage and, of course Sir Thomas, you do sit very high in the councils of the King and the House of York. They do . . .' Osbert paused.

'Continue.'

'Well, people do wonder why the countess cherishes your son so fervently even though he bears your name and you are so furious against her.'

'Fervently?' Sir Thomas retorted. 'You say that's how they describe it? She cherishes him so fervently?'

'Yes, my Lord. Master Christopher, like his noble father,' Osbert was now almost gabbling, 'is intelligent, courtly and highly skilled. The countess is a lonely woman married to Sir Henry Stafford who lies mortally ill at their manor in Woking. The Countess Margaret visits him rarely, though she does send him letters, presents and medicine.'

The Recorder put a hand up for silence even as his nimble brain pondered the possibilities. He knew only too well the true reason for Christopher's closeness to the countess. She had supported him unstintingly through his mother's grievous sickness. He hated to concede this, even to himself, but he believed that Countess Margaret Beaufort viewed Christopher Urswicke as her own beloved son and Christopher responded in kind. The Recorder closed his eyes and quietly reflected on all of this.

'Yes,' he murmured, 'there are possibilities here, dramatic possibilities.' The Recorder listed them, not ready as yet, to create a chronicle, a story which would account for everything. What were the main items of this? The countess fervently cherishing Christopher Urswicke? Christopher Urswicke falling under suspicion by some of the same countess's supporters? The possibility that, in their eyes, Christopher Urswicke was a turncoat. Sir Henry Stafford lying mortally sick at Woking, all alone, bereft of his wife even though she despatched gifts and medicine to comfort him? 'Oh yes,' the Recorder breathed, 'this rich crop could yield a generous harvest!'

'My Lord?'

Sir Thomas opened his eyes and beamed down at the scrivener. 'You also work with Master William under the sign of The Red Keg near St Paul's, yes?' The scrivener agreed. 'And Master William produces broadsheets?'

'Under licence, my Lord.'

'My licence.' The Recorder gleefully rubbed his hands. 'And I also issue licences for him to post his broadsheets at the Cross and on the Standard in Cheapside. Very well, Master Osbert.' Sir Thomas pointed at the table. 'Let us be busy. I will dictate certain conclusions to you under the title of "The last and true confession of Guido Vavasour, self-confessed rebel and traitor, before he was taken out for lawful execution, as the aforesaid Guido confessed in the presence of witnesses in the King's own Tower of London." Now . . .'

Osbert hastened to obey. Once he had stretched out a sheet of parchment and readied both quill pens and inkpot, Sir Thomas began to whisper what he wanted copied down. The Recorder spoke softly but clearly. Occasionally Osbert would glance up fearfully but the Recorder simply patted him on the shoulder and told him to continue. Once he had finished, the Recorder carefully read the confession. 'Such rich possibilities,' he repeated. 'Of course, this needs a little more attention. We need to create a story which flows and convinces but, at the moment, there's no haste.'

'My Lord?'

'Yes Osbert.'

'My Lord, these so-called witnesses?'

'Why Osbert, you and the two scavengers. Who can gainsay that?'

'The prisoner. I mean, if he is to be arraigned before King's Bench or the justices at the Guildhall?'

'He is a rebel, Osbert, a traitor, caught red-handed perpetrating his hideous treasons, there's no reason for a trial. He had indicted himself.'

'He has a tongue.'

'Very perceptive. So come, come.'

He led the scribe across the torture chamber, calling the scavengers to join him. They all gathered around the prisoner stretched out on the rack. Vavasour glared up at the Recorder.

'God curse you, Thomas Urswicke,' he grated. 'God curse you and yours. You attack the countess without and your son from within. Two Judas men, father and son more fit for a hanging then Hell than any city felon . . .'

The Recorder abruptly lunged, fast as a striking viper. He punched the prisoner in the face, two savage blows which drew blood.

'Very well, very well.' Sir Thomas fought to control his breathing. 'Master Osbert, continue the punishment.'

'My Lord?'

The Recorder snapped his fingers at the scavengers and pointed at the prisoner. 'Remove his tongue!' Sir Thomas spun on his heel and walked back to the table where he refilled the pewter goblet. He popped a piece of cheese into his mouth and drank the wine, listening to Vavasour's screams turn into a horrid rasping. The Recorder then walked back and glared down at the prisoner.

'Sir, you think you are so knowledgeable, so judgemental, so clear on everything.' Vavasour could only open his mouth, all bloodied and torn to make the most heart-rending sounds. 'You are a traitor caught in your crimes,' Sir Thomas declared. 'There is no need for a trial. You will be despatched to the gallows. But, Master Vavasour, I will ensure that you die a wiser man than you are now. So listen carefully.' The Recorder turned to Osbert

and the two scavengers. 'A moment, sirs, a moment to myself and
the prisoner.' The three men walked out of earshot. The Recorder
watched them go, then leaned down and whispered heatedly into
Vavasour's ear. He repeated what he had said then straightened
up, smiling at Vavasour who could only glare back. The Recorder
waggled his fingers in farewell. 'Master Guido we are finished.
I have no further use for you except to arrange your hanging.
Till then . . .'

Margaret Beaufort, Countess of Richmond, sat in the high-back
chair in her bedchamber which stood on the first gallery of her
elegant riverside mansion. The room, like everything in the house,
was exquisitely refined, be it the blue and gold arras hanging
against the pink-washed walls or the thick, deep scarlet turkey
rugs which almost covered the highly polished elm-wood floor.
The gold-edged four-poster bed, tables, aumbries and small cabi-
nets, caskets and coffers were a dark oaken-brown, their polished
wood gleaming in the fluttering light of a host of beeswax candles
placed on spigots around the room. The fragrance of the pure
melting wax mingled with the perfumed smoke curling from the
small herb pots and braziers, their glowing charcoal sprinkled
with the dust of crushed flowers plucked and prepared the previous
summer. Margaret, garbed in grey like a nun, her thin, expressive
face framed by a snow-white wimple, slowly threaded amber
ave beads. She stared intently at the two men seated before her;
these were her council, the only men she could really trust.
Christopher Urswicke, dressed in dark jerkin and hose, the collar
of his cambric shirt pulled high under his clean-shaven chin. A
good-looking, almost beautiful young man, Urswicke had an
open, smooth, boyish face, blue-eyed and sweet lipped. He looked
much younger than his twenty-six years, an impression height-
ened by his tousled auburn hair. Urswicke sat languidly, his cloak
and warbelt laid over a coffer, his spurred riding boots placed in
the tiled window embrasure next to those of his companion,
Reginald Bray. The latter was close faced with deep hooded eyes.
Bray was swarthy, even sallow, his beard and moustache closely
trimmed, his hair, black as a raven's wing, tied neatly in a queue
behind him.
    Margaret continued to sit and stare as she let her sharp mind

turn over the business in hand. She was confident that this chamber was sealed. No eavesdropper could lurk. No Judas man hungry for reward could slink close, hungry for any juicy tit-bit to pass on to his masters. God knows there was enough for them to feast on: as Margaret had conceded to these two confidants, she was steeped in treason and the danger of discovery and punishment hung over her like the executioner's axe. But that did not deter Margaret. She recognised the times and the place. This was not the hour or the occasion for sharp sword-play and blood-soaked conflict. No, this was the time for intrigue, plot and counterplot, deceit and deception. She must wear masks and move cautiously as she threaded her way through a murderous maze to celebrate her vision, her dream of a Tudor, her son, enthroned at Westminster wearing the Confessor's crown as his right.

'Mistress,' Urswicke cleared his throat, 'Mistress we are here . . .'

'Yes, yes, we are here, my friends, in close and secret council.' Margaret drew a deep breath. 'Christopher, Reginald, what we say here, what we will discuss is high treason which could incur all the dire and dreadful penalties of the law. Of course,' Margaret smiled thinly, 'if what we plot is successful, then it will not be treason. So let us begin. Today is the eighteenth of October, the year of our Lord 1471, the Feast of St Luke the Evangelist. Autumn has come and the horrors of last summer are past. Here in this kingdom the House of York reigns supreme. Edward the warrior King is supported by his Woodville wife and a host of henchmen, be it his wife's wolf pack or the likes of Hastings, Howard of Norfolk and the rest. Edward so far has kept the support of the city and the kingdom and, above all, Holy Mother Church, who views Edward as sitting on the right hand of the power, God's anointed, vindicated by battle. In the meantime,' Margaret tried to keep the bitterness out of her voice, her raging anger against what was, when it should be so different, 'we of the House of Lancaster now eat the hard bread of disgrace and sip the bitter wine of exile. Lancaster has been depleted. My kinsmen, Beaufort of Somerset and the rest are no more. The bloody defeat at Tewkesbury saw to that. The same is true of possible allies, such as Neville Earl of Warwick, the self-styled Kingmaker, killed outright at Barnet. The true King, my son

Henry, now shelters in Brittany, the guest of Duke Francis who
will keep him safe. What I say is true – yes?'

'Undoubtedly, mistress,' Bray replied. 'Our enemies wax
powerful.'

'But York is not so strong,' Urswicke retorted. 'True, Edward
is supported by his henchmen, in particular Richard of Gloucester.
But the other brother,' Urswicke smiled bleakly, 'George of
Clarence is as treacherous as they come. He sees himself as the
rightful King of England, France,' Urswicke flailed a hand, 'and
whatever.'

'We shall come to him in a while,' Margaret murmured, sifting
through the documents piled on the small chancery table to her
right. 'In the meantime, we shall plot. My son Henry is in exile
with his uncle Jasper. He has few friends and even fewer allies.
The rest, well they have gone into the dark.' Margaret lifted her
ave beads. 'God rest them.'

'And God bless us.'

'Yes, Reginald, but let's give God a little help. Now, as you
may know, a cohort of Welsh horsemen joined our array just
before Tewkesbury, a battle group which assumed the name of
the Red Dragon. A logical choice,' she shrugged, 'as they all
came from Wales. They were about twenty in number. All mailed
clerks, young men who had studied in the halls of Oxford or
Cambridge. Many of them were secretly patronised by me. I
provided money and purveyance. They are totally loyal to the
Tudor cause.'

'I have heard of these, fierce fighters but . . .'

'Listen, Christopher, they joined Somerset's army and, before
the Battle of Tewkesbury, they gathered in a local church
where they took a solemn oath to fight as a battle group under
the standard of the Red Dragon. They also swore to seek out and
destroy Edward of York and his two brothers Richard and George.
Especially the latter who, as you well know, joined the House
of Lancaster and then just as blithely betrayed us to return to the
bosom of his family.'

'They failed . . .'

'Christopher, I assure you, it wasn't through lack of trying
and, because of that, they are specially hated by York. Now some
of the battle group were killed in the slaughter. A few fled the

kingdom whilst the rest went into hiding. Recently, with my support, they emerged from the shadows and took sanctuary in a number of churches across London.'

'Some, however, have been caught and slain, including those two men stabbed and hanged at Walton.'

'Yes, Reginald. One of my son's most trusted allies, De Vere of Oxford brought them from La Rochelle in Brittany to land in Essex.' Margaret shrugged. 'You know this and the outcome. Two of them were taken and killed.'

'I wonder how,' Urswicke interjected tapping the hilt of his dagger, 'I really do. And, why my father, Recorder of London and one of York's most loyal henchmen in the city, should be involved. My father the guildsman,' Christopher added bitterly, 'locksmith, cabinet-maker, councillor, alderman. Oh my father has climbed the greasy pole and never once slipped. What was he doing there?' Christopher paused, rocking gently backwards and forwards. Bray watched him from the corner of his eye. Christopher Urswicke had never forgotten or forgiven how his dissolute father, with his ever so handsome face, ready smile and sweet tongue, had driven his wife, Christopher's mother, to an early grave. Or that is what Christopher passionately believed, as he did that Margaret Beaufort had done all in her power to assist Christopher's mother, especially during those last mournful days of sickness.

'Father against son,' Bray murmured, 'son against father: that's what this kingdom has come to.'

'No my friend,' Urswicke replied sharply, 'my father and I would be daggers drawn even if we met, though I doubt if we ever will,' he added dryly, 'on the streets of Paradise.'

'Does he know the truth of this situation?' Bray demanded. 'I mean . . .'

'No, no.' Urswicke shook his head. 'Only our mistress and your good self know the truth. You see Father thinks I am like him. I have created my own God in my own heart, namely myself. Consequently, I have no loyalty, no real allegiance, no firm commitment except to my own advancement, be it at his expense or anybody else's, including yours, mistress.'

'Now,' Margaret smiled, 'I know the truth, Christopher, and that, my friends, is what we are now pursuing.'

'My father,' Urswicke declared, 'is Recorder of London, one of the Crown's most important justices, yet he led a comitatus from London across the wilds of Essex to seize four men.'

'Because York trusts him,' Bray countered. 'Edward and his ilk realise Essex is not as warm in its support for them as it should be, that's one of the reasons De Vere chose Walton as a landing place.'

'And so did I.' Margaret moved the ave beads from one hand to another. 'You saw those two men die barbarously. Your father, Christopher, realised how important those four men were and their loss is a grievous blow. But, that's not enough. Somebody betrayed us, even though I kept such information to myself until the last moment. I did not even share it with you until I had to.'

'You told us to be at a certain place on a certain night,' Urswicke retorted. 'And so we were. You informed us that four retainers of your beloved son would come ashore at Walton-on-the-Naze. We were to meet them and bring them to London.'

'And of course you must now wonder why?'

'Certainly, since our return yesterday.'

'You encountered no trouble Reginald, I mean on your journey back?'

'None, mistress. So tell us what that was all about?'

'The battle group – the banner of the Red Dragon, were a cohort of friends. A few of these escaped to join my son in Brittany. They became close, loyal guards of my beloved son. Now the leader of the cohort was a Welshman, Gareth Morgan, a mailed clerk trained in the law, a former member of the Middle Temple. Morgan was born and bred in the House of Tudor. A good friend of my beloved husband.' Margaret swiftly crossed herself. 'Morgan left a family in Wales, I believe his mother and daughter still live there. Anyway, Morgan joined Lancaster's retinue and was caught up in our disastrous defeat at Townton some ten years ago. Morgan was taken prisoner by a cohort of mercenaries fighting for York. These were led by a truly nightmare soul, a freebooter known as Zeigler who'd soon won a hideous reputation for his ill-treatment and abuse of prisoners. Zeigler loved nothing better than to comb the battlefield for enemy wounded and, when he did, God help those poor souls. Zeigler was a man to be truly feared.'

'Yes, yes I have heard that name,' Bray murmured. 'Tales and stories from old soldiers. Apparently Zeigler was a true blood-drinker with a deep hunger, a sharp appetite for deaths, other people's.'

'And Morgan?' Urswicke demanded.

'During the battle of Townton, some ten years ago, Morgan was captured by Zeigler who thrust him into a bear pit. The beast was not one of those placid, trained creatures that dance to the reedy tune of a pipe. No, no! This was a huge, ferocious animal. Morgan was severely mauled. He was only saved by a priest visiting the tavern where Zeigler had set up court. The priest intervened. He was no ordinary cleric but a royal chaplain patron-ised by the House of York. Austin Richards.' Margaret pulled a face. 'We will meet that name again. Richards carried York's seal and used his power so Morgan was pulled out of the bear pit. He had suffered multiple wounds, particularly to his face, where some of the flesh had been clawed away. A local wise woman, a leech worked a miracle. Morgan survived. He recovered, though ever since then he wears a specially woven mask over his face.'

'And now?'

'And now, Christopher, Morgan has taken the title Pembroke after the lands we Tudors hold and where his family farmed. Pembroke is now both his home and his title. He is a most fervent adherent to the House of Tudor. A soul, kinsman Jasper trusts implicitly.'

'And he and the other three were sent with messages to you?'

'No, Christopher, they were despatched to help extricate their comrades from England. Pembroke led the Red Dragon Battle Group. After his cohort was shattered at Tewkesbury, its members, including Pembroke, fled for their lives. He and others reached safety but the rest, about six in number, went into hiding until the furore of the recent conflict subsided. A few days ago, at my insistence while you were away at Walton, the remaining members of the battle group broke cover and, as I said, took sanctuary in different London churches.' Margaret paused to sip from a goblet on the table beside her. 'I have told you this already but it is important. I am using what influence I can to arrange that all five sanctuary men . . .'

'I thought you said six?'

'Ah, I shall come to that, Christopher,' she replied brusquely. 'I have petitioned the Bishop of London that all five, being sanctuary men, are under the protection of Holy Mother Church. Accordingly, they and any more of the battle group who take sanctuary should be allowed to leave England safely and securely on the understanding that they never return on pain of death. Of course,' she breathed, 'they will return, not by themselves but in an army led by my son.'

'And, if all goes well,' Bray demanded, 'where will all these sanctuary men muster?'

'In four days' time, in the courtyard of All Hallows Church near the Tower. They will then be escorted out of the city, across Essex, to the same place you recently visited, Walton-on-the-Naze.'

'And who will be their escort?' Christopher smiled bleakly. 'My father and a cohort of his bully boys from the Guildhall?'

'In a word, yes. The sanctuary men, as we should now call them, will be escorted through Cripplegate, along Mile End to Bow Church, then take the trackways across the fringes of Epping Forest towards Colchester: their destination is the disused and derelict royal manor of Thorpe. After that, it's a short walk to Walton which provides a natural inlet, good clear water and is fairly safe whatever the tides. On the Feast of St Simon and Jude which, as you know falls at the end of the month, the Breton merchantman *The Galicia*, under its master Savereaux, will appear and despatch a boat to take them on board.' Margaret heaved a sigh. 'I have negotiated all this with the Bishop of London's principal henchman Archdeacon Blackthorne.' Margaret held up her ave beads so they could see the crucifix attached to the end of the chain. 'Thank God Holy Mother Church so jealously and zealously guards its privileges, and that includes the right to sanctuary. Moreover, not only are these survivors of the battle group sanctuary men, but three of them are tonsured clerks having received minor orders and, as such, are subject to church courts rather than those of the Crown.'

'Yet they are not truly safe?' Urswicke's question hung like a noose in the air and the countess's face betrayed her own agitation. She just sat back in her chair, as if listening to the faint sounds of her mansion bounded on the south by the busy river and to the north by a tangle of narrow runnels leading into the city.

'They are not safe,' Urswicke repeated. 'Their departure will be regulated by the most stringent ordinances. If any, or all of them, try to leave their designated route, clerks or not, they can be killed on sight.'

'True, true.' The countess sighed.

'Why are these men so important?' Bray demanded.

'Oh, for many reasons. They are mailed clerks, skilled in both the chancery and the tourney yard; they support my son without reservation. They hail from families in Wales who foster and cherish loyalty to the House of Tudor.' Margaret sat, head down, then glanced up. 'Surely, gentlemen, in this dark vale of bitter tears, such experience, such loyalty must be treasured? All of them have been declared "utlegati" – beyond the law, wolfsheads worthy of immediate death.' She shrugged. 'They live deep in the shadows, not even you are acquainted with all of them. Some you have met, others come and go as quietly as a watch in the night. They are more Lord Jasper's people than mine. However, what we all hold in common trust are the God-given rights of my son Henry. We need to get such men safely back to him.'

'And you can do all this,' Christopher asked, 'despatch these men out of the kingdom and not incur York's displeasure?'

'I've already incurred that for being who I am and what I do. But, in essence, I am doing nothing wrong except petitioning Holy Mother Church to protect certain retainers who have legitimately invoked its protection. Oh, York may fume and threaten but so what? They would love to kill the retainers of the Red Dragon, annihilate a battle group which threatened their King. They will undoubtedly strive to seize any opportunity for mischief. However, if they cannot do this, they will at least rid the kingdom of such an enemy, and that is where you, Christopher, will play such an important role. I want you to accompany these sanctuary men to Thorpe Manor. I want you, as much as you can, to protect and sustain them. I may well accompany you. I have yet to decide that. Finally, and most importantly, I want you to keep a sharp eye on your father Sir Thomas; I do believe he will lead this sorry procession out of London.'

Urswicke nodded in agreement: his father was cringingly loyal to York. Sir Thomas would love to take the credit for ridding the kingdom, one way or the other, of men so valued by the House of Tudor. He would adorn himself in his fur-lined woollen robes and lead this procession out of the city, but to what? Oh yes, Urswicke reflected, his father would seek any opportunity to settle scores with the Countess Margaret.

'You do realise,' Bray spoke up, 'and I am sure Christopher thinks the same, that this will not flow smoothly?'

'Oh yes, oh yes,' Margaret murmured. 'I don't believe Sir Thomas will travel through the autumn countryside just to say farewell. Something will happen. Some mischief is being plotted: some bloody conclusion to all this. But, for the life of me, I cannot decide what.'

'I should go too.'

'No Reginald, I need you in London on other business that's come upon us. Christopher, you will need your sharp mind and keen wits but you will be helped. Two men escaped the ambuscade at Walton. Pembroke and Guido Vavasour. They became separated. God knows where Guido is hiding but Pembroke made his way to London and now hides deep in the city. Naturally Pembroke's despair has deepened. There is no doubt that the disaster at Walton was plotted. Pembroke, like Vavasour, has little confidence in anyone. Now,' Margaret pointed to the hour candle flaring under its copper-topped glass case, 'Pembroke will soon be here. So let me continue. I mentioned six of the Red Dragon Battle Group but there are now only five. Last night Jacob Cromart, a leading member of that cohort, a mailed clerk highly skilled in the use of secret ciphers, was found murdered, killed by a crossbow bolt to his heart. This murder occurred in a church, St Michael's near the Thames, where Cromart had claimed sanctuary.

Cromart's death is truly mysterious. The parish priest, Parson Austin, was roused in the middle of the night by someone tolling the tocsin. The good parson hurried down to his church. He unlocked its main door and went inside. The bell had stopped tolling but he could find no one responsible for that. Indeed, the church was deserted except for a felon, Ratstail, who'd also claimed sanctuary. Parson Austin found Ratstail cowering in an enclave. He searched his church and could detect no sign, no evidence of a weapon or of any struggle. Most mysterious, all the doors of the church were either locked or bolted from the inside. So how could an assassin enter, commit murder and then slip away like a shadow?'

'There is no secret entrance or loose postern door?'

'None. Both the priest and Ratstail were in agreement on that.'

'And the corpse?'

'Found lying in a puddle of his own blood in the sacristy. Cromart had evidently gone out to visit the jake's hole and returned. But, there again, the priest found the outside door to the sacristy firmly locked and bolted from within.'

'And this Ratstail?'

'A hapless felon, a pickpocket. He was all jabbering and frightened.'

'And how do you know all this, mistress?'

'Oh, I invited Parson Austin here. He came earlier in the day. I made out that Cromart was a distant kin of my late husband. A glass of Alsace, a bowl of sweetmeats and a few coins had him chatting like a sparrow on a branch. A good man. As I have said, he saved Pembroke. A priest who has served as a royal chaplain, a close adherent of the House of York, though he was pleasant enough to me. He also informed me about your father, Christopher, not to mention other lords of the Guildhall,' she paused, 'you will undoubtedly hear more of this.'

'Mistress?'

'Well, Cromart's death is mysterious. How could a sanctuary man be murdered in a church where the doors are all locked with no sign of an intruder or a weapon? He also mentioned that Cromart's belt had been taken.'

'His belt?'

'Yes. And I do wonder if Cromart's assassin was searching for the Dragon Cipher.' Margaret looked away as if she didn't want to hold Christopher's gaze.

'Mistress?'

'The Dragon Cipher,' she replied, staring down at the floor, 'is a memorandum written in secret writing describing our power in Wales and elsewhere. Strips of parchment which list which churches have weapons stored, which families support us, which officials would show us favour, the most suitable port or harbour for incoming war cogs, the availability of food in what season and at what time. In other words, Christopher, a clear and distinct picture of who and what we could rely upon when my son returns.'

'And does it exist?'

'Cromart's killer certainly believed it does but I do not want to comment on the cipher. What is also puzzling is that York too must answer the question: who wanted Cromart dead? And, of course, York and all his minions in this city are under deep suspicion of being involved.'

'Oh Lord and all his angels,' Urswicke chuckled quietly, 'I see your logic, mistress. Who profits from Cromart's death? York certainly does.'

'According to Parson Austin, your father's retainers ransacked St Michael's but they discovered nothing amiss. No secret entrance whilst our good pastor assured them that all was as it should be on the night Cromart was murdered.'

'What about Ratstail?'

'A hapless felon incapable of using a crossbow?'

'How so?'

'Ratstail has been caught far too many times putting his hands where they shouldn't be, so three fingers on both hands have been savagely nipped. He could hardly hold a dagger let alone an arbalest. Christopher,' she continued, 'I want you to visit Parson Austin and see for yourself. You will do that?' She gazed earnestly at this young but highly talented clerk whom she regarded as dear as any son.

'Of course, mistress.'

'Thank you.' Margaret paused. 'And so we come to more recent news.' The countess took a sip from her goblet. 'Richard Neville, Earl of Warwick, was killed earlier this year at Barnet fighting for the House of Lancaster. Warwick's earldom is the greatest in the kingdom; fertile, prosperous estates stretching the length and breadth of this country. Now Warwick was once the most fervent supporter of York until the latter chose to ignore his advice. However, before this, Neville did enter a marriage alliance with York which cannot be annulled, his daughter Isabel being married to George of Clarence. Warwick died without a male heir. And so,' she gestured at her two henchmen, 'we all know that Clarence now lays claim through his wife Isabel to the entire Warwick inheritance.'

'And that is being challenged by Richard of Gloucester,' Christopher declared, 'who wants to marry Warwick's other daughter Anne and so claim half of the Neville estates as his new wife's dowry.'

'Both brothers,' Bray declared, 'are daggers drawn, though they know their elder brother the King will take no nonsense from either of them.'

'Well,' Margaret declared, 'what I suspected might happen, indeed Christopher, you warned me about this, Anne Neville has disappeared. Poor girl!'

'Yes, yes.' Urswicke nodded. 'Poor girl indeed! Anne Neville is powerless. Her father died a traitor, the one thing which saved her was Isabel's marriage to Clarence. Nevertheless, Anne was left vulnerable, a mere court lady in her sister's household.'

'And now she's gone,' Bray intervened, 'Gloucester cannot marry her nor, more importantly, lay claim to any portion of the Neville inheritance. But where can she be? Has she been murdered by Clarence and his evil shadow Mauclerc?'

'He wouldn't dare,' Urswicke retorted. 'Edward the King would have Clarence's head on the proverbial platter. Never mind her father, Anne Neville is a high-born noble lady. She is not to be slaughtered like a pig in a flesher's yard. Moreover, Edward of York has a soft heart for the ladies, even more so for Warwick's brood. We mustn't forget that Warwick and Edward were once the most loving of brothers. If Clarence murdered Anne Neville, he would go into the dark.'

'I agree,' Margaret declared sharply. 'I know something of this which I cannot share with you at the moment, I think that's best. Anyway,' she sighed, 'we must foster the story that Clarence has abducted the Lady Anne and that only God knows her true fate: forced incarceration either in a lonely convent here or across the seas, perhaps a desolate priory deep in the Irish countryside. Heaven bless the poor woman!'

Margaret pointed to a triptych on the wall venerating the three great archangels of heaven, Michael, Gabriel and Raphael. 'Believe you me,' she murmured, 'whatever her situation . . .' Margaret's voice was now hardly above a whisper, as if she were

talking to herself. Urswicke felt a slight chill of fear. Something
had seriously disturbed the countess. She was wary, no longer
expressing herself in her usual blunt, forthright manner. She
seemed reluctant to talk to them; even their journey to Walton
had been shrouded in mystery. Only now were they learning what
was really happening. 'Yes, yes,' Margaret recollected. 'Whatever
her situation, Anne Neville will need all the help of heaven. She's
already a broken woman after the violent death of her father, his
corpse and that of his brother being exposed naked in St Paul's.
Anne watched her father fall like a star from heaven. Now she
has no real protector. I do not know if she wants Gloucester's
protection, Anne is nothing more than a timid mouse, a virtual
mute after the ordeal she has been through. But,' she added
slowly, 'I am sure she will be safe.'

'And what is all this to us?' Bray demanded.

'York fishes in troubled waters,' Urswicke replied. 'And so
can we. Mistress, we have our spies across the city, the street
swallows, that legion of grimy urchins, the House of Beggars,
the Guild of this and that.' Urswicke grinned. 'All the poor alley
worms, who see everything though they are never seen themselves.' Urswicke rubbed the side of his face. 'Anne Neville was
of slender build, slim, golden-haired with a rather peaked face
and, if I remember any distinctive feature, it was that golden
hair. Quite singular. We shall search . . .'

'No Christopher, you have other business. Reginald will deal
with this amongst other matters.'

'If the Lady Anne has been abducted,' Bray murmured, 'it
must be Clarence. He has everything to gain.'

'From the little I have heard,' Margaret replied, 'Clarence is
volubly protesting his innocence. But, there again, he would,
wouldn't he?' Margaret grinned impishly. 'Oh, rest assured, I am
only too pleased to stir this pot of mischief.'

'Could Richard of Gloucester have abducted her?'

'No, I don't think so,' Margaret pointed at her devilishly shrewd
steward, 'but when Christopher leaves you must conduct a hunt,
a true search for her so it appears that we do really care.' Margaret
broke off as a bell tingled, sharp and clear throughout the house,
signifying that someone had been admitted into the hall below.
Margaret held a hand up for silence. The chamber door opened

and a retainer hurried in to kneel beside the countess and whisper a message.

'Oh very well.' The countess smiled. 'Despite the stench, bring our guest up here. But fetch a sheet.' She gestured at the empty chair next to Urswicke. 'Yes, bring a sheet to cover that.'

The servant hurried out and returned with a strangely garbed visitor. Urswicke judged him to be fairly young, though older than himself. The man was dressed in shabby and deeply stained leather jerkin, leggings and stout-laced boots. He had night-black hair streaked with lines of white so it looked like the fur of a badger. However, what was most remarkable was the soft leather mask which covered his face with finely stitched apertures for eyes, nose and mouth. The mask was like a visor fashioned out of the costliest Moroccan leather, so carefully moulded it seemed to be part of the stranger's face. Urswicke stared as the man knelt beside the countess, lifted her hand and kissed her finger rings before rising to greet Bray and Urswicke.

'Good to see you.' The stranger's voice was soft, melodious with a slight lilt. '*Pax et bonum*, my friends.' The eyes behind the mask seemed to twinkle. 'I am so very sorry that both my comrade and I were unable to meet you at Walton-on-the-Naze but, as you know, we had to leave more swiftly than we would have liked.'

The man laughed, patting his jerkin, and Urswicke tried to ignore the fetid stench from their visitor's dirt-caked leathers. Bray simply coughed and pinched his nostrils. Their visitor seemed not to be the least perturbed as he sat down on the chair now covered by a sheet.

'You'd best introduce yourself,' Margaret murmured.

'My lady, I am delighted to. I was held over the baptismal font as Gareth Morgan but now I rejoice only in the title of my seigneur, Jasper Tudor. My name is Pembroke.' He made himself more comfortable on the chair. 'You have visited the principality?'

'I have been.' Bray gestured at Christopher. 'Both of us have been to Pembroke on the countess's business, a prosperous, fertile shire—'

'Not now,' the visitor interrupted, 'not while its God-appointed lord shelters in exile in Brittany.'

'Hush now.' Margaret lifted the small hand-bell from the

chancery table beside her and rang it. When the retainer reappeared, the countess ordered some fresh Alsace and a platter of small pastries. Once served, they all ate and drank, the conversation being rather desultory about the weather and the imminent approach of winter. Only when the platters had been removed did Margaret softly clap her hands.

'So gentlemen, I sit with three of the very few souls I trust. So let us listen to you, Master Pembroke. My friends here know your story about leading the battle group, your exile abroad and especially the horrors inflicted upon you. How you are a hunted man, indeed York has marked you down for total annihilation. May God deliver you from that.' Margaret raised her goblet in toast. 'You tell them in your own words what happened. Reginald and Christopher were meant to receive you and escort you safely into London. But, of course, that did not happen.'

'The countess,' Reginald declared, 'asked us to travel deep into Essex and be at Walton on the eve of St Edward the Confessor, with the further advice that if nothing happened we might well have to return on the following night, the actual feast day of that great King. We did not know the why or the wherefore except that a war cog would swing in close to the coast and four men would come ashore. We were to meet them and lead them safely into London for the countess's use. God knows why,' Reginald glanced swiftly at the countess, 'we were not given the reason.'

'Reginald, you know why I acted as I did. If you had been caught you would have been questioned, tortured. You know how it is.'

'We sheltered for a while in some ruins,' Urswicke declared, 'a ghostly place with its hollow, empty passageways deep in the wilds of Essex's lonely fields. We gave the lantern signal then moved into the sand hills to watch events unfold.' Urswicke paused. 'So what happened that night?' He demanded. 'You were hardly on the beach when those horsemen appeared as if summoned by a trumpet? Now I have learnt something myself since returning to the city. I have made careful enquiries. You know those horsemen were led by my father, the Recorder Sir Thomas?' Urswicke didn't wait for an answer. 'Apparently my father led his comitatus out of London the day before you landed. I met some of the ruffians involved in The Katherine Wheel, a

Cheapside tavern much frequented by those who work at the Guildhall. The comitatus, according to them, rode swiftly into Essex to a lonely tavern out on the heathland, close to an old beacon station which provides a clear view of the sea. They sheltered in The Owlpen, just after sunset on the night you landed. We too were waiting, hiding deep in the gorse on those sand hills. Good sailing weather,' Urswicke continued, 'and lantern light, be it from ships close by or from the coastline, can be clearly seen. Now we saw Oxford's cog draw close, its bum-boat lowered,' he gestured at Pembroke, 'but you know this better than we do.'

'We had a good journey from La Rochelle,' Pembroke retorted, 'sound, safe sailing to Dordrecht, where we sent messages to you, my Lady, providing precise details about the time of our landing and where.'

'Safely received,' Margaret murmured. 'Do continue.'

'We judged that we would reach the Essex coast either before or on the actual feast of Edward the Confessor. We honestly hoped it would be the former, and so it was. *The Glory of Lancaster* is a powerful war cog. Our passage through the northern seas was peaceful enough, though Oxford was wary of Flemish pirates in the pay of York. We slipped through the straits of Dover and closed in, hugging the coastline till we made landfall. We used lanternhorns to alert our friends.' Pembroke pointed at Urswicke and Bray. 'Your good servants, mistress.' Pembroke touched the mask on his face. 'The rest you know.' He continued, 'I could not believe what happened. We left the ship's boat, staggered up the beach and the horsemen were upon us.'

'Two of your comrades were captured,' Urswicke declared, 'you and one other, Guido Vavasour I believe, escaped. How was that done?'

'My friend, remember the moon was full, the light very strong, the horsemen milling about us. We fought back as hard as we could.' Pembroke tapped his leather mask. 'I truly think it was this. Horses can be so easily frightened by the unexpected. They were excited after their furious gallop and the violence which ensued. To put it bluntly, my face frightened them. I am sure that's what happened. The horses shied away, their riders tried to control them. In the confusion, a gap appeared. I fled through it followed by Vavasour. If you recall, he was a swifter runner than myself.' Urswicke just shook his head.

'Well, whatever,' Pembroke continued. 'We reached the sand hills. The loose shale along the banks made it easy for us to climb but not for any horseman. We clambered up and lost ourselves in that sea of gorse. Mounted men would find it nigh impossible to push their horses forward at the dead of night. Once scratched by those thorns, the horses would rear and throw their riders. However, you must have seen all this, you were close by?'

'We were.' Urswicke turned to face Pembroke more directly. 'And afterwards?'

'My friend, I have hunted by moonlight through thickly steeped Welsh valleys. Vavasour is no different. We could find our way forward. Both of us carried good coin. We parted. We thought it would be best to join the constant stream of travellers going into the city. An easy enough task. Vavasour went into hiding; perhaps he's with his brother Robert.'

'Robert,' Margaret intervened, 'is also a member of the Red Dragon group, although his name never appeared on the proscription list. He continues to hide in the shadows, a good friend and supporter, a man with keen wits who has successfully avoided any ensnarement.'

'So you hid?' Urswicke demanded.

'You are quite the interrogator, Master Urswicke?'

'My name is Christopher.'

'And my question still stands, sir?'

'I am just curious, mystified by events. I mean,' Urswicke leaned forward, glancing quickly at the countess, 'I am deeply surprised at how my esteemed father seemed to know the exact date, the precise time and the actual location of your landing. Not only was Sir Thomas acutely aware of what was happening, but so were those two war cogs which came sailing over the horizon. And, in the end,' Urswicke spread his hands, 'on that particular night the countess's plans were seriously disrupted in such a short space of time. Nor must we forget the six unfortunates who lost their lives: the rowers of that boat and your two companions.'

'True, true,' Margaret agreed. 'But listen, Christopher. First,

Oxford's ship *The Glory of Lancaster* is well known. Fishing smacks, herring boats and other crafts would have kept him under sharp scrutiny. Secondly,' she sighed, 'I might be to blame . . .'

'Mistress?'

'Well, once the members of the Red Dragon Battle Group found sanctuary in churches across London, I visited them. I have that right: their lord is a close kinsman of mine whilst even prisoners awaiting execution can receive visitors. And, of course, I could dispense charity, alms, if not to them, at least to the different parishes providing such former servants shelter and sustenance. Naturally, I met each of the sanctuary men. I spent a day, the very same you and Reginald left London for Walton. I was desperate to give these loyal retainers some hope: whispering swiftly in parables, I told them that Pembroke and three of their party would be making a landfall in Essex within a few days. I informed them of the date, the place and the hour. I trusted all of these men. They had fought valiantly for our house. Yes Pembroke?'

The masked visitor nodded vigorously.

'One or more of these may be the traitor,' Bray murmured. 'If one of them did betray us, they certainly had time enough to inform the Guildhall so the Yorkist lords could despatch a comitatus into Essex. Pride of place,' he added, 'was given to your father, Christopher. He must be the guiding hand in all of this.'

Urswicke could only stare bleakly at his mistress.

'We are all trapped, caught out by the traitor within,' the countess whispered. 'And now Jacob Cromart has been murdered.'

'Who was he?' Urswicke turned to Pembroke. 'I mean, you were his comrade. You probably knew him better than any of us here?'

'A mailed clerk. A true warrior. Jacob was highly skilled in ciphers, secret messages, and all the hidden tricks and clever devices of the chancery. I needed to speak to him. When I returned to London, I bided my time. I found my own hiding place and sirs, with all due respect, I would prefer to keep its whereabouts secret, even more so because of this enemy within.'

'What business did you have with him?'

'My business, Master Christopher.'

'So who would kill Cromart? I mean, if it was one of his comrades they would have to leave sanctuary.'

'London teems with paid assassins,' Bray declared, pulling himself up in his chair. 'One, two or even a legion of them could be hired, though the real responsibility lies with York. Such an explanation is logical. Our enemies have removed a prominent clerk, a fervent adherent of the House of Tudor.'

'But if they are accused,' Urswicke replied, 'that would be highly embarrassing. If the Bishop of London discovered who was responsible; he, she or they, however powerful they may be or whoever patronises them, would incur the full wrath of Holy Mother Church, excommunication with bell, book and candle.'

'Aye, and that's the rub.' Margaret dabbed her mouth with a napkin. 'Allegations are one thing, proof is another.'

'Yes, yes, I agree,' Urswicke replied. 'Mistress, you told us that Cromart's belt had been stolen?'

'Ah,' Pembroke declared, 'my Lady, you have told them about the cipher?'

'My friend, I have.' Margaret again lowered her head, refusing to meet Urswicke's gaze.

'So, it's this cipher the assassin is looking for? Mistress, don't you know who holds it?'

'Christopher, the cipher exists, but God only knows if it's held by one of the Red Dragon Battle Group or someone else.'

'Do you know?' Urswicke turned back to Pembroke.

'No, I do not. But, my Lady, we must alert my other comrades, otherwise their sanctuaries will become coffin chambers, housing nothing but their murdered remains.'

'That could be very dangerous for you,' Urswicke retorted. 'Where you stay can remain a mystery, but surely you attract dangerous attention with that mask?'

'Not with this one,' Pembroke replied, bending down to open the small sack he'd brought with him. He drew out a crudely devised satyr mask and placed this over the mask he always wore. Urswicke smiled, Bray softly clapped his hands.

'We put on masks,' Urswicke declared, 'to face other masks. But you use one to hide the other.'

'Easy enough.' Pembroke put the mask back into the sack.

'Once I leave here, I am a member of the honourable Guild of Dung Collectors who, as you know, wear such masks to protect their faces as well as to proclaim who they are! How many of you would willingly approach a dung collector reeking of filth. No, no, we are left well alone. I have my barrow, my shovel and I can move around streets without let or hindrance.'

'True, true.' Urswicke smiled at his visitor. 'A man of great cunning, Pembroke. No one would ever suspect you.'

'To hide in full sight,' Margaret declared, 'to hide in full sight,' she repeated, 'one of my maxims because it always proves successful.'

'My Lady,' Pembroke patted his leather jerkin, 'gentlemen, my comrades sheltering in other churches must be warned.'

'They have been already,' Margaret replied. 'I have a trusted courier, a messenger and well-known member of my household. Fleetfoot.'

'Ah yes,' Urswicke declared. 'Well named. Swift and cunning as any lurcher . . .'

'He was once a member of a mummers' guild.' The countess smiled. 'A master of disguise. Fleetfoot has been busy on my behalf. He has visited the other five sanctuary men and informed them of Cromart's mysterious slaying. But, rest assured Master Pembroke, my two henchmen here must also help in the preparations for our departure.'

'And you,' Urswicke demanded, 'Master Pembroke, you cannot continue to hide. There is no profit in it for you?'

'I certainly don't intend to.' Pembroke's voice became mocking. 'Indeed, I am going to seek sanctuary myself at St Michael's. And why not? Parson Austin is friendly to me, very well disposed. You have told them about my former life, mistress?'

'Of course.'

'I will be safe there.' Pembroke patted his jerkin. 'The good parson will keep special vigil over me. And, who knows, I may have words with Ratstail, discover anything I can about Cromart's death. But I won't do this immediately. Once tomorrow has come and gone, I will become a sanctuary man. But first, I intend to watch Zeigler hang on the great gibbet over Tyburn stream.'

'What!'

'Oh yes, Master Christopher, the monster responsible for this.'

Pembroke touched his mask with his gloved fingers. 'Zeigler, that horror from the very bowels of Hell, will be strangled tomorrow morning. I intend to be as close as possible to watch the very last beat of his heart.'

'How is this?' Bray leaned forward. 'I understand Zeigler was a Yorkist captain who enjoyed an infamous reputation for ferocious cruelty?'

'Once the war ended,' Pembroke retorted, 'Zeigler was freed of his indentures. He drifted into the city as a freebooter, a mercenary. He joined a gang of rifflers who, quite recently, attempted to plunder a warehouse in Queenhithe. During the attack two watchmen were killed. Zeigler was captured, summarily tried before the justices at the Guildhall, found guilty and sentenced to hang. He is, at present, languishing in Newgate, but his execution is tomorrow. I will watch him choke to death then I will take refuge in St Michael's.'

'And you think you will be safe there?' Urswicke demanded.

Pembroke rose to his feet. 'As I said, perhaps I can discover something during my stay in St Michael's. After all, it won't be for long, we are to leave soon for the coast. So,' he extended a gloved hand for Urswicke and Bray to clasp, 'God willing, we shall meet again just before the Angelus bell in the courtyard of All Hallows by the Tower.' Pembroke bowed and left, Urswicke closing the door behind him.

'Now there goes a strange soul, a man with no face so what of his heart?'

'Full of loyalty to me and mine, Christopher,' the countess replied. 'A man who seethes with hate for York and all his works.' Margaret abruptly rose and Urswicke wondered why his mistress was so agitated and distracted. In fact, she had been for days before she despatched them into Essex. She had just confided in them, showed them great trust, but Christopher believed she was still holding something back and wondered why this was, what business could it be? True, the countess and her son lived in constant danger and the threat and menace against them seemed to be closer and greater . . .

'It's time we left as well.' Bray rose and picked up his cloak and warbelt. Urswicke did likewise. He was fastening them on when the door was flung open and a maid, all a fluster, her white face framed by night-black hair, bustled into the chamber. She abruptly stopped and stared at the two men.

'I am sorry, mistress,' she stammered, 'but I thought your visitors had left. A man came, a courier from the Guildhall.'

Margaret almost snatched the scroll from the maid's hand and peremptorily dismissed her with a sharpness Urswicke had rarely seen. The maid fled, slamming the door behind her as the countess broke the blob of red seal wax. She unrolled and read the scroll, crossing over to one of the glass-filled windows. She groaned and let the letter fall into the window seat.

'Oh Lord have mercy on us,' she whispered. 'I suspected as much.' She picked up the letter and beckoned her henchmen closer. 'It's from your father, Christopher. Sir Thomas Urswicke, Recorder of London, he will definitely escort the sanctuary men from All Hallows to Thorpe Manor. After that, they are to make their own way to any waiting ship. Secondly, Sir Thomas has, in his infinite wisdom, decided that not only will our five sanctuary men be escorted into exile, but certain other malefactors and miscreants will join them and so rid this city of troublemakers. God's teeth,' she breathed, 'your father, Christopher, is cunning! Only he knows what mischief he will arrange along the way.'

'It certainly gives him the opportunity to watch Pembroke and the rest,' Urswicke added bitterly. 'Heaven knows what spies and assassins will join our unholy pilgrimage, if you can call it that.'

'It makes sense, mind you,' Bray declared. 'I can see the cruel logic in Sir Thomas's decision. In his eyes, Pembroke and his coven are dyed-in-the-wool traitors. Your father would love to curry favour with York by annihilating Pembroke and his coven once and for ever; perhaps he plans to do this on the journey to Thorpe.'

'Mistress?' Urswicke queried. 'You have gone silent.'

'Of course I have, Christopher. I have made my decision. I must get a message to Adam Blackthorne, Archdeacon of London. Yes, yes, I will ask for his permission to accompany these sanctuary men across Essex to Thorpe Manor. After all, those who sought sanctuary were retainers of both my late dead husband and my close kinsman Lord Jasper Tudor. I doubt if Blackthorne will refuse. I mean no harm. I pose no threat and he will be the richer for it.'

'What happens,' Bray demanded, 'if we get these people safely aboard ship? If Sir Thomas has spies and assassins joining our sanctuary men, they will not be too happy at a long voyage through the Narrow Seas down to La Rochelle. Moreover, they could still pose a danger . . .?'

'True, true,' the countess agreed. 'What we must do is ask the master of *The Galicia* to keep a close eye on this cohort and let them go ashore at the first available port along the coast of France. So gentlemen,' Margaret rose, 'we are finished for the while.'

PART TWO
'See Fulfilled The Angel's Warning!'

U rswicke and Bray left the countess's riverside mansion. Cloaked and hooded, hands not far from the hilts of their swords, they pushed their way through the surging city crowds. Despite the weather with all the signs of approaching winter, the streets were thronged with sellers and buyers as well as those who flocked through the city gates for a day's distraction. The dung carts were out. The week's trade was drawing to a close so as much filth as possible was being cleared from the streets in preparation for the day of rest. Cesspits, lay stalls and jake's pots had to be emptied. The filthy, reeking sludge was being loaded on to great carts which would empty their vile contents into the cavernous sewers close to the Fleet and Walbroke rivers and, if these were full, the deep-dug cesspits beyond the city walls. The stench was truly offensive and the nosegay sellers were doing a roaring trade so the good citizens could thrust their faces into the soft, wet herbs, a welcome relief from the reek of the streets.

Bray and Urswicke walked purposefully, yet wary of the swinging shop and tavern signs creaking just above their heads. They were also vigilant about the upper windows of the dwellings on either side and the rain of slops hurled from these into the streets below. People cursed and shoved each other for the safest path through this midden heap of sheer foulness. Merchants, guildsmen, prosperous priests and clerics garbed in taffeta, damask, thick furs and the finest leather, rubbed shoulders with bare-arsed beggars, whining whores and complaining cripples. Apprentices, hot-pot girls and boys, spice scullions and pastry patters threaded their way through the crowds offering trays of different foods. People bought items, clinking coins into the tray, ignoring the bailiffs whipping a meat-pie man who had tried to sell cat meat as the juiciest beef. Alehouses, taverns, beer booths and wine shops offered a range of different drinks. Tavern masters and their scullions bawled for trade, competing against the raucous din of the streets and the constant clanging of church bells. Others had flocked into the city eager to make a pretty penny. A conjuror stood on a plinth boasting how he could make his pet monkey disappear for a coin. The conjuror became involved in a furious shouting match with a city wit who offered two pennies if the conjuror could follow his monkey. Curses were exchanged, blows threatened, but the King's peace was strictly maintained. City bailiffs in their coloured liveries patrolled with clubs and whipping canes. Turnkeys led lines of boisterous miscreants, now sobered up after being doused in the freezing water of a horse trough. These peace-breakers, soaked and shivering, were being dragged down to the city clinks, gaols or stocks.

Bray and Urswicke turned into a crossroads where soldiers wearing the colours and insignia of York, be it the royal arms, the Bull of Clarence or the White Boar of Gloucester, milled about a three-branched scaffold. Apparently felons guilty of breaking the King's peace by rifling a merchant's house had been summarily tried and hanged. The dangling bodies still quivered, in their final death throes. At the foot of the scaffold friends and relatives waited to take the corpses. Others had also gathered: robbers hoping to snatch the dead men's belongings, pathetic though they may be. These shoved and pushed at the wizards, witches and warlocks who also clustered close as they regarded those who had been hanged, be it their flesh or their clothing, as a source of great power in their dark rites. A macabre nightmare scene. Urswicke just stood staring at the gallows as he recalled those two unfortunates, their bodies dangling on the gibbet at Walton. Urswicke plucked at Bray's sleeve.

'Come,' he whispered. 'Let us rest for a while. This tangle of streets has jarred my mind.'

Bray glanced at Urswicke and noticed how the young clerk's face had paled. Sharp of wit and keen of mind, Bray realised that Urswicke sometimes found it difficult to thread the streets of London. A dark maze, as he once called them, fraught with danger and the haunt of nightmare souls. On occasion, Urswicke would even panic, and Bray believed that such anxieties had now surfaced.

'Follow me,' he whispered.

Bray led his companion down a narrow street to The Rose and Crown, a smartly decorated tavern with a pillared entrance where a watchman stood on guard. He let them through into the sweet-smelling taproom; its beams decorated with white sacks containing meats and other foodstuffs so they could be dried by the smoke curling from the great-mouthed hearth as well as the savoury fragrances from the kitchen to the right of the roaring fire. A young spit-boy sat in the inglenook. Now and again he turned the spit and basted the meats roasting there with spices and herbs. Urswicke and Bray, their mouths watering at the savoury smells, took a table in the corner where they could keep a sharp eye on both the taproom and its different doors. They ordered a capon cooked in white sauce, with strips of crispy pork from the great hunk of meat decorating the spit, along with blackjacks of home-brewed ale. They ate and drank in silence. Urswicke, now much restored, leaned across the table as he cleaned his horn spoon on the napkin.

'Reginald, our mistress . . .'

'What about her?'

'Well, I concede her troubles have deepened. We left London some days ago. We travelled into Essex, sheltered there for a while before going down to Walton. Well, you know what happened. We returned to London to report nothing but failure. Our mistress is truly distraught. Two of her most loyal retainers have been executed. Two others fleeing for their lives, whilst another has been mysteriously murdered in sanctuary at St Michael's. More importantly, and indeed this is vital, a traitor, an assassin lurks deep either in her household or that of her kinsman Lord Jasper Tudor.'

'Or in both.'

'True, Reginald. And yet there is something else troubling her. I know that.' Urswicke paused and sipped at his ale whilst warning Bray with his eyes. Two dung collectors had wandered in, their faces hidden behind the usual grotesque masks. The men took these off and began to argue with the watchman who'd followed them in. Both men claimed they didn't care if they stank, they were hungry officials of the city and demanded to be served, only then would they leave. Minehost became involved and, during the ensuing altercation, two pedlars slipped into the taproom. Both men were young and shabbily dressed, each had a tray of geegaws on a cord slung around their necks. Urswicke ignored the dung collectors, who had followed minehost out of the taproom, whilst he closely scrutinised the new arrivals, the deep hoods on their cloaks now pushed back. The pedlars sat down whispering to each other. Urswicke's wariness deepened. Never once did these men look across at either him or Bray. Pedlars, wandering tinkers, were always hungry for trade, and would accost anyone, anywhere at the drop of a hat. He also noticed how their cloaks were bulky and wondered if both men wore warbelts beneath.

'Christopher? You were saying?'

'Oh, Reginald,' Urswicke shifted his gaze from the pedlars and smiled at his companion, 'our beloved countess. I appreciate she has sustained a grievous setback to her plans. I also realise that her husband, Sir Henry Stafford, lies mortally ill in their manor at Woking. But there is something else nagging at her, disturbing her peace of mind, fretting that great heart of hers. But what? Some other worry she has not shared with us? Is she being threatened? Does some great danger lurk close by?'

'Of course it does. I am sure Margaret Beaufort, Countess of Richmond, is never far from the mind of York. They would love to do her mischief but, to all appearances, she is a noble, lonely woman. She may act like a little cat but, in truth, she is a great lion. She walks a lonely path but, as for what troubles her?' Bray shrugged and got to his feet. 'I don't know, Christopher. However I must first visit the jakes.'

Urswicke watched his companion go. He lifted his tankard, swilling around the dregs of ale and glanced quickly across. Bray had left through a narrow postern door. Urswicke immediately tensed as one of the tinkers rose and ambled across to the same door. A short while later, his companion followed. Urswicke quietly cursed: his suspicions had been aroused and he should have shared these with Bray. He rose, strapped on his warbelt and slipped across the taproom. He quietly opened the postern door on to a deserted cobbled yard which stretched down to the jake's closets at the far end. There were three of these: those at either end had their doors flung open, the middle one was closed. The two assassins, and Urswicke recognised the tinkers as such, had slung back their cloaks and drawn both sword and dagger. They were waiting for Bray to come stumbling from the closet. They expected him to be fumbling with his points while trying to rearrange belt and cloak. A clever assassin's trick. Bray would be totally unprepared for the ambuscade awaiting him. He would virtually walk on to the blade points of his killers.

'Good morrow my friends,' Urswicke called out. 'How can I help you?'

Both assassins spun round, going into a half crouch, shuffling forward, sword and dagger out. They separated, one from the other as they edged forward in that macabre dance of professional street fighters, veteran dagger men. Urswicke adopted the same stance, closely watching his opponents. The one on his left seemed to be the most aggressive. Urswicke darted forward, sword blade flickering, dagger ready for when they closed. His assassin blocked the parry and moved slightly away. The other assassin was now creeping closer. Suddenly the door to the jakes was flung open and Bray, realising what was happening, charged out, weapons at the ready. The assailant to Urswicke's right turned but then slipped and Bray drove his sword deep into the man's chest. Urswicke closed with the other assailant. He got beneath his guard and slashed with his dagger, a searing cut which deeply gashed the man's entire belly. The assassin collapsed to his knees, dropping sword and dagger as he toppled silently to one side. Urswicke and Bray immediately searched the belongings of both men but, apart from heavy purses which Bray and Urswicke immediately pocketed, there was nothing else.

'Hired killers,' Bray grated. 'Nothing to show the who, the why or the wherefore.'

One of the attackers groaned and Urswicke turned him over. The assassin was dying, eyes fluttering, teeth chattering. He gagged on his own blood as he glared up at Urswicke. 'It was not you,' he whispered. 'Not you.' He then shuddered, body trembling as he gave one last deep breath.

'What did he mean by that?' Urswicke murmured.

'God knows, Christopher, but let us leave as quickly and as quietly as we can.'

They left the corpses sprawled in the deserted yard and

slipped out of The Rose and Crown. Bray was his usual taciturn self. Christopher felt unreal after the abrupt, deadly violence of the recent affray. He gazed fearfully around. Surely other assassins lurked nearby? They must be followed, pursued by that host of enemies who quietly and incessantly threatened his mistress.

Now and again, Urswicke would pause and gaze back down the ill-lit, slime-ridden runnel, searching for some dark shape or darting shadow. Bray would pluck at his sleeve whispering that they were safe, yet Urswicke remained wary. The places and people he passed seemed unreal, as if in a dream; flitting images like dark clouds before his eyes: a whore being pilloried in the stocks to raucous shouts and insults. A bailiff playing his bagpipes as a woman stood in a pillory being pelted with muck and rotten fruit. Next to this, a tooth-drawer pulled with his pliers whilst his patient, tied to the chair, screamed in agony. A group of men-at-arms dragged a felon along the street, tugging at the ropes as if the man was a horse. The ghostly white faces of beggars and cripples touting for alms seemed to reflect his own fears with their popping eyes and gaping, toothless, red-gummed mouths. A lunatic danced frenetically in a tavern doorway, shouting abuse at a puppet master who was trying to stage the gruesome murder of a merchant in Lothbury. Shouts and cries echoed eerily. Chants and curses mingled, as did the different processions making their way through the streets: wedding parties, funeral corteges and the pompous rituals of different guilds as they processed all solemn to their favourite shrine. Urswicke's mood did not lighten when they reached St Michael's, a dark stone, ancient church, forbidding and sombre with its narrow lancet windows, crumbling cornices and crudely carved gargoyle faces. They went up the mildewed steps towards the battered main door. City bailiffs guarded the entrance. Bray and Urswicke showed their passes 'issued by the Chancery at the intercession of Margaret Countess of Richmond'. They entered the musty porch; Urswicke gazed around and shivered.

'A haunt of ghosts,' he whispered, 'and here comes its keeper.'

Parson Austin, thin and bony, his pallid face all puckered, came hastening down the nave. He introduced himself in a gabble of words, gesturing around as if the murky nave really did house a true menace waiting to spring. 'Never before,' he gasped, 'never before has this happened.'

'What, Father? What did truly happen here the night before last?' Urswicke nodded towards the crudely carved rood screen, its entrance now guarded by city bailiffs.

'I am concerned,' the parson wailed, 'you see these bailiffs, sirs, they will be gone soon. The Guildhall says they can't afford a constant watch.'

Urswicke nodded understandingly. 'But, Father, my question still stands, what did happen here?'

'Well, well.' The priest rubbed sweat-soaked hands on his black robe. Urswicke noticed that this was of the finest wool. Silver rings gleamed on the parson's fingers whilst the collar of the white shirt was of the best linen. A shepherd who looked after himself, Urswicke reflected, though, this was also the man who'd saved the hapless Pembroke from Zeigler's cruelty. The parson kept turning round. Urswicke touched him gently on the hand.

'Ah yes, ah yes.' The priest licked his lips. 'Well, the church was locked and bolted that night and, before you ask, sirs, my sexton accompanied me. He saw me turn the keys in every lock as well as draw the bolts.' Parson Austin led them back to the main door and the postern gate beside it. 'I held the key to the main entrance. I locked it and when the alarm was raised, the bell tolling the tocsin, I came in,' he pointed at the main door, 'through there. I confess I was all fearful but I am no coward, sirs. I served as a royal chaplain in the Duke of York's array.'

'Yes, yes I understand you did. We learnt from the Countess Margaret that you saved a Welshman from a bear pit. Some cruelty plotted and planned by a miscreant called Zeigler.'

'Ah yes him.' The priest rubbed his hands together. 'Zeigler was and is a great sinner. I am pleased to learn he has been taken up and lodged in Newgate. He's ripe for hanging and ready for Hell.'

'And you saving that poor Welshman?'

'God save us, Master Urswicke, you would have done the same. I was also accompanied by a cohort of Cheshire archers. Zeigler did not wish to clash with them. I did what I could. I drew the poor man out of the pit and lodged him with a leech,

a local wise woman. After all,' he smiled thinly, 'I am a priest,
I could not pass by.'

'Of course, but let us go back to the night Cromart was
murdered.'

'Ah well. I opened the door, locked it behind me and hurried
over here.' He led them over to the narrow entrance to the bell
tower. 'I went in to see who was tolling the tocsin. But . . .'

'The bell had stopped tolling?'

'Yes it had. A real mystery because there was no one, no one
at all, so I hurried down to the sanctuary. Ratstail was cowering
in the corner, Cromart lay sprawled in a puddle of his own blood
on the sacristy floor. I clearly remember checking the door
leading out to the jake's pit, it was both locked and bolted from
within.'

'Impossible!'

'Master Bray, I agree. All the doors were locked and bolted,
apart from the main one. There is no tunnel or secret passageway,
no hidden door here in St Michael's. So it's all a great mystery.'
The priest, still muttering to himself, led them down the nave,
through the rood screen and around the high altar to the place
of sanctuary in the apse. The ruffian whom Parson Austin introduced as Ratstail was a shabbily dressed little man with thick
uncombed hair and straggling moustache and beard. He simply
lifted a hand in greeting from where he sat on a stool in the
shadows. Urswicke glimpsed the mangled finger stumps of each
hand.

'That man,' he whispered to Bray, 'would find it difficult to
turn a key, let alone prime and loose an arbalest.'

Parson Austin, still whispering to himself, beckoned them
forward. They left the enclave of mercy and crossed to the sacristy,
a long, dusty chamber with tables down one side and battered
aumbries on the other. Parson Austin hurried to the far end. He
unbolted and unlocked the door, flinging it open so they could
see the tangled gorse and bramble of God's Acre. Urswicke
walked out and stared across the ancient cemetery, a sea of
wooden crosses and stone plinths hiding behind and beneath the
wild scrubland which seemed to cover this mournful house of
the dead. Urswicke turned and stared at the jake's pit dug into
an enclave between a buttress and wall of the church. He then

returned to the sacristy where Bray and Parson Austin were in deep conversation about the murder.

'According to our good priest here,' Bray patted Austin on the shoulder, 'he did the same as we have done now. He came into the sanctuary and around the altar. Ratstail, or whatever he likes to call himself, was cowering in the enclave. Cromart lay dead in the sacristy. More importantly, Ratstail knows nothing because he claims he neither saw nor heard anything amiss.'

'It's possible,' Urswicke tapped his boot on the floor, fingers playing with the hilt of his dagger, 'but let us see.' Urswicke went and crouched beside Ratstail. The felon peered back through matted hair, wiping his dripping nose on the back of his dirty hand. He acted frightened and cowed but Urswicke held the man's stare, catching the gleam in those cunning, narrow eyes. The clerk was not convinced of this man's innocence. Ratstail was a typical child of the slums. In his world, only one person existed, namely himself.

'What happened here, Ratstail, the night Cromart was murdered?'

'I was asleep,' the man grated. 'I have told everyone the same. I was fast asleep until that bloody bell began to ring loud and noisily. I awakes and up I jump. I was frightened. I shouted for Cromart. No answer at all. So,' Ratstail became even more excited, though Urswicke still suspected the man was a mummer and all this a mere game he played, 'I could not find him so I went into the sacristy then I saw him, he just lay soaked in his own blood. Of course,' Ratstail's shorn fingers fluttered to his lips, 'I was afeared so I came back here and crouched, waiting until Parson Austin arrived.'

'No, no, no.' Urswicke edged closer, glancing over his shoulder at Bray who was deep in conversation with the priest about the doors and windows to this church. Urswicke turned back. He pushed his face closer. 'Ratstail, I don't believe you. You saw a man lying dead. I suspect you are a sneak thief amongst sneak thieves. Didn't you go through his possessions, his wallet, his purse? Now, if I accused you of that, others would accuse you of breaking sanctuary, and where would that leave you? Eh?' Ratstail gazed fearfully back. Urswicke took a penny from his own belt wallet and held it up. 'All I want is the truth. Tell me it and you can have this, as well as my solemn word not to say anything.'

'I found him there. I went through his pockets but found nothing. See, it was missing . . .'

'What was?'

'Cromart's belt, he wore one of good leather, broad and finely stitched with a purse wallet and an empty dagger sheath. But sir, I swear this here in the presence of the Blessed Sacrament, the belt was gone and I did not take it.'

'Did you tell the priest?'

'Of course not! He'd only accuse me of stealing it.'

'And that evening, after nightfall, when Parson Austin locked this church. Did you notice anything amiss, out of the ordinary?'

'No, no. Cromart kept to himself. Though, on that night, he seemed very restless, complaining of belly pains but,' Ratstail shrugged, 'apart from that, nothing.'

Urswicke studied Ratstail's face. He believed the felon was telling the truth but he did wonder if there was more. Urswicke tossed the coin, patted Ratstail on the shoulder and rose to his feet. He walked back around the sanctuary where Bray joined him.

They thanked the priest and slowly made their way down the ghostly nave. Now and again, Urswicke paused to gaze into the murky transepts or to study the vivid wall paintings depicting Michael Archangel's constant battle against Satan and the powers of Hell. One scene caught his attention, two fiery-haired demons pursuing a soul along a deep, flame-filled gully.

'Pursuit and capture, Reginald,' Urswicke murmured. 'Just like us and all the mystery which surrounds our lives. We are about to enter our own dark valley.'

'Christopher?'

'Reginald, we have, God forgive us, just killed two men, albeit in self-defence. We do not know why they attacked us, though we know that this city houses a legion of those, great and small, who hate our mistress. Anyway, now we are here in this church where one of the countess's most loyal henchmen, a member of the Red Dragon Battle Group, has been mysteriously murdered.' Urswicke's voice dropped to a whisper. 'Ratstail has confirmed what the countess told us. Cromart's belt was indeed stolen, but,' he stared around to make sure they were truly alone, 'that is only part of the mystery. Why was it stolen? Is our assassin searching for the so-called Dragon Cipher?' Urswicke pursed his lips. 'How did the assassin enter and leave a church which, according to all the evidence, was firmly locked both within and without? Who did sound the tocsin? The assassin? And, of course, why was Cromart killed now, close to the day when he was supposed to be exiled from England? So many questions but one thing really puzzles me.'

'The involvement of York?'

'It's logical. Cromart was important, he may have carried the cipher. York would love to seize that, as well as kill one of the countess's loyal retainers. Is that why the assassin cloaked Cromart's murder in such mystery? To confound and confuse? Yes, that may be the answer. The finger of accusation can be pointed at York. However, for my father or anybody else, it's a case of much suspected and nothing proved. True, Archdeacon Blackthorne may be angry and suspicious, but there is no real evidence that York is responsible, apart from the mere logic of the situation. Nevertheless, York was running a risk, though perhaps it was worth it . . .' Urswicke broke off at the rising clamour from outside. The postern door crashed open and Sir Thomas Urswicke, Recorder of London, garbed in the finest livery of the Guildhall, swaggered in: the silver bells on the spurs of his brocaded riding boots tingling like bells to announce his presence.

'Christopher, my beloved son.' Sir Thomas took off his gauntlets and – his jovial, smooth face all smiles – extended his hand for Christopher to grasp: Bray he totally ignored. 'My beloved son. Despite the circumstances, so good to see you. I heard you were here.'

'Dearest father, I am sure you can guess why, and you?'

Sir Thomas tapped his boot against the paving stone until the bells on his spurs jingled. 'Do you know something, dearest son, I hate this benighted church. But come, our masters await . . .'

Urswicke made himself comfortable on the narrow chair he'd been ushered to around the fine oak table in the council chamber of the great White Tower. Next door was the Chapel of St John the Evangelist; this was the very heart of London's formidable fortress and the centre of royal power in the city. His father, who now sat opposite him, had been most insistent that his son join him. On their journey to the Tower, Christopher didn't even bother to ask his father how the Recorder knew that he was in St Michael's – those bailiffs guarding the church must have informed the Recorder immediately. He glanced across. Sir Thomas was full of himself, constantly preening, touching his chain of office as he smiled across at the countess who also had been summoned. Christopher had met her in the atrium below and she had warned him with her eyes to be prudent, quickly lifting a finger to her lips as a sign to say as little as possible and be wary about what he did. Not that Christopher would ignore such advice. He was now in a house of war where Edward of York slouched in his throne-like chair playing with the rings which dazzled his fingers, or touching his finely coiffed golden hair and neatly cropped moustache and beard. Standing at over six foot, a superb horseman and God's own warrior, Edward, with his golden hair, glowing skin, full mouth and merry blue eyes, certainly deserved the compliment of being the handsomest man in the kingdom. He was fresh from the hunt and dressed in a costly leather jerkin, leggings and cambric shirt, his silver-stitched warbelt slung over the newel of his chair.

On the King's left sat George of Clarence, who looked like his royal brother except his good looks were marred by a fat, red-tinged drinker's face, his full lips twisted into a perpetual pout or sneer, his blue eyes ever restless, which accounted for Clarence's constant finger-tapping on the table. On the King's right, next to Hastings, Edward's henchman and constant companion in lechery, sat Richard of Gloucester, the youngest of his family. Richard bore little resemblance to his two brothers with his lank, reddish hair, which framed a white-peaked face and wary eyes, although when he relaxed and smiled, Richard could be as charming as anyone. Both royal brothers were garbed like the King though, as with all who entered the royal chamber, they had to surrender their weapons and warbelts to the chamberlain on guard outside.

Urswicke stirred in his chair and glanced at the others. Gloucester's henchman, the effete-looking Francis Lovel, sat next to Clarence's constant shadow Mauclerc. This henchman from

Hell was garbed as usual in black which, in Urswicke's judgement, matched his soul. Mauclerc had a wolfish face, his slanted eyes ever shifting, his pock-marked cheeks and chin as cleanly shaven as his head. Mauclerc looked what he was, a true bully-boy who more than fulfilled the verse from scripture of a soul who feared neither God nor man. Mauclerc was now deep in conversation with Urswicke's father, though now and again those cruel eyes would shift to study either Christopher or the countess. Mauclerc would then give that cold smile and return to discussing troop movements with the Recorder, who seemed more interested in furtively watching the King.

'Mistress?' Christopher leaned closer to the countess. 'The weather is still good and messages from your manor at Woking keep us well advised.' Christopher spoke clearly as if in ordinary conversation. In truth, he was conveying a message garbed in a parable, that matters outside were under control whilst the so-called messages were both himself and Bray who would inform her later about what they had discovered. Margaret nodded in agreement and gently patted Urswicke's arm.

Christopher leaned back in his chair as the door opened and a cleric, garbed in grey-furred robes, was ushered into the chamber. From his days as an apprentice clerk in the Inns of Court, Urswicke immediately recognised Adam Blackthorne, Archdeacon of London, a priest with a reputation of being most hot-tempered. He was indeed a hatchet-faced cleric who zealously guarded and enhanced all the power, pomp and privileges of Holy Mother Church. Blackthorne knelt and kissed the King's fingers then took the chair offered to him. Once the servant had left, Edward asserted himself, clapping his hands and inviting Blackthorne to intone the '*Veni Creator Spiritus*'. The Archdeacon did so in a harsh, ringing voice, glaring at everyone as if he expected to be challenged.

Christopher kept his face suitably schooled and glanced around. The council chamber was opulent with gorgeous tapestries, gleaming oak furniture, silver and gold spigots, pots and vessels. Dozens of pure beeswax candles flared, providing light as well as a delicious fragrance. Urswicke, however, knew that sudden, bloody violence was only a breath away. Death lurked nearby, one shadow deeper than the rest and all the more frightening because of it. Christopher would never forget the blood-letting after Tewkesbury and the Yorkist treatment of the Lancastrian Prince Edward. That young man had been taken into a chamber like this, and drawn into an argument. The subsequent confront-ation had ended with the Yorkist lords gathering around the Lancastrian heir and plunging their daggers time and again into their rival's body. The same could happen here. Clarence was volatile and Gloucester would be quick to defend himself: their respective henchmen, unswerving in their loyalty, would be quickly drawn in. The Yorkist court was magnificent, centred around the King; courtiers basked in his smile as people would the warm light of summer. Nevertheless, a darkness could descend and close in swiftly to trap the unwary and unprepared. Even his mistress the Countess Margaret wasn't safe. Edward the King might have a softness for 'the ladies', but he would accept oppos-ition from no one. Archdeacon Blackthorne might gabble his prayers, but Urswicke doubted if the Holy Spirit could even find a foothold in this chamber.

Once the archdeacon was finished, a deep stillness descended. Edward drummed his fingers on the table top, staring around, as if memorising every face. He then visibly relaxed. He clapped his hands and welcomed them all, especially the countess and the archdeacon. Edward sketched the briefest bow to both of them then clapped his hands again.

'So,' the King smiled, 'to business. We all know about the traitorous and blood-seeking battle group calling itself the Red Dragon. God has annihilated that treacherous tribe of traitors. I understand only about seven survive . . .'

'Even fewer now.' Thomas Urswicke, full of smug pride, leaned against the table and stared adoringly down at the King who had elevated him to knighthood.

'Excellent!' The King chose to ignore the interruption. 'I understand, Sir Thomas, that we executed two of this brood at Walton, though another pair escaped, Guido Vavasour and Gareth Morgan, who styles himself Pembroke. Guido Vavasour, I under-stand, has now been captured hiding in the cellar of a tavern called The Hangman's Noose. Well named because that's where he will end up.' He laughed at his own joke, beating the table, nodding at the others to join in and they all happily obliged.

Christopher just smiled, trying neither to catch his breath or turn to stare at the countess. This was dire news. Urswicke knew something about this pair of loyal brothers. Guido Vavasour and his brother Robert were two of Margaret's most trusted couriers; men deeply skilled in both disguise and deception, they could mislead any pursuer with consummate skill. Loyal agents who could slip in and out of the kingdom and across the Narrow Seas in all sorts of disguises. Moreover, the two brothers never carried documents which might incriminate them, but memorised messages that they could faithfully recall. Guido had been one of the four who had landed at Walton; he too had escaped and, like Pembroke, slipped quietly into London to hide. So how had he been captured? And his brother Robert . . .? Christopher broke from his reverie as the King continued praising his 'good and faithful servant, Sir Thomas Urswicke'. The King paused as Archdeacon Blackthorne raised a hand to speak.

'Your Grace,' he intoned, 'the safety and the security of the Crown is the constant prayer of my master and the other bishops. We pray day and night for your prosperity and that of your family. We do not support treason of any kind. You are God's appointed King. However, this meeting is not to discover what banner these rebels may have followed, the threats they may have issued or the dangers they pose. No, no your Grace. Let us face the facts. Survivors, remnants of this battle group, have slipped into this city and sought sanctuary in churches across London. One of these fugitives, Jacob Cromart, was foully murdered the night before last in St Michael's. Someone not only committed murder, but did so in a church and shattered the protection Cromart had the right to expect. Whoever is responsible for Cromart's death has indeed committed a heinous offence.' The archdeacon's words hung in the air like a sword.

'I have assured your bishop, indeed anyone who has business with the church of St Michael's.' Edward's voice was now a lazy drawl, a dangerous sign, a clear warning that he was not to be confronted or opposed. 'I, the King, have told your good bishop that the House of York,' he gestured round, 'neither me nor mine, had anything to do with Cromart's death. You must remember, and even the good Countess will attest to this, Cromart may have been a retainer of this person or that but he was still an adjudged traitor. He was put to the horn and declared an outlaw to be killed on sight. Believe me, Master Blackthorne, if Cromart had fallen into our hands, his death would not have been so swift.'

'Very good, your Grace,' Blackthorne muttered. 'But your servants will pursue this matter? The Bishop of London demands certain answers. Sanctuary has been violated, a man cruelly slain close to the Blessed Sacrament. Sacrilege, blasphemy. The malefactor will be pursued?'

'Day and night,' the Recorder sang out. 'I assure you, Master Blackthorne, this matter is never far from our thoughts.'

'And the other sanctuary men?' The archdeacon purposefully ignored Sir Thomas's sarcasm.

'They are to be escorted to Thorpe Manor. A royal residence now partly derelict and desolate. However, the manor does provide some shelter and can be a place of residence. More importantly,' Sir Thomas smiled falsely, 'it's only a short walk from Thorpe to the coast. The sanctuary men must make such a walk where they will meet a bum-boat despatched by a Breton cog, *The Galicia*, under its master Savereaux. Countess Margaret, I believe both that vessel and its captain are well known to you?'

'Yes, yes. Savereaux is well regarded by Duke Francis and a man I trust, a most skilled seaman. I understand he has done service in many battles at sea. An experienced mariner, I am sure he will bring his ship in as close as possible. Once the sanctuary men are aboard, they will be safe.'

'Will they now?' Sir Thomas's question was just above a whisper.

Urswicke kept his head down. Savereaux's *The Galicia* was not only part of the Breton fleet but a cog which had already performed excellent service for Countess Margaret in giving safe and secure passage to those who had fled England after the disaster at Tewkesbury. Savereaux could be trusted implicitly, yet Christopher secretly wondered about the menace behind Sir Thomas's question. What was his snake-like father plotting?

'They will be safe, Sir Thomas?' Margaret seized the opportunity to wring a pledge from the Recorder here before both Crown and Church.

'They will be safe,' the Recorder murmured, 'as long as the sanctuary men keep to the established route, do not try to escape and observe all the rules and rituals laid down by canon law. If they do that, they have nothing to fear from us. However, if they choose to ignore what is clearly proclaimed, they will be summarily executed.' Again, the false smile. 'Let us hope,' Sir Thomas's good humour faded, 'indeed, let us pray that the sanctuary men observe our edicts so we can banish them for good from this kingdom.' He flailed his hands. 'Let us wash them away like dirt down a sewer.' The Recorder leaned across the table staring hard at the countess. 'They will suffer permanent exile on pain of death.' Sir Thomas Urswicke preened himself then stared down at the King, who nodded imperceptibly. The rest of the royal retinue, his two brothers included, murmured their approval.

'And I will ensure that these men,' the countess's voice was hard and brittle, 'observe all the rituals. Indeed, I shall accompany them.' She delicately raised one gloved hand. 'I do have some obligations to these men.'

'Madam, be careful. They are retainers of your kinsman Jasper Tudor, an attainted traitor.'

'My Lord of Clarence,' Margaret retorted, 'they are also kinsmen of my late and beloved husband Edmund. I do have certain obligations to them.'

'They are still traitors.'

'My Lord of Clarence,' Margaret half smiled, 'surely you know – we know – that treason is a moveable feast? What is treason on Monday can be something else by Friday. Times change, as do people. Do they not, my Lord?' She stared meaningfully at this royal brother who had blithely betrayed his own family, kith and kin on more than one occasion. The King put his head down, one hand covering the side of his face. Richard of Gloucester smiled coldly whilst the other royal henchmen stirred restlessly.

'Praise the Lord!' Archdeacon Blackthorne swiftly intervened. 'Madam, you have our permission to accompany your sanctuary men. But I will also send my own representative, Parson Austin Richards, parish priest of St Michael's: his church has been polluted by Cromart's murder and needs to be reconsecrated. The church now stands open and may continue to serve the parish, but Parson Austin was responsible for Cromart and he may wish to redeem himself by ensuring that the remaining sanctuary men stay safe. Moreover, Parson Austin has seen royal service: he is also most knowledgeable on the issue of sanctuary, its rights and privileges. You have no objection, Sir Thomas?'

'No, none at all.'

Christopher caught a look between his father and the King and wondered what mischief Sir Thomas was stirring. Charming, pleasant faced, courteous and amiable, Christopher knew that such virtues were only a veneer. Sir Thomas was as treacherous as any snake: a man who, in the spirit of malicious fun, had betrayed his nearest and dearest one by one. No one was safe, be it Christopher's mother, whom he tortured and abused with his constant dalliance around other women, or his relationship with his so-called allies at the Guildhall. If any of those posed a danger, Sir Thomas would strike and send former friends and allies to the scaffold without a second thought.

'In which case . . .' The Recorder rubbed his hands, staring down at the King as if searching for guidance. Edward just nodded. 'In which case, one final matter,' the Recorder cleared his throat, 'or rather two. The traitor Guido Vavasour has been captured, taken up and interrogated, we have told you this. We are also searching for Vavasour's brother Robert as well as for Gareth Morgan, who styles himself Pembroke. Both men may well, as our net closes in, choose to seek sanctuary, but we shall see. However, as I have already informed you, mistress, his Grace has also decided to clear the city churches of as many sanctuary seekers as possible. So when our cortege,' he smiled at his oblique reference to a funeral procession, 'gathers in God's Acre at All Hallows by the Tower, they will be joined by five other felons destined to be transported across the Narrow Seas. Your Grace,' the Recorder bowed towards the King, 'that completes our business.'

'I agree.' Gloucester's voice was hard and clipped as he pushed himself away from the table. 'We do have other business, pressing business which, your Grace, demands your attention and, indeed, most of those gathered around this table.'

'Yes, yes of course.' Edward spoke quietly, as if to anticipate and prevent any trouble. Clarence was already bristling with arrogance, puffing himself up like the peacock he was.

'Lady Anne Neville,' Edward leaned forward, elbows resting on the table: the King's mood, as was customary, had abruptly changed. He was no longer the charming prince but the warlord, a warrior King intent on preventing a bitter power struggle between his two brothers.

'Lady Anne,' Gloucester snapped, 'has gone missing. Five days now. She was,' he pointed an accusatory finger at Clarence, 'in your riverside mansion.'

'I agree, she was,' Clarence retorted. 'And then she disappeared. Lady Anne was seen cowled and cloaked near the buttery going out through the garden door. A brief description of something she did quite regularly. She certainly left and has not been seen since.'

'An accident? Some mishap?' Hastings, who seemed to be asleep, now stirred himself.

'Or abducted?' Lovel retorted.

'And why do you look at me, sir?' Clarence half rose, but then sat down again as the King beat upon the table.

'The situation,' Edward paused and took a deep breath, 'is clear to all, though it could give rise to misinterpretation. You, George, are married to Isabel, daughter of Richard Warwick. He died leaving no male heir, but two daughters. If Anne Neville does not, cannot plead for her inheritance, then Isabel, and that means you, dear brother George, inherits everything. Whilst you,' Edward pointed at Gloucester, 'my loyal and faithful brother, have asked for the Lady Anne's hand in marriage.'

'And the common allegation being levelled,' Clarence loudly declared, 'is that somehow me or mine are involved in Lady Anne's disappearance.' He glanced at Mauclerc, and Urswicke caught the fury in Clarence's face. 'Tell them,' he grated.

'We have searched the city.' Clarence's henchman shook his head. 'We have the lady's description, quite distinctive, golden-haired of slim, slender build. Our retainers have scoured the taverns, the alehouses, any place where she could be imprisoned.'

'As have mine,' Gloucester interjected. 'Nothing.' The duke's usual pallid face was now mottled in anger.

'Whilst I,' Archdeacon Blackthorne spoke up, 'have written to all nunneries, convents and any other cloister-communities demanding that they immediately report any attempt to intrude a young woman into their house.' He shrugged. 'Again, nothing.'

'Your Grace,' Countess Margaret demanded, 'I deeply regret Lady Anne's disappearance, as I do the hurt and division it has caused.' Urswicke could only marvel at his mistress's calm and reasonable response for, deep in her heart, the countess would like nothing better than these three brothers to be at war with each other. 'Your Grace,' she repeated, 'given all that, why have I been summoned here?'

'Invited,' the King retorted. 'Madam, you are our honoured guest, or whatever I suggest. There was the business of Pembroke and Vavasour and your presence was important because of that. As for this matter.' The King pointed at Sir Thomas Urswicke.

'The Lady Anne,' the Recorder declared, 'always spoke highly of you, Countess Margaret. In addition, we also know that you have many, how can I put it, faithful admirers across the city.'

'Men and women devoted to my late husband Edmund.'

'And his son Henry, now sheltering in Brittany?'

'You may well be correct, Sir Thomas.'

'In which case,' the Recorder continued cheerily, 'we ask you to use your good offices to make enquiries amongst them about Lady Anne. After all,' the Recorder spread his hands, 'His Grace the King has been most magnanimous in dealing with the matter of the sanctuary men, and his Grace will strive to sustain such favour.'

'Especially if you aid us in this matter,' Gloucester interjected. 'I assure you, madam, as I have before, you also enjoy my protection and good favour. I am anxious about your present husband, Sir Henry Stafford. Indeed I will do all in my power to ensure that, if that unfortunate man dies, I will work unceasingly for your welfare. So, do we have your support in this matter? I ask you bluntly.' Gloucester paused. 'Will you come to the assistance of this hapless, innocent young woman?'

'I surely shall,' the countess retorted.

Christopher glanced quickly at his mistress as he detected a hint of mockery in her reply.

'In which case,' Clarence declared, 'this present business is finished and we have reached an accord. Dear brother,' Clarence extended his hand for Gloucester to grasp, which he did, albeit reluctantly, 'I swear dear brother,' Clarence intoned, 'I swear by all that's holy that I have no knowledge of the whereabouts of Lady Anne Neville.'

Gloucester nodded in agreement and Edward extended both hands to cup those of his two brothers. Urswicke watched this drama intently. He wished Bray was present, to study and assess what was happening, but the countess's steward had been ordered to stay with other lackeys in the atrium below. Urswicke turned to the countess but she made no sign, lost in her own deep thoughts. Urswicke was genuinely mystified. Anne Neville had disappeared. Most of the gossip would point an accusing finger at Clarence who had so much to gain from that young woman's disappearance. Nevertheless, Urswicke was not too sure, watching that perverse prince, Urswicke was certain that Clarence, probably for the first time in his life, was actually telling the truth.

The meeting ended, the royal brothers deep in conversation with the Recorder. Straining his ears, Christopher was certain he heard something about what was happening below outside the White Tower.

'Come.' Margaret rose, proffering her hand for Christopher to take. 'My friend,' she whispered, 'this masque, this mummery is not yet over. Whilst we have been here, they have been preparing something for us. I wager it is not pleasant. Some threat, some warning, some menace . . .'

They followed the others out of the chamber and down the great, sweeping steps into the bailey, which stretched around the soaring White Tower. Bray joined them, slipping beside the countess as silently as a shadow, nodding at Christopher but then looking away, face impassive to watch the drama unfolding around them. The day was drawing on. A biting breeze blew rain into their faces. The royal party had moved to stand at the foot of the great execution platform erected between the Tower and the grey-stoned, grim-looking Chapel of St Peter in Chains. Sir Thomas caught sight of them. He raised a hand, smiled and strolled across, as if welcoming them to Yuletide festivities. Christopher realised that this stage had been set on their behalf. The soaring, three-branched scaffold, the noose dangling from one of its arms, the gibbet ladder resting against the main beam and the red-masked executioners. The hangmen, garbed in bottle-green leather, waited patiently at the foot of the ladder, holding wrist cords in their gauntleted hands.

'Vavasour,' Sir Thomas breezed, 'Vavasour the traitor is to be hanged, swiftly condemned by the justiciars. His Grace and his brothers wish to witness the well-deserved execution of a traitor who committed himself to the destruction and extermination of the entire House of York.'

'Tried and found guilty before the Guildhall justices.' Mauclerc, who'd followed Sir Thomas across, declared gleefully, rubbing his hands and gazing malevolently at the countess.

'God rest the poor man,' she whispered.

'Sympathy for a traitor, madam?' Mauclerc taunted.

'No sir. Compassion for another human being. But you wouldn't know what that was, would you?'

Mauclerc took a step forward, his hand falling to the warbelt he had just strapped on. Any further conversation was stilled by the braying of war horns and the ominous beat of a drum from the dark caverns beneath the White Tower. A door was flung open. The horn blowers, with the drummer between them, all garbed like the Figure of Death, came up the steps. This macabre cortege was followed by two of the hangmen's apprentices dragging a prisoner with ropes tied tightly about him. The man's hair and beard were dirt-clogged. As he came into the fading light, the prisoner raised his head, mouth gaping to reveal a bloody mess where his tongue and teeth had been. Urswicke grabbed the countess's elbow and steadied her as she whispered a prayer. Urswicke quietly cursed. Bray kept silent, just gently rubbing his mistress's arm as if this would dispel all these terrors. The countess called out. 'Guido.' The prisoner turned towards the countess; he opened his mouth to speak but could only make a chilling, rasping sound.

'Lord have mercy, Christ have mercy, Lord have mercy,' Margaret murmured, staring at the pathetic relic of what had once been Guido Vavasour, a jovial, dashing young man with quick wit, a prodigious memory and courtly ways. Guido, despite the pain of his shattered mouth, recognised the countess. He broke free of his guards and, before they could seize him, he knelt at the countess's feet, straining at the ropes around his chest. He raised his hands, bound at the wrist, fingers splayed to cover his face. He then repeated that chilling, rasping sound of a voice which could not be understood, of words that could never be formed. His captors pulled at the ropes but Vavasour still persisted, hands raised, fingers splayed, as if he wished to hide his ravished face, eyes gleaming frenetically between the gaps. Vavasour was eventually dragged away to the foot of the steps and pushed up onto the execution platform. Here the hangman freed the prisoner's wrists to bind his hands behind his back. Vavasour no longer resisted. He was thrust up the ladder, the executioner clambering alongside him to drape the thick noose over his head and tighten it fast around his throat.

Sir Thomas Urswicke had also climbed onto the platform and in a loud carrying voice proclaimed how 'Guido Vavasour, a self-condemned, malignant traitor, a malefactor, an outlaw who had fought under the treasonable banner of the Red Dragon and so committed himself to the destruction of our noble King Edward . . .' The Recorder spoke swiftly and, once he had finished, gestured at the drummer who began to slowly beat his tambour. The drumming rose to a crescendo and stopped. The hangman swiftly descended the gibbet ladder then gave it a twist, so Vavasour was left dangling and kicking in the air. The countess did not watch: she bowed her head reciting the 'De Profundis', whilst Urswicke watched Vavasour kick and twist until at last he hung still.

'So die all traitors,' the Recorder proclaimed, staring down at the countess. 'Such will be the fate of all who plot against our noble King . . .'

Christopher Urswicke stared into the dancing flames leaping so fiercely in the hearth of his mistress's bedchamber. He watched the logs split in the heat and the fire burn the small leather pouches of dried herbs so puffs of fragrant smoke curled out to sweeten the air. Urswicke eased his feet, now free of the boots which, with his cloak and warbelt, stood on a coffer behind him. He glanced to his right. Countess Margaret was still deeply withdrawn after that brutal execution, as well as the news Urswicke had related about the murderous attack upon them in The Rose and Crown, followed by their visit to St Michael's. They had left the Tower soon after Vavasour's death,

openly ignored by the Yorkist warlords: these clustered around
the Recorder, offering their congratulations whilst toasting
Vavasour's corpse with goblets of hot, spiced wine. Margaret
and her henchmen had hastened down to the quayside and hired
a barge to take them along the riverbank. They disembarked at
the water-gate of the countess's mansion and hurried up here,
silent and very subdued. During their journey, Bray had hardly
uttered a word, sitting in the barge, his sallow face laced with
sweat, lost in his own thoughts. Only then did Urswicke recall
a story that Bray had once been half hanged, the cord mark
around his throat remained hidden though the bungled execution
had seared his soul.

'Lord have mercy on his soul,' Urswicke prayed, wanting to
break the ominous silence.

'Why did they remove his tongue?' Bray abruptly asked. 'Poor
Vavasour. He must have been tortured in the dungeons beneath
the White Tower, a true hell-hole. I understand the walls are
decorated with pincers, pliers, hand-clasps and other instruments
of torture. They must have used those to shatter Vavasour's mouth.
But why remove his tongue?'

'A fitting punishment, or so they think, for the messages
Vavasour used to carry, as well as a filthy mockery making him
unable to plead. But,' Margaret crossed herself, 'now he's gone,
past all pain. God rest his soul. So . . .'

The countess leaned forward, once again welcoming Pembroke,
who'd arrived only a short while earlier. The fugitive had slipped
like a ghost through the water-gate. He'd been ushered up to the
countess's chamber where, with his boots and dung collector's
mask off, he now relaxed, stretching his hands towards the hearth
or, now and again, touching the delicately crafted mask hiding
his face.

'My good friend Pembroke,' Margaret declared, 'you now
know the fate of poor Guido. So, where is his brother Robert?'

'God knows, madam.' Pembroke straightened in his chair. 'He
and I move like will-o'-the-wisps; indeed it's the best way, the
only way.'

'Who do you think betrayed Guido?' Urswicke demanded.
'Who knew where he was hiding?'

'No one did,' Pembroke replied. 'Nobody in this room knew

where Guido lurked, or indeed, where I lie hidden, that's the way we arranged it. Vavasour and I would meet at a certain time in St Paul's graveyard near the Cross. If one of us didn't come, then fine, we would wait for the next time. Yet, despite all this,' Pembroke drew a deep breath, 'I concede York seems to know more than he should. There are whispers, Christopher, that your father the Recorder heads a secret chancery council, authorised under the King's privy seal, to receive and deal with all information about their enemies both within and without. Madam, they are hunting us. They have already inflicted great damage on the Red Dragon Battle Group. Only I and five others remain.'

'I agree,' Margaret sighed, drawing a set of ave beads from her belt pouch, 'and I have deepening suspicions about what might happen on our journey to Thorpe. The Recorder calls it "a cortege" and I wonder if it really will be a funeral for our sanctuary men. As for those others joining us, I am sure, as God lives, that at least two of them will be Yorkist spies. Our future certainly looks bleak.'

'Mistress, you may be correct.' Pembroke shuffled his feet.

'Speak,' Margaret declared.

'I went down amongst the dead men,' Pembroke referred to those denizens of the twilight who prowl by night and hide by day, 'I have drunk ale with the Vagabond king and his princes including the Vicar of Hell, the Parson of Purgatory and the Keeper of the Gates. You know who these are?'

'Lords of the underworld,' Christopher retorted. 'They rule the slums, the mumpers' castle, stinking cellars, and all the other havens of Hell where the city mob lurk like a ravenous pack waiting to break free.'

'They are all of one mind,' Pembroke declared, his voice thick with emotion. 'Lancaster is finished. Those of our persuasion who once hid now sue for pardon. Men are ripe for betrayal and treachery. York's spies cluster like flies over a turd. We cannot be sure of those we deal with.' Pembroke shook his head. 'You know that Parson Austin Richards once served in York's retinue and was well rewarded for it?'

'We have learnt that,' Bray replied.

'Ah yes, but did you know that Ratstail, that cowering,

frightened felon, is deeply suspected of not only being a sneak thief but an informant, well paid and protected by the Guildhall?'

'Sweet heavens,' Bray whispered. 'So Ratstail could have had a hand in Cromart's death.'

'Yes, yes I agree,' Urswicke declared. 'Hence the mystery. How could Cromart be murdered behind closed doors? Ratstail might have allowed the assassin to slip in and out. Who knows, Parson Austin may have also been involved.'

'Whatever,' Pembroke warned, 'I suggest both men cannot be trusted. Perhaps I will discover more when I take sanctuary in St Michael's. But, until I am ready, I will go back into hiding. Robert Vavasour said he would contact me when we met this morning. I told him that I would be here until the Vesper bell tolled. I believe it has. I thought I would receive some message from him but it would seem otherwise. It's best if I go.'

'You are still going to watch Zeigler hang?'

'Of course, Christopher.'

Urswicke stared at the eerily masked man and thought about what had happened since he'd landed in England. Urswicke recalled the beach at Walton-on-the-Naze, the moon-washed sea, the horsemen milling about, Pembroke and Vavasour fleeing for their lives, that's where all this mystery had begun. Now Vavasour was dead whilst Pembroke was in mortal fear of his life. No wonder he brought such dire warnings! Lancaster's cause had been grievously damaged.

Urswicke also understood the countess's deepening despair. Her son was in exile, her war captains either dead, imprisoned or, like Oxford, forced into exile. York was hacking at the very roots of Lancaster's tree. The countess had confided how the surviving members of the Red Dragon Battle Group were valuable retainers, men she could trust, yet they too had been reduced to nothing. York was hunting them like a ferret would a rabbit. Was it just the destruction of these retainers or something else? On their return from the Tower he had asked the countess if Vavasour and, more especially Cromart, might have carried the Dragon Cipher. But the countess had simply shaken her head. Urswicke wondered what was truly eating at his mistress's soul. She had become taciturn and evasive, almost as if she did not trust the world and himself included. Of course, the horrors she had just witnessed would only sour her mood. Yet there was something about that macabre masque at the Tower which intrigued him. Urswicke could not forget the hideous vision of Vavasour, fingers splayed across his face, forcing those heart-chilling sounds from his wounded, bloodied mouth. Why did Vavasour do that? What was he trying to say? Was he begging pardon, or for something else? Why was he so desperate? Urswicke stared around. Bray sat silent. The countess had her eyes closed, threading the ave beads as if reciting the rosary. Pembroke coughed as he played with a clasp on his tarred jacket. He tapped his feet as if ready to speak but paused at a knock on the door. The countess's new maid, Edith as Urswicke had learnt, opened the door and, timid as any mouse, stood rubbing her fat stomach which strained against the fustian gown she wore.

'What is it, Edith?'

'Mistress, a street swallow,' Edith paused to pat at her night-black hair, 'he left this for you.' Edith held out a small scroll. The countess rose, snatched it from her hand and summarily dismissed the maid, locking the door behind her. The countess peered at the small, honey-coloured scroll.

'The docket,' she declared, 'provides my name and dwelling, but this is for you.' She walked over and handed it to Pembroke who tapped the parchment.

'It's from Vavasour,' he murmured. 'Robert deliberately mixes up my name. Now I am Gareth Pembroke.' He broke the blob of sealing wax, read its contents and passed it to Urswicke. 'Christopher, you may find this interesting.'

'The Devil's Cellar in Darklin Street,' Urswicke declared. 'Robert wants to meet you, something urgent to impart. You had best go.' Pembroke rose to his feet. 'Gentlemen, do you wish to accompany me? I would certainly appreciate your presence and protection.'

Both men agreed. They made their farewells of the countess and left her mansion. There was no sign of the street sparrow who'd delivered his message and promptly disappeared. Darkness had fallen and, as they made their way through the labyrinth of stinking streets and runnels, Urswicke sensed how the city had changed to greet the night. This was the hour of the knife, the garrotte and the club. London's underworld had opened its gates to disgorge all the nightmare predators on to the city streets. An eerie silence had descended, shattered by the sounds of the night; dogs howled from their kennels, cats scratched and scrabbled at the steaming midden heaps in their frenetic hunt for the vermin who sloped dark and humped across their path.

Flashes of light illuminated dire scenes: a whore standing in a doorway, skirts all hitched; two urchins, skeletal and fearsome, one pushing an old man in a wheelbarrow whilst the other carried a clacking dish. A beggar fondling his dog and the watchers, silent as ghosts, men and women who waited, studying whoever passed. These hunters of the night were keen to seek a weakness yet wary less their prey turn predator. Strange, eerie sounds carried. Voices called. A child screamed followed by the drunken roar of some oaf. They passed gibbets and scaffolds where corpses hung naked and blotched. Foul smells polluted the air. At times, the runnels they passed down became needle-thin, winding between houses so ancient they now leaned over to close off the alleyway below. Urswicke felt as if he was going down tunnels into even deeper darkness. Few lights burned. Doors and windows were firmly shuttered. Sinister forms emerged out of the darkness but three men, fully armed with weapons drawn, proved warning enough and the shapes receded.

They reached a small cobbled square; on the far side stood The Devil's Cellar, a thin, narrow building tightly wedged between two derelict mansions. Nevertheless, despite its shabby appearance, crumbling masonry and flaking paintwork, the tavern's taproom was genial enough. A fire roared in the hearth and minehost was merrily serving ale and platters of hot food from the buttery table. Pembroke approached him. The taverner didn't seem at all perturbed by the mask. Urswicke glanced around and smiled. No wonder, he concluded, the customers who thronged there were all members of the Guild of Dung Collectors who now sat, masks removed, drinking and celebrating the end of a day's work. Pembroke turned and beckoned at his two companions. He led them across into the corner of the taproom and up a sturdy set of stairs to the gallery above, a long, gloomy passageway where only one lanternhorn flickered. The place reeked of urine, despite the pots of crushed lavender which hung on the walls either side.

'Robert's chamber is at the far end,' Pembroke whispered, 'it overlooks the stable yard.'

They went down the gallery, Pembroke leading the way. He knocked on the heavy door and, when there was no response, drew his dagger, beating its pommel hard against the wood. Again, no reply. Pembroke then crouched down and inserted the point of the stiletto into the keyhole. He glanced up at his companions.

'The key is turned. Something is very wrong.' Pembroke became agitated. 'If there is, God help us. We cannot stay long here.'

Urswicke immediately hurried back along the gallery. He went down to the taproom and had urgent words with the taverner, who turned to a square wooden frame hanging on the wall to the side of the buttery table. This contained rows of keys, each under a garishly painted number. Minehost chose one, shouted at two of his customers, dung collectors, bellowing that one of them should bring his mallet. They returned to Vavasour's chamber. The taverner inserted the key but was unable to make it catch. He pushed at the door but it held fast.

'It's locked and bolted from within. By all that stinks, something is wrong.' He beckoned at the dung collectors and, at his insistence, the one carrying the mallet began to pound the door whilst the taverner hurried down to the stable yard. He returned all breathless to declare how Vavasour's chamber had one small window which looked as if it was fully shuttered with no sign of any light. The pounding on the door continued. The dung collectors, taking it in turns, crashed their mallet against both the keyhole and the top of the door until an entrance was eventually forced, the door breaking free to hang loose on its leather hinges. The taverner had fetched and lit two large lanternhorns. Urswicke took one whilst minehost carried the other into Vavasour's chamber. It was dark, cold and musty. No candle flared, whilst the charcoal in the chaffing dish was mere dust.

The taverner raised his lanternhorn and moved deeper into the chamber, the shifting light caught the gruesome scene. Robert Vavasour lay sprawled against the far wall, head thrown back, across his chest and belly a dark blotch of dried blood which had poured from the crossbow quarrel driven deep into his heart.

A truly killing blow. Death would have been swift. Urswicke pushed himself past the taverner to squat and examine the corpse even as Bray, muttering under his breath, snatched the lanternhorn and began a search of the chamber.

'Nothing.' Bray came to crouch beside Urswicke. 'Nothing, Christopher. A few paltry possessions, clothing, weapons, but nothing of note.' Bray pointed to the dead man's jerkin hanging open. 'Look, Christopher. Just like Cromart, there is no belt.'

'Why should the killer take Vavasour's belt?' Urswicke glanced up at Pembroke.

'I don't know,' came the hissed reply. 'Perhaps the killer was searching for the Dragon Cipher.'

'It could be, or it might be something else. God knows how the assassin got in and left. That window is too small and the door was locked and bolted.' Urswicke made a face and stared around the chamber. 'A true mystery,' he murmured.

'We cannot stay.' Pembroke leaned down. 'Christopher, mine-host has to alert the watch. The sheriff's men will soon be here and I must be gone. I strongly suggest you do likewise. So, until we meet again.' Pembroke lifted a hand and slipped out of the room. Once again Urswicke and Bray searched both corpse and chamber but could discover nothing significant. The taverner came hurrying back to warn them the watch would soon arrive. The taverner was now not so merry but nervous and agitated, his fat face sheened with sweat. Urswicke strongly suspected that minehost had a great deal to hide, be it contraband in his cellars or some of his customers who would not wish to attract the attention of the sheriff's men.

'You'd best go, you'd best go,' the taverner wailed.

'Hush now.' Urswicke grabbed the man by his sleeve and thrust a coin into his hand. 'This chamber,' he demanded, 'had no secret or hidden entrance?' The taverner shook his head. 'And the window?'

Urswicke crossed to the shutters.

'Firmly barred,' the taverner declared. 'Open them, sir, and see.'

Urswicke lifted the bar, raised the hooks and pulled back the two wooden boards; the window they concealed was nothing more than a square gap, certainly not big enough for anyone to crawl through. Moreover, it was covered by oiled parchment which, despite the dirt strewn across it, stretched unbroken.

'The killer,' Bray hissed, 'must have come through the door.'

Urswicke picked up one of the lanternhorns and inspected the door, its lintel, hinges, lock and bolt clasp; the latter had been torn away, the clasp hanging loose, the bolt twisted. Urswicke kicked aside the shards of wood and other rubbish which littered the floor and crouched down to scrutinise the lock and its key. Both of these had been buckled by the hammer blows of the two dung collectors, who'd returned to the taproom for the free ale the taverner had promised. Urswicke continued his inspection. He was certain the door had been properly secured and sealed. The bolt clasp had been shattered loose so it must have been drawn across, whilst the key appeared to have been turned. Yet all this only deepened the mystery, for how did the assassin leave?

'Christopher,' Bray urged, 'we must go. The sheriff's men must not find us here. I do not want to be arrested on suspicion of being involved.'

'And yet we are, Reginald, deeply involved. Who is responsible for this? Who knew Vavasour was here? Pembroke only learnt it when we did. So what happened here?' Urswicke snapped his fingers, beckoning the taverner close. 'What happened here?' Urswicke repeated.

'Nothing happened here,' the taverner retorted. 'You see what I do. The man, my guest,' he gestured at the corpse, 'arrived in my tavern late this afternoon. He bought a stoup of ale and a platter of hot food. He ate and drank by himself. He hired a chamber. I gave him the key and up he went. After that,' the taverner pulled a face, 'nothing, nothing at all. He was no trouble. Sometimes they are. They get drunk and begin to smash the furniture or cause a nuisance, that's why I always hold a second key to each chamber. But this guest was fine. I saw nothing untoward. I've been busy, you see. The Guild of Dung Collectors assembles here. Today was a frenetic one before Sunday comes. The tavern's lay stalls, cesspit and jakes must be cleaned so my tavern smells nice and clean.'

'And this man had no visitors?'

'Not that I saw. I saw nothing, I heard nothing, and I know nothing about this man's death.'

'Impossible!' Urswicke glanced around the chamber. In truth, this was really nothing more than a sealed box: there was no entrance except the door and that had been securely locked. Nevertheless, the assassin, armed with a crossbow, crept in here to kill Vavasour. How and why was a mystery. Urswicke chewed the corner of his lip as he stared at the corpse: he'd met Vavasour before, a soldier, a skilled dagger man, so why hadn't Vavasour resisted? Yet there was no evidence that he had, and why was this?

Christopher Urswicke relaxed in his private chamber on the first gallery of his mistress's riverside mansion. He'd kicked off his boots and put his cloak and warbelt on a wall peg. He'd made himself comfortable on a chair close to the narrow hearth with Bray sitting beside him. Both men were lost in their own thoughts, staring into the fiery red coals as they searched for an answer, a way forward through the murderous maze they had entered. They had left The Devil's Cellar just a hop and a jump before the sheriff's men arrived. They'd kept to the shadows, hurrying along the streets to report everything to their mistress. The countess, her face all severe, had listened carefully. Once they'd finished, she'd raised her head, eyes welling with tears: she blinked these away and sat praying for the souls of both Guido and Robert Vavasour.

'Good and faithful servants,' she whispered. 'They will be sorely missed and how many more will there be?' She turned and stared fearfully at her two henchmen. 'How many more?' she repeated. 'God help us but are we finished? Is this where it will end? My son, a forgotten exile in Brittany and I, an ageing countess. So,' she picked up a psalter from the table beside her, 'dark thoughts, I concede. But leave me now. Leave me to my prayers.'

They quietly left the chamber, both of them wondering what the countess meant. Bray coughed and drew himself up. 'Our mistress's mood is like our own.'

'Little wonder,' Urswicke replied, 'Sir Henry Stafford is close to death and she is watched day and night by the House of York, even here. For all we know, Edith the maid could be in the pay of the Guildhall.'

'Oh I agree. The likes of Clarence would love to strike at her. But so far they have no evidence to indict such a well-born, highly respected lady whilst her marriage to Sir Henry affords her the protection of the Duke of Buckingham, with all the power and prestige of the Staffords. They cannot strike directly so they hunt those who support her, Cromart, Vavasour and the rest, including us. The countess is correct,' Urswicke paused, 'it's a matter of logic. They intend to execute or murder Pembroke and the rest of the sanctuary men. I am not too sure how many will reach Thorpe Manor or live to board *The Galicia.*'

'I agree,' Bray retorted. 'This murderous masque is reaching its conclusion. Our mistress's retainers are being slaughtered so why should the sanctuary men be spared . . .?'

'Very well, very well.' Urswicke's tone turned brisk. 'Let us be logical. First, York wants Pembroke and his coven utterly destroyed. My father the Recorder has taken personal responsi-bility for seeing these sanctuary men out of the kingdom in accordance with all the published protocols and procedures of canon law. Indeed, Holy Mother Church, apart from our own sharp wits, is the only defence we have. My father must not alienate the Church. Archdeacon Blackthorne, through his emis-sary Parson Austin, will watch what happens like a hawk does a wheat field. Parson Austin may well be in the pay of York, but he's a cleric and, I suspect, deeply fearful of offending his priestly superiors.'

'Let's pray,' Bray murmured, 'that Pembroke can safely watch Zeigler hang and afterwards reach sanctuary.'

'Oh I am sure he will. Pembroke is redoubtable, resolute and resilient. What concerns me is how my father intends to destroy him and the rest, for he has surely set his mind on that. But he can't do it here, not in London or Essex. So what happens?' Urswicke felt a surge of excitement. 'Oh yes Reginald, what happens if York's allies, God knows who, are waiting for them at sea?' Bray nodded in agreement. 'This game has been played out before,' Urswicke declared. 'De Vere's ship managed to escape but if they'd trapped and sunk it, that would have been a disaster. Now what happens if York intends to do the same again? Our sanctuary men board *The Galicia*, but they are never allowed to leave. Flemish pirates close in. *The Galicia* is sunk and all aboard are killed or drowned. Edward of England, like Pilate, washes his hands in public and claims to be totally innocent. Yes, that's where they will strike so we must, if we can, plot our moves at sea.'

'Is that possible?'

'Certainly! So,' Urswicke leaned over and grasped Bray's arm, 'let us describe the tribe of troubles which surround us. Primo, our mistress is deeply worried, concerned, withdrawn. We know some of the causes for this but, I suspect, not the full truth. Secondo, kinsman Jasper and her beloved son Henry hide in exile. They are safe enough in Brittany. However, if York can do them a damage, he will. They live constantly in the shadow of the axe, the sword or the poisoned cup. Tertio, the countess has her allies. However, most of these hide deep in the grass here in England or drink the bitter dregs of exile. Quarto, our mistress has, or had, a chain of messengers with her exiled son, envoys such as Pembroke and Vavasour; these are all links in a chain, former members of the Red Dragon Battle Group, and they are being betrayed or murdered. Cromart and the two Vavasours are proof enough.'

'Whilst their deaths remain shrouded in mystery.'

'Deep and tangled,' Urswicke agreed. 'Cromart was murdered in a sealed, locked church, Vavasour in a shabby tavern chamber. Quinto, who is this Judas man? We must not forget the intelligence we have received, that Parson Austin and Ratstail may well be in the pay of York. Did they collaborate in the killing of Cromart? Did they have a role in Vavasour's death? A shifting scene, Reginald. We are staring into a mist of murder.' He paused at a loud rap on the door and a servant entered.

'Master Christopher, there's a messenger from the Guildhall. He says he's been despatched by your father Sir Thomas.' Urswicke glanced at Bray who just shrugged.

'Show him in.'

A short while later the courier, wearing the livery of the Guildhall, much splattered with mud, walked into the chamber, sketched a bow, and handed Christopher the new woollen robe he carried and a clinking leather purse.

'What is this?' Christopher declared.

The man pulled a face. 'Gifts from your father, master.' The courier closed his eyes. 'Sir Thomas said you looked tired and dishevelled when you last met so he sent these gifts to ease your discomfort.' Christopher was on the point of refusing when Bray coughed, shaking his head imperceptibly. Christopher took the proffered gifts.

'Inform my noble father,' he declared, 'that I am grateful for his kindness and charity. Tell him that, as always, he has touched my heart.'

The man bowed and left. Bray crossed to make sure the door was closed. 'Beware of Greeks bearing gifts,' he declared, 'but in this case, the Recorder of London. Christopher, I truly wonder why?'

Urswicke put both cloak and purse on a stool, rubbed his hands and stood for a while, eyes half closed. 'I am suspicious,' he murmured, 'what does my noble father intend?' He gestured at the purse, which had a white rose crudely stitched on either side. Urswicke smiled. 'White rose, red rose, whatever rose, there certainly is a malignant canker at the heart of ours.'

'I agree,' Bray retorted. 'What we confront is shrouded in a fog of deceit and treachery. Your father sends you gifts. I would give everything I have to discover how your father knew when and where those men would land at Walton. I have been thinking, Christopher, do you think he had a hand in those two hired assassins who tried to kill us?'

'Yes, though what did one of them confess when dying?' Urswicke tapped his foot against the floor. 'What did he mean when he muttered something about the attack on me was not intended? Ah well, Reginald,' Urswicke pointed to the hour candle, 'we must sleep and rise early. I also want to watch Zeigler hang.'

PART THREE

'Oh What Fear Man's Bosom Rendeth'

All of London seemed to be of the same mind as Urswicke and Bray. Early next morning, after the Jesus mass had been celebrated, the great bell of Newgate began its mournful, hollow booming, proclaiming that a hanging was imminent and a sinner's soul was to be despatched to God for judgement. Merchants and their wives, garbed in furs, ermine and other fine fabrics, cordovan leather warming their feet and beaver hats and caps protecting their heads, gathered to watch. They moved in a shimmer of jewellery along Cheapside into the Shambles, the great slaughter yard and fleshers' market which stretched close to the grim, grey-stone prison. Newgate truly was a house of iron, with its narrow caged windows and well-guarded, steel-studded postern doors. Other citizens, shopkeepers and traders closed their stalls. They left their apprentices, armed with cudgels and clubs to guard their premises. These would be under strict instruction to watch the shadow-dwellers, the knights of the dark, the masters of the cut and the snip, the conjurors and confidence tricksters who now swarmed out of their reeking cellars and stinking dens, hungry for a quick profit. Beadles and bailiffs also thronged around the great stocks, thews and pillories set up before the prison. These officials, armed with white wands deliberately splintered, their pointed ends sharpened even further, moved amongst the multitude of miscreants, keen-eyed and ferocious as they hunted the sneak thieves and pickpockets.

Other groups had also assembled; the Guild of the Lost Souls, pious men and women who gathered on execution day, to pray for those condemned to die. Friars of the Sack, who had a unique apostolate to prisoners, chanted psalms or recited the rosary. All of these rubbed shoulders with a coven of warlocks who flocked to the scaffolds searching for relics for their own macabre rites. Of course, the cold weather, the frost and the biting breezes whetted appetites. Taverners and ale masters touted for business along with the wandering cooks, hot-pot girls and other servitors. All of these threaded their way through the noisy, surging crowd offering spiced meats, mulled wine and other refreshments. Urswicke and Bray, cowled, cloaked and muffled against the nipping breeze, pushed their way through to a vantage point where they could clearly see the massive iron-studded front of Newgate. The great bell had now fallen silent. The crowd waited patiently for the huge, soaring prison gates to open and the execution cart emerge on its journey to the scaffold over Tyburn stream.

Urswicke stood watching, distracted by the thoughts milling about in his head, eyes half closed as he recalled that sombre sacristy in St Michael's where Cromart had been slain. He reflected on what he and Bray had discussed the previous day. Had the parish priest and Ratstail been involved in that murder? Yet neither of these appeared to have a hand in Guido Vavasour's capture or Robert's mysterious murder in that tavern chamber. And would Pembroke be safe? Urswicke opened his eyes and took a deep breath. He must be more vigilant. He opened his belt purse and paid a chanteur who'd occupied a stone plinth in a fruitless attempt to entertain the crowd with stories about visitors from the mountains of the moon. The fellow cheerfully took the coin and stepped down so that Urswicke, one hand on Bray's shoulder, could climb up to survey the crowd. He reasoned that Pembroke, garbed and masked as a dung collector, would have risen early and secured a place close to the barrier which stretched up to the doors of Newgate.

Urswicke studied the front line of the crowd, the best place to catch a view of the notorious riffler before he danced in the air. Urswicke was sure he glimpsed Pembroke standing in front of the barrier where the prison cart holding Zeigler would pass on its way down across Holborn Stream and up to Tyburn. Urswicke narrowed his eyes in concentration. Yes, was that Pembroke? The dung collector turned his head and Urswicke smiled, it was his man! He then realised that Pembroke was not alone but accompanied by two ladies, both garbed in grey like nuns from the House of Minoresses outside Cripplegate. Both these women turned. Urswicke could not distinguish between them but Pembroke was certainly their companion, coming in between the two or moving around so as to converse with one then the other. Urswicke also noticed something amiss and felt a shiver of apprehension. The crowd was noisy and colourful, the air rich with a variety of smells and different sounds. People gossiped, prayed, cursed and laughed in a swathe and surge of colour. Yet a subtle change had occurred. Well-armed, battle-harnessed men, garbed in boiled leather with warbelts slung over their shoulders, had emerged from the nearby alleyways. Undoubtedly rifflers, they wore blood-red neckerchiefs proclaiming the colours of their particular gang.

'Rifflers,' Urswicke murmured, patting his companion on the shoulder. 'I suspect they are the same pack Zeigler hunted with.'

'In which case there could be trouble. Rifflers do not usually watch their comrades hang. I am surprised they have appeared here to be scrutinised and studied by the sheriff's men.'

Further conversation was stilled by further booming of the great prison bell, a chilling, sombre proclamation of what was about to happen. The iron-studded gates creaked open. The tolling became more incessant, the bell's clamour echoed by shrill, piercing trumpet blasts as the sheriff's men filed through the gate. Behind them, a group of executioners led out the death cart, pulled by four great dray horses, caparisoned in black, shiny leather. The cart, decorated with red-black ribbons, was in fact a huge, moving cage, capable of carrying at least a dozen prisoners, but this morning there was only one. A giant of a man, his head and face were completely shaven whilst he was garbed in a filthy white death gown. Many condemned men just crouched and cried, but not this prisoner.

'Zeigler the riffler,' Urswicke murmured. 'He certainly looks the part.'

Zeigler stood grasping the bars of the cage. He greeted the shouts and catcalls with his own litany of abuse. He spat, shook his fists and banged the bars. Urswicke watched the crowd. The rifflers, garbed in their red neckerchiefs, now clustered together like a shoal of fish, pushing their way through the mob close to the rear of the death cart.

The sheriff's men, no more than a comitatus of sixteen, were also growing alarmed. Some drew swords. The serjeant leading one of the dray horses came back to remonstrate with the growing cohort of rifflers who now threatened to surround the cart completely. At the same time, Urswicke glimpsed a dung collector, garbed in flapping leather, a mask across his face, reach the side of the cart. Urswicke was sure it was Pembroke, yelling curses at the prisoner who now ignored his fellow rifflers to pound against the bars of the cage and scream abuse at his tormentor. The growing clamour drowned what was being said during this furious confrontation. The execution party now turned, going up towards the Inns of Court. The cart slowed down then stopped and the red-garbed rifflers attacked. They swept aside the hapless guard and cohort of executioners. Four of the rifflers, armed with hammers and iron bars, battered at the door of the prison cage. Pembroke, realising what was happening, turned and vanished into the surging crowd, which now panicked as the violence erupted and spread. Urswicke clambered down and grabbed Bray by the arm.

'Let us leave,' he urged. 'There will be no hanging this morning.'

Later that day, Urswicke and Bray squatted in the sacristy of St Michael's. They sat on the floor, their backs to the great wooden aumbries. Pembroke, dirty and dishevelled after his hasty flight through the city, sat opposite.

'So you fled Newgate and sought sanctuary here?'

'Master Christopher, that's obvious.' Pembroke's voice carried a touch of laughter.

'And your confrontation with Zeigler?'

'A litany of curses were exchanged. I told him who I was. How I'd pay good money to watch him strangle in the air. He remembered me well, though he mocked that he could not recall my face.'

'And his escape?' Bray demanded.

'I understand it was successful. He must be hiding deep in a cesspit, some city sewer as filthy as he is.' Pembroke shook his head. 'What a pity! To watch him strangle would have been some reparation for the grievous wound he dealt me.'

'Aren't you suspicious?' Urswicke queried. 'I do wonder if he was meant to escape.'

Pembroke just glanced away and, despite the mask, Urswicke sensed the man's fury at what had happened.

'Will you pursue him?' Bray asked.

'How can I?' Pembroke beat a fist against his leg. 'How can I, a fugitive, a sanctuary seeker? I dare not go down amongst the dead men to hire an assassin. I just pray that one day I will meet Zeigler this side of Hell. But, as for his escape?' Pembroke shrugged. 'You both know, indeed it is well recognised, that prisoners escape, scaffolds and gibbets are stormed. However, I cannot say if the sheriff's men were involved in some conspiracy. I, I . . .' His voice trailed away.

'Tell me,' Urswicke urged, 'why did you seek sanctuary here? I have asked this before but, bearing in mind what has just happened,' he gave an abrupt laugh, 'Zeigler could very well come here.'

'And you have answered your own question, Master Christopher. First, despite Cromart's murder, St Michael's still enjoys the right of sanctuary. Secondly, as you know, Parson Austin saved me from Zeigler. He has a sympathy and compassion for me which I would be foolish to ignore. Thirdly, Parson Austin, I understand, is to accompany the sanctuary men to the coast and I am pleased to continue under his protection. Fourthly, if matters go awry, St Michael's stands by the river. It lies at the heart of a tangle of narrow runnels along which, if I have to, I could flee. You know how easy it is to get lost in such a maze. Finally, this is where my good friend and companion Cromart was murdered. I just wonder if he hid something here in a crevice in the wall, a gap between the flagstones – though, I admit, that would be a rare possibility.'

'And when you reach Brittany?'

'Gentlemen, let me first check that Ratstail is not eavesdropping.' Pembroke rose and walked to the door. He drew back the bolts and went into the sanctuary. He returned a short while later, shaking his head. 'This church,' he exclaimed, 'is locked and bolted from within. However, my good comrade Ratstail is certainly not someone who lurks deep in the shadows. He claims to have heard sounds. According to him, he went to investigate. He stood in the entrance to the rood screen, he is certain that he saw a shape flitting between the pillars along the north transept.'

'And?' Urswicke demanded.

'When Parson Austin welcomed me here, he personally assured

me that all entrances were sealed. He used the postern at the far end near the font to leave and enter the church. At my insistence, he handed me the key to lock ourselves in. Now, as far as I am concerned, when I safely reach Brittany . . .' Pembroke paused at a rapping on the sacristy door.

'Sweet heaven!' Bray exclaimed. He rose and opened the door. Ratstail stood there, all a-quiver, pointing back across the sanctuary. In the dim light Ratstail looked a truly pathetic sight and Urswicke wondered if such a witless creature could be in the pay of York.

'There is someone in the church,' Ratstail whined, 'I feel it. I see dark shapes. Master Pembroke, good sirs, I am greatly afeared.'

Urswicke rose.

'Let's search the church,' Pembroke murmured, 'then we will have peace.'

They crossed the sanctuary. Bray marched down the nave towards the main door and the entrance to the bell tower. Urswicke crossed into the murky transept. Pembroke searched the equally dark south transept, the only light being that piercing the narrow lancet windows along the outside walls. They moved around the church trying the devil's door, the corpse door and the ancient postern once used for lepers. Yet, like the others, they were secure, their rusty keys thrust deep into battered locks. Urswicke thought he heard a door open and close, but this old church constantly creaked, its timbers groaning as if they found the stone too heavy to support. Urswicke joined Bray outside the bell tower: his comrade had gone up the steps inside so Urswicke checked the main door and returned to the sanctuary. He went around the altar and almost stumbled over Ratstail's corpse. The felon lay sprawled in a widening pool of blood. Urswicke shouted for the others. He then crouched down and scrutinised the crossbow bolt embedded deep in the felon's throat, shattering flesh and bone it had gone so deep. 'And your purse?' Urswicke whispered. He quickly searched the dead man's ragged clothing and found his tattered wallet: this contained the penny Urswicke had previously given him, but also, surprisingly, two good silver pieces which Urswicke swiftly pocketed. Pembroke and Bray joined him, both murmuring prayers as they knelt beside the corpse.

'How?' Pembroke's voice was muffled by his mask which he quickly readjusted. 'How?' He repeated. 'None of us is carrying a crossbow and with this mask I would find it hard to prime, aim and loose one.'

Bray just shook his head in disbelief.

'Ratstail may have been telling the truth,' Urswicke declared. 'He believed someone was lurking in the church.' Urswicke crossed himself. 'Leave the corpse, Ratstail is beyond our help. Let us search this place.'

They did but it proved fruitless and, once they'd finished, they gathered before the rood screen.

'No weapon!' Urswicke exclaimed. 'No sign of an intruder or anything left by the assassin.'

'They will blame us,' Pembroke exclaimed bitterly. 'One or all of us. We are the only ones here. But look at me,' Pembroke beat the dirty, deeply stained leathers he wore, sending up gusts of reeking dust. 'Gentlemen,' he pleaded, 'search me, search the church. There is no weapon.'

'No need,' Urswicke replied, patting Pembroke on the shoulder, staring into the fear-filled eyes peering through the slits in the mask.

'A true mystery,' Bray whispered. 'There must be, there has to be another entrance into this church. What other explanation can there be?'

'There's no logic to it,' Urswicke agreed. 'We saw or heard nothing untoward. No click of the arbalest, no cry or indication of any resistance by Ratstail, yet he was murdered – why?' Urswicke demanded. 'Why was it so important to kill that pathetic little man?' He pointed at Pembroke. 'You say that Ratstail may have been an informer, a spy in the pay of York?'

'Ratstail was a master of deceit and . . .'

Pembroke fell silent at a rattling down the nave, a pounding on a door followed by cries and shouts. Urswicke excused himself and hurried down the church, the hammering came from the devil's door in the north transept. He hastened across, turned the key and the door was flung open as Parson Austin, accompanied by a group of men armed with cudgels, swept into the church.

'Good morrow, Father,' Urswicke stepped back raising both hands. '*Pax et bonum*. Why all this tumult?'

'Why indeed.' Parson Austin, carrying a morning star, a battle mace, stepped closer. He lifted the ugly spiked club. 'Being a priest,' he declared, 'I cannot carry a sword, but this will be defence enough against any mischief. Well,' he indicated with his head at the shabbily dressed men thronging around him, 'we believe there is mischief. Is all well here?'

'Ratstail has been murdered, a crossbow bolt to his throat.' Urswicke's reply provoked an outcry from the parish council, which Parson Austin stilled by raising his hand.

'And the perpetrator?'

'God knows,' Urswicke retorted and, beckoning the priest closer, told him exactly what had happened. The parson heard him out, nodding in agreement, gesturing at his parishioners to remain silent, now and again shifting his grip on the morning star.

'Ratstail may have been correct,' the parson declared. 'I was meeting my council in the parlour of the priest's house, its windows overlook God's Acre. Two of my parishioners glimpsed movement in the cemetery. It usually lies desolate but, according to them, a door swung open and closed. Perhaps it was the corpse door; they also glimpsed a figure running at a half-crouch through God's Acre. So,' he lifted his club, 'I donned boots and cloak and told my parishioners to join me. Ah well, I'd best see the corpse.'

Ordering his parishioners to stay where they were, the parson accompanied Urswicke up the nave. The priest nodded at Bray and Pembroke then went to stand over the corpse. Parson Austin sniffed then crossed himself before going into the sacristy where he put on a stole and took the phials of sacred oil and holy water from their coffer. He returned and swiftly administered the last rites, anointing Ratstail on the forehead, above his staring eyes and the corner of his bloodied lips. Urswicke watched closely. Parson Austin, he sensed, was certainly not what he appeared; the ageing, venerable, even ascetic parish priest. He carried that morning star like a veteran and, on occasions such as this, walked with the slight swagger of a seasoned soldier. Parson Austin, he reasoned, had been a man of blood. The priest glanced up and caught Urswicke's stare.

'A grim business, my friend.' The priest got to his feet and raised the morning star. 'You were watching me intently?'

'I was just wondering, you are a former soldier?'

'Master Christopher, you know what I am. I once wore York's livery. I served the present King's parents, Duke Richard and his wife Cecily, the duchess.' The priest's harsh face broke into an icy smile. He walked forward and clasped Pembroke on the shoulder. 'I left York's service shortly after I rescued my comrade here from Zeigler.'

'You call him comrade?'

'And rightly so. I relieved a soul in distress. I helped him to become his handsome self. Didn't I, Gareth?'

Pembroke, chuckling to himself, just bowed in mocking deference.

'And now Zeigler has escaped,' Bray declared, joining Urswicke. 'Rumour says he might take sanctuary.'

'Just a rumour,' the parson retorted. 'Tittle-tattle spread by Zeigler's criminal companions. I believe the villain will be hiding deep in the filthy shadows of this city. Ah well, I have a fresh corpse to take care of as well as a further report for Archdeacon Blackthorne. Indeed, apart from myself, I wager he will be the only one to mourn poor Ratstail, another soul slain in sanctuary . . .'

Urswicke and Bray made their farewells and left the church. Pembroke assured them that he'd be safe enough, though Parson Austin insisted that until Pembroke joined the rest at All Hallows on the following Monday, three of his parish council would stand guard in the church whilst others would mount close watch on all doors. Urswicke and Bray walked across to the lych gate. They were busy discussing what had happened when a dirty-faced Friar of the Sack, his ragged robes flapping, came slipping and slithering over the frost-hardened grass. The friar waved his clacking dish then paused to do a brief dance, moving from foot to foot as he extended his begging bowl towards them.

'Alms for the poor,' he whined, lips curled back to reveal blackened teeth. 'Have pity, good sirs. Just one penny for a loaf, stale though it might be?' Urswicke opened his belt purse. 'Oh do put the coin in, Master Christopher.' Urswicke glanced up in surprise. The friar pushed his face closer. 'Our mistress needs you.'

'Lord and all his angels,' Urswicke grinned at the false friar and turned to Bray, 'you don't recognise him?' Bray just gaped.

'Fleetfoot. It's Fleetfoot.' Urswicke studied their unexpected visitor from head to toe. 'Fleetfoot, my friend, you are a master of disguise.' Urswicke dropped the coin into the clacking dish. 'And this time you have truly surpassed yourself. I would never have guessed.'

'As those do who try to watch and follow me,' Fleetfoot murmured. 'They are truly confounded and confused. They wait for me and never see me. This morning I am a simple Friar of the Sack begging for alms. So sirs, give me another coin and I will be gone.'

Now Bray dropped a penny into the dish.

'And your message?' Urswicke demanded.

'Simply this. Our mistress needs to have urgent words with you in her secret chamber.'

'Why?'

'I simply deliver messages, Master Christopher.'

'What is wrong with our mistress?' Urswicke stepped closer, with another penny for the outstretched clacking dish.

'I simply deliver messages.' Fleetfoot raised his hand in benediction and walked away.

Urswicke and Bray watched him go then strode down the tangled runnels leading to the river. They hired a powerful wherry with six oarsmen and a tiller guide and clambered on to sit in the canvas-covered stern. The barge cast off, keeping close to the bank as its crew skilfully plotted their way along the busy river lanes. Here, fishing smacks, bum-boats, skiffs and other wherries fought the powerful current as the tide surged backwards and forwards. Banks of dense mist rolled and retreated, parted then closed again, to block sight and deaden sound. Beacon lights glowed in the poop and stern of most vessels. Vigilance had to be sharp and constant. The Thames was now a surging tide of ice so any mishap would be fatal. Urswicke tried to relax, peering round the canopy, staring out across the waters. Two Flemish carracks caught his eye; both vessels, formidable warships, were now coming in to dock at Queenhithe. Urswicke watched the great carracks turn, one after the other. If he served at sea, Urswicke would be most wary of such ships. The Flemings, despite the banners they raised proclaiming they came from this port or that, were close allies of York. In a word, they were pirates who often waged war on York's behalf, leaving Edward and his council to protest their complete innocence over any outrage the Flemings caused. He wondered if the two carracks now closing in on the quayside were the same ships which had tried to trap *The Glory of Lancaster*? Did their presence in a London port signify more danger?

Urswicke chewed his lip. Soon the countess would leave London, the sanctuary men going before her across the lonely fields of Essex to Thorpe Manor and then on to meet *The Galicia*. Urswicke realised the journey would be fraught with dangers, but once they took ship, what then? Urswicke sat back in his seat. The barge was now struggling against the turbulent river. To distract himself from the sickening rise and fall, the violent lurching of the wherry, not to mention the pervasive stink of rotting fish, Urswicke crossed his arms, closed his eyes and reflected on what he'd seen at St Michael's. The church locked and bolted from within, Ratstail sprawled with that ugly wound to his throat. Other memories stirred. Vavasour, fingers splayed against his blood-encrusted face, that horrid sound, the grunting from his shattered mouth. 'So much death,' he whispered. 'So much treachery.'

'Christopher?' Bray was shaking him. 'Christopher, thank God we are here . . .'

The countess still seemed very subdued and withdrawn when she met her two henchmen in the chancery chamber next to her bedroom. She sat in front of the hearth, Bray and Urswicke either side, and listened to their report. Now and again she would interrupt with a question or a muted exclamation.

'And here?' Urswicke asked, 'when we arrived your chamberlain and servants seemed cowed and frightened. I glimpsed Edith your new maid sitting at the buttery table all tearful?'

'Clarence and Gloucester visited me and brought their henchmen with them, a coven of real blood-drinkers. Mauclerc, in particular, is a violent wolf of a man. He is a killer born and bred. Christopher, you know that?'

'As I know that one day I will have to kill him.'

'A hard task,' Bray grated. 'Mauclerc is a man of blood to his very marrow. As our mistress says, a ferocious wolf in human clothing.'

'Wolves can be caught, trapped and slain.' Urswicke picked up his goblet and sipped at the mulled wine. 'What did they want?'

The countess simply tapped her brocaded slipper on the floor, lost in thought. 'Christopher, there was someone else.' She glanced sideways at him.

'My father?' Christopher felt his stomach lurch as he always did on those occasions when Sir Thomas and the countess were closeted together. Clarence and Mauclerc may hate the entire Tudor family but Sir Thomas? He dwelt in a deeper darkness. Christopher sensed that his father would like nothing better than the utter annihilation of the Tudors, and that he'd claim the credit for doing so. It was not just a matter of politics. The countess had supported the Recorder's lady wife during her most malignant last sickness. Christopher believed his mother had confessed things about her husband which not even Christopher knew. Matters which would provide a clearer view of the true nature of Sir Thomas's soul and the malice which bubbled there. Christopher also sensed that his father feared Margaret Beaufort, Countess of Richmond, but Christopher could never discern the reason why. Did Margaret hold information about Sir Thomas which would blacken his name and reputation in the eyes of York? Had Sir Thomas, when the star of Lancaster had risen so bright and powerful, wavered in his allegiance?

'What did they want?' Bray repeated Urswicke's question.

'Oh, they brought news about the fresh slaying in St Michael's and, of course, Zeigler's successful escape. I do wonder about that.'

'Mistress?'

'Well, Zeigler was a riffler, a dagger man, a bully-boy, but he was also York's bully-boy. I just wonder if his escape, flight and successful concealment were arranged by his former masters.' She smiled. 'But, there again, that's just a thought.'

'But why should York arrange that now? Zeigler was indicted, tried, found guilty and sentenced to hang. Why would York allow such a malignant to escape?'

'I don't know the reason, Christopher, I truly don't. Anyway, as regards the Devil of York and his two brothers, they are still searching for Anne Neville. They have virtually ransacked the city and even despatched couriers into the surrounding shires.'

'And they came to you for help?'

'Yes and no, Christopher. Of course they all hate me, my son even more so. However, they have reached the conclusion that Anne has been kidnapped and they believe this is the work of so-called traitors, adherents of the House of Lancaster.' Margaret stilled their exclamations, raising her hand for silence. 'My friends, don't be so impetuous,' she continued, 'such an allegation is logical enough. Anne Neville is the daughter of the great Earl of Warwick who died fighting for Lancaster. She is also a very rich heiress, or potentially so, a prize we would all like to capture.'

'Oh no,' Bray breathed, 'do they think you have kidnapped her? Abducted Anne to be sent abroad, even for possible marriage to your son? Is that possible, that they hold you responsible?'

'Well, they did not specifically accuse me,' the countess played with the ave beads laced around her fingers, 'they were more insistent that others could be involved, hinting slightly that I may know something and that, perhaps, I could be of more help.' She sighed loudly. 'Anne Neville is personable and wealthy: her disappearance is mysterious. But how could I do such a thing in plain sight of them, surrounded as I am by their horde of spies? Of course, they heard me out and replied there was no evidence for my implication in Lady Anne's disappearance. Gloucester, in particular, begged me to lend an attentive ear to any rumour, gossip or tittle-tattle about the missing woman. I replied that I would do all in my power to assist Lady Anne.' The countess half smiled and closed her eyes. 'Gloucester,' she said, straightening her chair, 'has asked for my help before. On a personal basis, I think he likes me, which is more than I can say for your father, Christopher. Sir Thomas sat preening himself, watching me like a fat cat would a mousehole. Then he made the most astonishing observation about why I had decided to accompany the pilgrimage, as he mockingly called it, to Thorpe Manor.' The countess sipped from her goblet and carefully placed it back. 'Sir Thomas implied, yes, perhaps even more than that, that I might be thinking, even plotting, to flee the realm, to accompany the sanctuary men and so eventually join my son in exile. Of course, I just laughed at such a suggestion.' The countess blinked away the tears which abruptly brimmed in her eyes.

'And then what, mistress?'

'Christopher,' Margaret leaned across and squeezed her clerk's hand, 'he said such a possibility was understandable. How my son lived in constant danger and that if something dreadful should happen to him, I would want to be there. He was hinting – Christopher, Reginald – that whatever promises Edward the King may give about the life of my son, young Henry cannot be protected against the lone assassin.'

'My father has a wicked tongue and an evil mind!'

'I recognise that, as I do his implied threat, so I shall tell you why my mood is dark and withdrawn. Ironically Lord Jasper Tudor maintains the same. He believes we have a traitor in our household and that this miscreant, with the full support of York, is intent on removing the only threat to the Yorkist supremacy – my son Henry Tudor. Jasper believes it's only a matter of time before this lone assassin strikes.'

'But Prince Henry is guarded day and night?' Urswicke said, then shook his head in disbelief at his own response. 'Concedo,' he murmured, 'what I say is of no help. We all know how assassins are trained in the use of the knife, the poison cup, the crossbow. But, of course, we could always strike first,' Urswicke hotly continued, trying to curb his anger against those who would dare threaten a woman who was so precious to him.

'And there's the rub,' the countess murmured. 'Of course York does not trust me but they have nothing to accuse me of. I am not too sure what moves they are plotting on the chessboard, whether they genuinely want my help or are trying to divide my household. Anyway,' she pointed at Bray, 'they look for any assistance I can provide in the search for Anne Neville. They have specifically asked for you, Reginald. When I leave for Thorpe Manor they want you to stay in London.'

'In a word I am a hostage,' Bray replied. 'If you fled, or even tried to, something sinister might befall me.'

'You may well be right but, be assured, I have no intention of fleeing. Stay in London, search for the Neville girl.' She laughed sharply. 'Much good will it do them. And there is a silver lining to this dark cloud, your stay is important to me. You and all those you pay will be our eyes and ears in this city.'

*   *   *

The riffler Zeigler made himself as comfortable as possible in the clean-swept cellar of The Dark Place, a comfortable two-storey tavern close to the river. Zeigler had fled there as soon as he was freed from the execution cart. The tavern master asked no questions but simply brought him down here, assuring him that the cellar was clean and Zeigler would be provided with all the usual comforts. Zeigler, frenetic with excitement after his escape, had demanded the services of a whore and, once satisfied, turned his attention to other matters. He had stripped naked, washed himself, then donned the brown woollen robe of a Franciscan friar that Joachim had brought. Zeigler now sat eating noisily, digging stubby fingers into a bowl of spiced pottage and taking generous gulps from a deep-bowled cup of wine the taverner had served.

'You are sure the whore can be trusted?' Zeigler spluttered in a spray of wine and food.

'You took her in the dark,' Joachim replied. 'And now she is in another cellar, sleeping off the wine I poured down her.'

Joachim, garbed like his leader, raised his goblet in toast. 'So you escaped, master?'

'I knew I would and now I am famous throughout the city.' Zeigler's piggy eyes, almost hidden by rolls of fat, gleamed in drunken satisfaction. 'Oh yes, we escaped,' he slurred, 'as I have done so many times.'

'Those sheriff's men,' Joachim laughed, 'they fled like coneys in a field, scurrying like rats down a sewer.'

'And so we are here.' Zeigler took another deep gulp of wine and stared around. 'I tell you, my friend,' Zeigler sniffed, 'I will be sorry to leave this city, its taverns, alehouses and brothels, but that is what our masters want.'

'It's been a hard season,' Joachim replied, 'a busy year, that fight at Tewkesbury, those blood-drenched fields.'

'I wish I had met him there.' Zeigler cradled his wine cup. 'I truly do.'

'Who?'

'Pembroke, of course. That malignant who hides behind a mask. If I had my way, and I surely shall, I intend to send Pembroke beyond the veil to join the rest of his treacherous coven. It's good to learn those bastards are being killed one by one. Pembroke too must die. I would love to drive my dagger deep into his throat.'

'And the others?'

'Oh yes,' Zeigler agreed, 'but did you see Pembroke, like some ragged-arsed urchin? He came to watch me die. A true coward who could act as brave as he wanted with me caged like a bear.' Zeigler laughed. 'Yes, like the bear I gave him to. I will hunt him down and I will strike. You saw those two women with him, yes?' Zeigler didn't wait for an answer. 'Mother and sister surely? Notice how they were garbed in the grey gown and white wimple of those pious bitches, the Minoresses. Well, they too must pay for what happened.'

'Master, Pembroke might try to hunt you.'

'He can't.' Zeigler laughed. 'Pembroke is now in sanctuary. What do we have to fear from him? I will take care of Pembroke and his ilk. I swear, Joachim, within the month, every traitor in the so-called Red Dragon Battle Group will be dead. I will kill them all. Yes.' Zeigler again drank from his cup. 'Then it will be home, but not before we make our fortunes in Brittany.'

'Master?'

Zeigler, full of himself, just shook his head. 'Joachim, I trust you as a brother, a true riffler like myself. A mercenary who has fought for York, yet I cannot tell you everything, but we shall be envoys. Yes, envoys.' Zeigler rolled the word around his mouth. He then laughed to himself, pointing at his henchman. 'Believe me, we are going to be envoys to the Tudor brat and, when we are accepted, we shall kill him.'

Reginald Bray made himself comfortable in the enclosed window seat overlooking the frozen garden of The Prospect of Jerusalem, which stood on the corner of Queenhithe quayside. He had dined well on roast beef cooked in a mustard sauce, a pot of stewed vegetables and a blackjack of strong ale brewed by the rubicund-faced tavern master. Bray had returned from All Hallows. He had made his farewells of the countess and Urswicke, solemnly promising that he would use the ever-attentive Fleetfoot as a courier between them. All messages would be conveyed by word of mouth or secret cipher. Bray had then watched the cortege assemble. Ten sanctuary men, shackled by foot and hand, squatting either side of the huge prison cart, a moving, barred cage with a small door above the tailgate. The prison cart was pulled by six massive dray horses caparisoned in the Guildhall livery though, at the countess's insistence, the carters were her own household, two sitting on the cart whilst a third walked on foot leading the horses. A dozen city archers were their escort under the command of Sir Thomas Urswicke. The Recorder, resplendent in his coloured robes, led the procession whilst Parson Austin rode alongside.

Bray had watched both worthies carefully and concluded that the priest and the Recorder appeared to be on the best of terms. The sanctuary men, however, were very subdued. According to the provisions of canon law, the churches they had sought refuge in had arranged for them to be shaved of all hair, both beard and face. The parishes had also supplied them with travelling clothes, a penny purse as well as a small wineskin and a well-baked loaf; the sanctuary men had eaten and drunk such sustenance immediately.

Bray approached the cart. He nodded at Pembroke, on either side of the masked man sat two of his comrades. Bray recognised some of these, individuals who had acted as messengers between Lord Jasper Tudor and his sister-in-law the countess. Veteran warriors, skilled mailed clerks, the surviving members of the battle group looked highly nervous. Bray could only lift his hand in a sign of friendship. He sensed their fearful wariness: their comrades had been brutally and mysteriously murdered and, for all they knew, they were on their way to secret, silent execution. They had no assurance that they would finish this journey or be allowed to board that ship and, indeed, even if they did, what guarantee did they have of safe passage?

After their last meeting with the countess, Bray and Urswicke had plotted every step of the journey these men would take. Bray was convinced that if danger threatened, it would definitely be at sea. He walked around the cart and stared at the other sanctuary men, a collection of thieves and felons, men who had been put to the horn and proclaimed as '*utlegatum* – beyond the law'. Despite their situation, these miscreants were of a more cheerful disposition, relieved to be free of their sanctuary enclaves and looking forward to freedom beyond the Narrow Seas. Bray had watched and waited as the procession left All Hallows, winding down the highway towards Mile End, Bow Church and then on to the road which cut across the fringes of the great forest of Epping towards the Essex coast. He raised his hand to the countess, who sat in her own covered carriage, and had a few parting words with Urswicke, who promised he would keep strict guard over their mistress, then they were gone.

'So let us reflect.' Bray leaned back against the cushioned chair, half listening to the faint sounds of The Prospect of Jerusalem. Shouts, cries, a scullion laughing in the kitchen, the soft music of a lute player, the murmur of three gamblers engrossed in their game of hazard and the shouts and cries of minehost and his scullions. Bray ignored these as he began to talk softly to himself, a mannerism both the countess and Urswicke constantly teased him about. 'The sanctuary men,' he whispered, 'probably include an assassin, a spy placed there by the likes of the Recorder. Nevertheless, Archdeacon Blackthorne will keep a sharp eye on proceedings through his envoy Parson Austin. Secundo . . .' Bray smiled as he realised he was imitating Urswicke. He lifted the blackjack and silently toasted his absent comrade. 'Countess Margaret has joined the cortege though she keeps her distance. The covered wagon she travels in is comfortable enough, with sound wheels, strong support; inside are cushioned seats, coverlets, provisions and chaffing dishes for the countess and her maid Edith. The carriage had been managed by her stable master, with Urswicke riding alongside. Countess Margaret,' Bray concluded, 'would be more than safe but the sanctuary men? York wanted them dead. 'Tertio,' Bray continued his whisper, 'the attack must be at sea. *The Glory of Lancaster* was nearly trapped trying to do the same as that Breton cog.' Bray recalled the two Flemish carracks he'd recently seen tacking into port. Often used by York, the Flemings sailed under their own colours. However, once they closed with their prey, they'd hoist the blood-red standard of war and the black banner of anarchy. So, what could he do? Never mind the Neville girl. Bray deeply suspected that all these issues would be resolved off the coast of Essex. Yet he had to stay in the city. He was undoubtedly being watched and followed along the streets. Bray sat supping his ale, wondering what to do next when he started at a knock on the screen door to the window embrasure. He rose, opened the door and stared down at the dirty-faced street swallow who raised a finger to his lips and beckoned him closer.

'It's a stranger, Sir Reginald.' The boy stumbled over the name. 'He's outside, he bears urgent messages.'

The street swallow turned and scampered across the taproom. Bray followed him out into the alleyway where a stranger waited, bold faced, his hood pulled back.

'Master Reginald Bray? Sir, if you would be so good as to follow me. Someone you know needs urgent but secret words with you.'

The man did not wait for an answer but turned and walked across to the mouth of a runnel. Bray followed. The stranger strolled into the alleyway then he abruptly turned, the dagger he had drawn cutting the air. Bray, his suspicions aroused, had already unsheathed his own blade. He feinted quickly to his left and thrust his dagger straight into his opponent's belly, cutting up before twisting the blade. The would-be assassin, mouth gaping, throat filling with his own blood, stood stock still before lurching forward, dropping his knife. Bray caught him by the front of his blood-soaked jerkin.

'You moved your hands too swiftly, my friend, and why should you put both of them beneath your cloak?'

He withdrew his dagger, struck again and let his attacker fall to the ground. Bray stared around. There was no one. The street swallow had disappeared. Bray rifled the man's purse and pockets but found only a few coins which he slipped into his own wallet. He then straightened up and walked swiftly down the alleyway.

'Yes, yes,' he muttered to himself, 'Reginald, my friend, it's time we disappeared, Master Fleetfoot will assist you. But first, we have a meeting with the hangman.'

Bray reached the iron-gated wall of Newgate prison and pulled hard at the bell hanging under its coping. He pulled again and again, listening to the harsh clanging till the postern door was flung open by the ill-kempt keeper who, by the look on his face, was full of fury and intent on mouthing a whole canticle of curses. Bray, however, simply pulled back his hood and extended his hand, which also held a well-minted piece of silver.

'My good Reginald,' the keeper grinned, 'how wonderful it is to look upon your face. You are most welcome.'

'My good Carrion-Crow,' Bray responded. 'I would like words with Tenebrae, the executioner appointed to hang the felon Zeigler, before the same sinner absconded to places still unknown. Hell must be disappointed, but the devil will have to wait. Tenebrae? I need to see him now.'

Carrion-Crow immediately became more wary. Stepping back into the darkness, he beckoned Bray to join him. 'A bad business,' the keeper intoned. 'Truly bad for business but, I can't talk about it. Tenebrae's your man.'

Carrion-Crow took the proffered coin, turned on his heel and walked down the passageway, a sombre, foul-smelling tunnel which seemed to be carved through a wall of rock. The stones above and below, as well as the walls on either side, glistened under their coating of wet filth. The lanterns did little to dispel the gloom. Cockroaches and a myriad of other crawling insects carpeted the cracked paving stones. The vermin clustered so thick they broke crisp and hard under Bray's booted feet. Rats and mice had made this their home. Cobwebs spanned every corner, stretching out like nets to catch their prey. The ominous silence of the gallery, a sinister stillness, was broken now and again by a shrill scream or some horrid invective echoing harshly through the darkness. They turned a corner. Carrion-Crow stopped before a bolt-studded door and clattered at the ringed handle until it swung open. Tenebrae the hangman, garbed completely in black, his capuchon pulled back, wiped his nose on the tattered shirt he carried in one hand and beckoned them in with the other. Carrion muttered something about being busy elsewhere and left.

The executioner kicked the door shut behind him. He peered at Bray and relaxed when his visitor held up a silver coin. The hangman gestured at Bray to sit on a stool next to him before a weak fire, its flames fluttering in the crumbled hearth. Bray made himself comfortable, refusing the offer of wine and ale. He'd vowed to never eat or drink in such a place, a filthy, sordid chamber with its dirty truckle bed, battered sticks of furniture and a heap of smelly clothes piled high between the two stools.

'The effects and possessions of those I have had the pleasure to hang.' Tenebrae grinned. 'Prerequisites of my high office, as our noble Recorder, God bless his trousers and all within them, describes these pathetic items. Well,' Tenebrae picked up a blood-stained pair of hose, 'their last owner won't be needing these, will he? Eh, Master Bray? I recognised you immediately, that's why I allowed you in. Steward of the countess, God bless her sweet tits.' He lowered his voice. 'My late brother fought for her kinsman, Beaufort, much good it did him. Killed hiding in a haystack. They pierced him like you would lance a fish.' He nodded at Bray's clenched hand. 'I will buy a juicy well-fed pike with the coin you are offering, but first, you want to buy something don't you? Certainly not this tawdry rubbish, so what?'

'You recall the morning Zeigler was meant to hang?'

'Yes.'

The executioner dropped the shirt he held, his face and voice more wary. 'How can I forget Zeigler? That dyed-in-the-wool son of Cain was more than ready for a hanging and fully set for Hell.'

'The escape was suspicious?'

'Of course. The sheriff's comitatus should have been stronger. Some horsemen would have helped but, there again, they were as surprised as I was at the number of rifflers who appeared. They reminded me of a horde of rats being disgorged by a sewer full of thundering shit. Remember Master Bray,' Tenebrae kicked the heap beside him, 'execution days are as common as fleas on a beggar's arse. The lords of the Guildhall simply under-estimated Zeigler's wickedness and the strength of his hell-born retainers. Zeigler escaped. Others, not many, have done the same.'

'Now on that morning,' Bray dug into his purse and brought out another coin, twirling it between his fingers, 'you do recall events? The execution cart left Newgate, people pressed around. However, on that particular morning, there was a man, a dung collector, his face all masked. He and his companions had fought their way to the front. This dung collector and Zeigler became involved in a furious argument, screaming curses at each other. The masked man, the dung collector, was accompanied by two women, garbed in grey as if they were Minoresses.'

'Ah yes, ah yes.' Tenebrae rocked himself backwards and forwards on his stool. 'I certainly do remember that. It's very rare for such an argument to take place, for insults to be exchanged. Usually it is loved ones clustering to make fond farewell.' Tenebrae licked his lips as he stared greedily at the coin Bray still held between his fingers. 'Of course it was obvious that Zeigler and this stranger, masked like a dung collector, truly hated each other.'

'And?'

'Well this stranger screamed how Zeigler had taken his face, whatever that means. And now, the masked man yelled, he was going to watch Zeigler strangle, that he would pay me to do it as slowly as possible.'

'Did he?'

'The masked man held a pouch up. I was at the back of the cart. I would have loved to have seized that purse, but by then I dared not move. The rifflers were surging all around us and, of course, I was frightened. If I took the purse and Zeigler was free, well he might have killed me before he fled.'

'And yet Zeigler and the masked man continued their tirade?'

'Yes.' He and the masked stranger were full of hate for each other.'

'So,' Bray flicked the coin at the hangman who, quick as a fly, neatly caught it, 'there was definitely bad blood between this mysterious man and Zeigler?'

'Undoubtedly Master Reginald but, after almost thirty years of war, men have grievances and grudges, a whole great cauldron of them, which they stir and stir: eye for eye, tooth for tooth, life for life. They invoke the blood feud and wage war against each other.' Tenebrae leaned closer. 'Look at our great ones, Master Reginald, John De Vere, Earl of Oxford, who has been offered pardon by our present King. You do know De Vere's reply?'

'That York killed Oxford's father and that he intended to never make peace with such enemies.'

'Precisely, Master Bray, you have it in one. So it is with Zeigler. Now his seizure and imprisonment here caused a great stir amongst the dark dwellers. You know he is half Flemish? That's his father, but his mother was Breton. Zeigler's father died early but his mother was seized and killed by freebooters who roamed the Welsh march; their abuse of Zeigler's family probably accounts for the man's horrid soul. Zeigler certainly has a special hatred for the Welsh and Tudor in particular.'

'And those two women?'

'Mother and daughter, or so I believe. Both garbed in the grey robes of lay sisters of the Minoresses with veil and wimple. They looked terrified but the masked man held them in thrall.'

'What more do you know about Zeigler?' Bray demanded. 'I mean as a hangman? You must listen to the tales and stories from the catacombs of London.'

'As I have said, Master Bray, Zeigler has Flemish blood. He is a mercenary well patronised by York. Indeed, I was very surprised to learn he'd been taken up, indicted and condemned. After all, he must have powerful friends both in the Guildhall and the palace of Westminster. What I do know is that don't be taken in by his bulk and bearlike ways. Zeigler is a street fighter, a true dagger man who has seen service both on land and at sea. He is also very cunning, not a master of disguise but he can dissimulate. One of his favourite games is to dress and act like a Franciscan friar, one of God's poor men begging for alms. He can become soft-voiced and dewy-eyed but he is still a demon incarnate. Now, he has a henchman Joachim, just as fit for Hell as his master. I glimpsed Joachim in the chaos surrounding the execution cart. I am sure that both of them are now safely and warmly ensconced in some rat-hole.'

'And the felon Ratstail who sought sanctuary at St Michael's?'

'Ah, our fumbled-fingered felon, now gone to God. Ratstail's hands were not as damaged as people think. He was still adept and skilled at picking a lock or purse. Ratstail was cunning, which is why he survived many a hue and cry. Indeed, he was most fortunate: others better than him have received my attentions at Tyburn. In the end, however, he still died violently.'

'Could someone like Ratstail have been in the pay of York?'

'Oh by the holy rope, Master Bray, Ratstail would be in the pay of anyone who gave him a coin.' Tenebrae then sketched a mock blessing in the air. 'And more than that, my esteemed visitor, I cannot say.'

Bray left Newgate and pushed his way through the crowds now milling across the blood-soaked shambles. The fleshers were still busy wringing the necks of geese, ducks, rabbits and other meats for the table. The air was riven with the terrified screams and final cries of these birds and other animals, the only real source of fresh meat during the winter season. The air was permeated with the distinctive tang of freshly spilt blood, the ground under- foot coated with feathers and discarded giblets, which a legion of beggars now fought over. Processions wound their way through the throng. Wedding guests, all festooned in their winter garments, singing, dancing and draining their deep-bowled goblets of wine. These mingled noisily with black-garbed, red-hooded funeral mourners who shuffled along behind different coffins, reciting the responses to the priest's constant plea for the dead.

Bray moved purposefully. He fully acknowledged he was being followed, if not by some hooded figure then by one or two of the flocks of street sparrows who darted along the narrow gaps between the many stalls. Bray felt an acute sense of danger. He recalled the two murderous assaults on him and wondered if these were all part of a well-laid plot to dig up and destroy the very roots of all those who supported Countess Margaret and her exiled son. Bray then wondered how his mistress and Urswicke were faring. As he crossed Cheapside, Bray glimpsed a finely carved statue of Our Lady of Walsingham standing on its plinth. He murmured a swift prayer to the 'Fragrantly beautiful Queen of Heaven' for the safety of the countess and those who served her. Now and again Bray would pause, as if to buy from a stall or listen to a storyteller fresh from Outremer chanting a tale about a strange creature which had the head of a hare, the neck of an ox, the wings of a dragon, the feet of a camel and so on. On this occa- sion Bray glanced around and caught two men at a nearby stall: they were studying him closely then quickly looked away.

Bray pressed on along Aldgate until he reached the grey stone convent of the Minoresses. He stood by the postern gate and pulled at the bell. The narrow door was flung open, a lay sister with a face as sour as vinegar looked him up and down from head to toe. She inspected his pass, sealed by the countess, before beckoning him in across the yard into the starkly furnished visitors' parlour. Bray was told to wait there and that the guest- mistress would be with him shortly. Bray had hardly settled himself on the narrow chair when Sister Isabella, as she introduced herself, swept into the room, all a-fluster at this unexpected male visitor. She sat down on a wall bench and peered across at Bray, her pallid face all wreathed in concern.

'What is this, what is this?' she exclaimed. 'What does the steward of the Countess Margaret want with us?'

'Sister Isabella, you have two ladies lodged here, Welsh women, their family name is Morgan. They were lodged here by . . .?'

'Alice and her daughter Beatrice,' the guest-mistress retorted. 'Been here for at least seven days. They were brought by their kinsman, a strange creature with a mask across his face. We never decided if it was to hide a most grievous wound or that he was what he appeared to be, a dung collector. Anyway, he said the two ladies had journeyed from their farm in Pembrokeshire. They were to lodge here until he returned to collect them.'

'And take them where?'

'Back to Pembrokeshire, I presume.'

'When?'

'I don't know. Master Bray, the masked stranger paid good silver, more than we asked. We take many lady guests here; they lodge in our convent and participate in our horarium. They attend chapel to chant the Divine Office and dine with us in the refectory. To ensure everything is appropriate, we insist that if they wish to share with us, they must dress like us.' She paused and smiled. 'God bless the two ladies, they are no trouble. They are as quiet and unobtrusive as church mice, which is rather strange because they seem to attract such attention.'

'Sister Isabella?'

'Well, Master Bray, you are here. Earlier in the day, just before the Angelus bell, two Franciscan friars, God's poor men licensed to beg on behalf of the poor. Well, they came here. One of them, the smaller of the two, stayed near the postern gate. Brother Damien, as he introduced himself, a great bear of a man, said he brought the most urgent messages for Mistress Alice and her companion. He was very charming, threading his rosary beads, praising our order—'

'And?' Bray interrupted.

'We escorted him to their chamber in the lady house reserved for our female visitors. In fact,' Sister's Isabella's fingers flew to her lips, 'I cannot recall him leaving, perhaps he is still there.' All a-fluster, the nun sprang to her feet. 'Perhaps yes,' she nodded at Bray, 'you'd best come with me.'

They left the visitors' parlour. A river mist had closed in to shroud the buildings, its wispy tendrils trailing across the pebble-dashed path they followed around to the guest house. They entered its welcoming warmth. Sister Isabella consulted the visitors' book displayed on a lectern. She then led him up the stairs, along the polished wooden gallery to a chamber at the far end. The door was on the latch. Sister Isabella pushed and swung the door open. She glanced in, then turned with a scream, a heart-chilling sound as the old nun sank to her knees. Bray brushed by her into the chamber to view the gruesome scene, two women flung back against the far wall to sprawl either side of the window. They lay like discarded dolls, their robes drenched in blood from the wounds in their chests, an arbalest bolt, embedded so deep only the stiffened feathers protruded. Sister Isabella scrambled to her feet and, hands waving, fled back down the gallery. Bray let her go. He swiftly inspected the corpses and stared around the chamber – panniers and coffers had been opened and searched. As the bells of the nunnery began to toll the tocsin, Bray expertly sifted through the documents and letters but found nothing of consequence. The assassin would have already combed whatever manuscripts the two women had brought with them, anything important or significant would have been removed. Bray stood listening to the bell as he studied the two corpses; they must be mother and daughter, comely in life but now . . .

Bray crossed himself, took a deep breath and left the chamber. The entire community had now been roused and Sister Isabella's panic had spread. Bray found it easy to shoulder his way through the throng. He reached the postern gate and slipped through it out of the nunnery. Once he'd walked some distance away, Bray stopped and looked back. The mist had thickened and provided good concealment, it would seriously deter those who dogged his every footstep. Bray was certain about what had happened at the Minoresses'. Two assassins had visited the convent. One had stood guard near the main gate, the other had tricked himself into that chamber and summarily murdered those two hapless women. He concluded, from what Tenebrae had told him, as well as from the brief description provided by Sister Isabella, that the two assassins were Zeigler and his henchman Joachim.

Bray, still trying to make sense of what was happening, slipped into a nearby tavern, allowing himself to relax in the warm darkness in the corner of the taproom. He bought a stoup of ale, sipped carefully, then wrapped his cloak about him; eyes half closed, he reviewed what he'd learnt. He was certain the killer was Zeigler yet that malefactor, despite the threat of being recaptured, had emerged from his hiding hole to commit murder and sacrilege. Zeigler was moving with confidence, displaying an arrogance, a certainty that he was protected, which meant his escape had probably been arranged but by whom? Had Zeigler been sent to murder those two women? Again, by whom? Or were the deaths of both women a logical continuation of his blood feud with Pembroke? That would be easy enough; Zeigler knew the city, he could find his way through the labyrinth of streets. On the morning of his planned execution, he must have also seen the two women garbed in the dress of a Minoress and so realised where they were lodged.

Bray supped at his ale. He recalled Archdeacon Blackthorne. York and his minions were determined not to upset that powerful churchman who would soon be informed of the sacrilegious murder of two innocent women sheltering in a London convent. 'Yes, yes,' Bray whispered to himself, 'York would not want to be tainted with the slaughter of such innocents in a sacred place. Zeigler the demon was acting on his own. So, what will he do now?' Bray took a deep breath then drained his tankard. 'A mist of mystery and murder.' He continued in a whisper. 'I am fogbound, like a vessel buffeted by both wind and sea.' Bray recalled those two Flemish carracks moving into berth at Queenhithe. And then, where would they go? Bray closed his eyes as he imagined Urswicke and the countess moving slowly towards the coast. A storm was gathering and he must prepare for it. 'It's best if I disappear now,' Bray murmured. He peered between the locked shutters. 'The day will soon be done,' he whispered, 'and we will all be for the dark.'

Bray rose, adjusted his cloak and warbelt; fingers tapping the pommel of his dagger, he left the tavern. He didn't tarry but strode through Aldgate and down a maze of reeking alleys to Queenhithe quayside. The river port was still busy with fishermen coming in before darkness fell and ships preparing to leave on the evening tide. Justice had also been busy and the three great gallows which soared up against the sky were decorated with the corpses of pirates and thieves sentenced earlier in the day. They'd hang there for the turn of three tides. The air stank of corruption, fish, salt, sweat and manure. The cobbles underfoot were slippery with all sorts of filth. Bray, his hood now pulled close and a muffler concealing the bottom half of his face, cautiously made his way along the quayside to where the two Flemish carracks, *The Sea Hawk* and *The Gryphon*, were berthed one after the other. Cresset torches had been lit along the quayside, braziers crammed with blazing charcoal provided more light and warmth. Despite the gathering dark and shifting mist, Bray had a very clear view of both the two-masted carracks with their high stern and poop. The steward had served in similar craft as a mercenary in the Middle Sea. The carracks were swifter than cogs, hulks and other merchant ships. 'Sleek wolves of the sea' was how one sailor had described them. Bray could only agree, yet he also recalled how vulnerable both vessels could be because of the armaments they carried.

Bray decided to stay and learn more. He kept hidden until he was satisfied that no pursuer dogged his footsteps. Once he'd established this, he found a shadow-filled recess and used this to scrutinise both ships. They were busy, their crews frenetically loading stores. Men, well-armed and harnessed for war, ran up and down the gangplanks and across the decks whilst others, nimble as squirrels, clambered up the mast to check the sails, cords and other rigging. Both vessels were well-armed. Bray took careful note of the small cannon, culverins and bombards on each of them, as well as the stout, heavy barrels used to store the black fire powder. Bray also noticed how the masters of both ships, along with their henchmen, stood at the foot of the gang-plank, talking to sailors passing backwards and forwards to other craft, be they merchantmen or fishing smacks. Bray smiled to himself. Both captains were trying to recruit, to bribe mariners to join their respective crews, a difficult task at the best of times. Most seafarers knew that these Flemish carracks were pirate craft, the profits of serving aboard could be great. However, if the dice rolled against them, the crew of such vessels would be shown no mercy, either cut down or summarily hanged.

Bray was about to move on when he glimpsed two figures on board *The Sea Hawk*, one tall and bulky, the other much shorter.

Both came up from the hold and hurried across the deck to a small cabin beneath the stern. Bray tensed. He was sure that the taller of the two, garbed in the earth-brown robes of a Franciscan, his head and face completely shaved, must be Zeigler, and the other was his murderous accomplice Joachim. Bray moved to keep them in sight. Zeigler entered the small cabin but his companion abruptly turned and scurried down the gangplank. Bray decided to follow the assassin as he made his way off the quayside into the tangle of alleyways which stretched up into the city. Bray hurried in pursuit, though at a discreet distance. The assassin had hired a lantern-carrier so it was easy to follow the circle of constantly bobbing light.

Bray's quarry eventually reached a crossroads and hurried across the cobbles to a tavern deep in the shadows. Only the occasional light peeped through the door and shutters of the squat hostelry with its garishly painted sign creaking on a post. The sign displayed a salamander with a beautiful blond-haired youth, naked as he was born, caught between the creature's jaws. Bray watched as the assassin knocked on the front door and was immediately ushered in. Bray stared around. An alehouse stood to his right, its narrow front window overlooked the square, providing a full view of The Salamander. Bray went into the ill-lit taproom; it was completely deserted. He sat down before the barrel which served as a table whilst he positioned the rickety stool so he could peer through the gap in the shutters and keep the main entrance of The Salamander under close scrutiny. The ale master, a greasy tub of a man, came bustling across, wiping fat fingers on a filthy apron. Bray pulled out his purse and placed silver coins on the table.

'You are keeping The Salamander under sharp observation?' the ale master asked.

'My business.'

'It's mine if you are a sheriff's man.'

'Why, is your ale watered or of poor quality?'

'Now, now sir.' The ale master smiled, his fat, greasy face creased in the falsest good humour. Bray tapped the table, the ale master wetted his lips as he gazed longingly down at the silver pieces winking in the poor light. 'If you are not the sheriff's man,' he whispered, 'I will do what you want.'

'Of course you will.' Bray pointed to the gap in the shutters. 'The Salamander caters for those who like young men, yes?' The ale master pulled a face. 'You know it does,' Bray persisted, 'and for having such information and for not sharing it with the sheriff's men, that could mean trouble. Yes?' The ale master's small, black eyes didn't waver. 'Even worse,' Bray continued, 'Archdeacon Blackthorne would be very upset to discover what you know and did not share with Holy Mother Church. Oh yes,' Bray tapped the side of his nose, 'Archdeacon Blackthorne is a close acquaintance. He has powerful friends at the Guildhall. It would be a pity if you were indicted,' Bray waved a hand, 'and, if you were found guilty, all this would be confiscated.'

'You also know about The Salamander?'

'No,' Bray countered, 'I have just discovered that and now I am wondering what to do with such information.'

'Sir,' the ale master wailed, though his eyes never left the silver coins, 'what do you want from me?'

'Does The Salamander have more than one entrance?'

'No, just the front door, though there are hatches at the back just in case the tavern is ever raided.'

'So the man I pursue will leave as he entered?'

'Of course.'

'Good, then this is what I want.' Bray beckoned him closer and spoke quietly and bluntly. The ale master made to interrupt and object but Bray, picking up the coins, told him to shut up and listen. Once he'd finished, the ale master nodded in agreement. He shouted for a scullion to watch The Salamander then took Bray out into the back yard of his establishment. He opened a trapdoor, lit cresset torches and led Bray down to inspect what was really a dirty stone box, its walls, ceiling and floor coated with filth. More importantly for Bray, the cellar was the haunt of long, black sewer rats which scampered and slithered about as if oblivious to the dancing cressets or those who carried them. Satisfied, Bray told the ale master to prepare the cellar, giving further instructions about what he wanted. Now assured of the ale master's support, Bray returned to his seat in the taproom where the sleepy-eyed scullion reported that nothing had happened and the man fitting Bray's description had not left the tavern opposite. Bray flicked him a penny and watched the boy climb the stairs to his garret.

Bray continued his vigil whilst the ale master, now his willing accomplice, did what was asked. The ale master was delighted with the two silver pieces Bray had handed over and fervently hoped that the mysterious stranger would hand over two more once this business was completed. Now and again Bray would rise to inspect the thick hour candle as its flame greedily burnt away the wax between the broad, red circles. He half dozed for a while, conscious of the ale master hovering behind him, ever eager to help. Bray wondered about Urswicke and how he was faring; he just wished that the skilful young clerk were with him now.

'Master?' Bray shook himself fully awake. 'Master?' The taverner was pointing to the gap between the shutters. 'The man you described, garbed in a brown robe . . .'

Bray peered through the slit: his quarry, much the worse for drink, had lurched out of The Salamander, its door slamming shut behind him. For a while the assassin leaned against the wall of the tavern, struggling to find a hold as he vomited and retched.

'Now,' Bray murmured, 'let us take him now.'

Accompanied by the ale master, Bray left the taproom. The square was deserted except for the cats hunting through the midden heaps.

'Can we help you, sir?'

The assassin turned to greet the ale master who repeated his request. The man staggered forward, eyes all blurred, face caked with vomit. Bray slipped around him and brought the cudgel down, a smacking blow to his quarry's bald pate, which laid him out across the cobbles. Bray and his accomplice dragged their victim over into the alehouse and out to the cellar in the yard beyond. They thrust him down the steps into the darkness. The chamber below had been well prepared with ropes to fasten Bray's quarry by wrist and ankle. Once their victim was stretched out, Bray tore off the brown robe along with the begrimed shift and loincloth beneath. Bray swiftly searched the robe to find a purse of coins, fighting rings for the fingers and a long, thin Italian stiletto. Bray handed these over to the ale master. He then asked for the lantern to be pulled closer and the taverner to leave.

Once he was gone, Bray took a bucket of icy water and threw it over the semi-conscious assassin: his victim stirred, mouthing curses. Bray threw more water over him.

'What is it?' The man, gasping and spluttering, spat out the dirty water. 'Who are you? What do you want?' The prisoner, his close-set eyes blazing with fury, mouth twisted in a snarl, tugged at his bonds until Bray punched him in the mouth.

'Where you are and who I am does not concern you,' Bray hissed. 'You, sir, are an assassin who slew in cold blood two innocent women in their chamber at the Minoresses, a mother and her daughter, Alice and Beatrice Morgan. For that you are going to die but you do have a choice.' Bray edged closer, dagger drawn, and sliced the man's calf. The prisoner screamed and writhed, tugging at the ropes which held him fast. 'You now know what I am,' Bray continued remorselessly, 'I am your death. Answer my questions,' he sliced the man's leg then waited for his victim's shriek to fade, 'I will cut you whenever I think you are lying or refusing to answer. So let us begin. Who are you?' Bray demanded.

'Joachim.'

'A citizen of this great city?'

'Yes.'

'A riffler?'

'Yes.'

'Your relationship with Zeigler?'

'I am his henchman.'

'Who organised Zeigler's escape?' Bray pressed on the knife.

'He did.' The prisoner screamed in protest. 'He did it, he did it, I swear. I visited him in the death cell, the Hell pit. You know the custom, the condemned can meet whoever they want. Zeigler,' Joachim gasped, 'Zeigler organised it all. He told us to throng around the cart and then attack and so we did.'

'I saw you on board the Flemish carrack.' Again, Bray cut then waited for Joachim's scream to fade. 'Who is Zeigler?'

'A Fleming. His mother was Breton. He is a freebooter. He fought for the House of York. Different battles up and down the kingdom.'

'And his quarrel with that masked man who styles himself Pembroke?'

'I don't know much about that. Some family feud which originated in Wales.'

'Ah,' Bray pressed the knife against the man's leg, 'and that's why Zeigler murdered those two women at the Minoresses'?'

'I know nothing.' The prisoner screamed as Bray pressed on the knife. 'It was all part of the blood feud. Zeigler saw them near the cart. He recognised who they must be and where they were staying, that was obvious by their grey garb. He wanted them dead.'

'And why were you and Zeigler on board the Flemish carrack *The Sea Hawk*?'

'We were to sail on it on tomorrow's evening tide.'

'Where?'

'I heard mention of the Essex coast. Walton-on-the-Naze.'

Bray withdrew the dagger. 'Joachim, Joachim,' he murmured, 'listen carefully. Just listen. Those great rats!' Bray kept rigidly still so the scrabbling and screeching of the foraging rodents could be clearly heard. 'Sewer rats, Joachim. Long and black and, when hungry, totally vicious. I could cut you again and again, gag your mouth and leave you here. You know what would happen. Such vermin are always hungry, ever ready for blood, eager for soft, warm flesh. They will be cautious at first but then the horde will close in. They will shred you.' Bray ignored Joachim's curses and groans. 'That's one way you can die, or I can give you the mercy cut, light candles for you in a church and pay a chantry priest to sing a requiem for your soul, if you have one. Anyway, the choice is yours. You are certainly going to die but how lies entirely with you. If you fail to answer my questions, or if I catch you in a lie, then I will be gone and leave you to all the horrors of this hell-pit. Ah well.' Bray made to rise.

'Stay,' Joachim gasped. 'What I have told you is the truth but Zeigler only shared a little.'

'He has powerful friends?'

'Yes, yes he must have.'

'So you think his escape was planned?'

'Of course, but Zeigler never spoke about that. He simply ordered me to organise the rifflers, attack the execution cart and that, once he was free, we would hide until we went aboard that carrack.'

'So Zeigler boards the carrack to go where? I mean, apart from Walton-on-the-Naze?'

'Across the Narrow Seas.' Joachim strained as an inquisitive rat slithered towards him, a swift, darting movement, the rodent eager to lick the trickle of blood seeping out over the filthy floor. Bray banged his dagger on the ground and the rat scampered out of the light.

'You see,' Bray whispered, 'their appetite is sharpening. The carrack? Swiftly now, time is passing.'

'Zeigler and I,' Joachim spluttered, 'were to go aboard *The Sea Hawk*. It leaves tomorrow on the evening tide. I learnt it was to take up station off the Essex coast. Zeigler mentioned something about a Breton ship being attacked and, after that, we would return to London then sail for La Rochelle.'

'Why?'

'I don't know. But he said the world would be turned topsy-turvy, that there was a task to be done. However, once this was finished, we would be well paid and given every comfort.'

'What task?' Bray tried to keep calm as he recalled the countess's dire warnings about the real dangers to both herself and her exiled son. 'What task?' Bray pressed on the dagger.

'The assassination of the Tudor, Edmund and the boy Prince Henry.'

'How was this to be done?'

'I don't know.'

Bray closed his eyes. He could answer his own question. Zeigler would inveigle himself into Tudor's household, an easy enough task. Not many of the Red Dragon Battle Group had survived and, if Zeigler's plot ran true to course, the group would cease to exist. Jasper and Henry Tudor had a cohort of loyal retainers but not many, being totally dependent on Duke Francis and the Breton court. Somehow or other, Zeigler would enter that court. He'd assume a false name and identity. He would carry forged passes and papers. Bray opened his eyes and felt a shiver of fear as he recalled those sanctuary men. What papers and seals did they carry? All of these could be filched from their corpses and used in Zeigler's plot. After all, the assassination of Prince Henry wouldn't take long, just a mistake, a time when the young prince was left by himself or when he went hunting.

Once the fox was in the hen coop, it would be difficult to remove it. Bray, his mind a whirl of thoughts, his heart gripped by a creeping fear, wondered what he should do? Riding out to inform the countess would not lessen the danger. Whilst Bray had other urgent business to do on Urswicke's behalf here in the city. In a sense the die was cast. The sanctuary men would, on the appointed day, be put on board *The Galicia* which, he was sure, would come under fierce attack from those Flemish carracks. The sanctuary men, and all those Bretons friendly to the countess's cause, would perish at sea. The House of York would weep hypocritical tears and publicly wring their hands, proclaiming that the outrage was the work of pirates and they were totally innocent of any bloodshed. Archdeacon Blackthorne could do little. York, Sir Thomas Urswicke in particular, would protest their innocence, demonstrating that they had safely escorted the sanctuary men to Thorpe Manor whilst they had no responsibility for Flemish pirates or Breton ships. *The Galicia* would be destroyed. Somehow Zeigler would slip into the Breton court and the Tudor household. Murder would be committed and then, and only then, would they turn on the countess in England. The Tudor cause would be finished. Supporters such as De Vere, Earl of Oxford, might well reflect on what the future could hold and act accordingly. Bray made his decision. Let York go hang in their search for the Lady Anne, he intended to disappear from London as swiftly as possible. He had to be on that Flemish carrack when it left tomorrow evening and Master Fleetfoot would certainly help him. Joachim stirred and moaned. Bray stared down at him. He recalled those two innocent women; the memory hardened his resolve as he gripped the dagger more firmly.

'Is there anything else you wish to confess?' Bray demanded.

'Mercy,' Joachim whimpered.

'Mercy indeed.' Bray leaned forward and expertly slit the man's throat with one swift slash.

Bray collected his possessions and left the alehouse. Sword and dagger drawn, he hurried like a flitting shadow along the dingy, stinking streets. The glint of lights from lanternhorns, hanging on their hooks beside some citizens' doors, caught the drawn shine of steel, a clear warning to the dark-dwellers to stay well away. A witch and her warlock made the mistake of darting

from their enclave. Bray whirled round, his dagger slicing the
warlock high on his upper arm, and both nightmare figures fled
shrieking. On one occasion he was stopped by the watch, six
burly bailiffs dragging a line of drunken roisterers, now much
sobered after being doused in a horse trough, to the city stocks.
The bailiffs demanded to see Bray's warrant and, satisfied with
the countess's seal, they let him pass.

As he entered deeper into the city, Bray realised the truth of
it all. The new Yorkist King was enforcing the peace, little wonder
that his mistress's despair deepened at the bleak prospect of a
resurgence by the House of Lancaster and the Tudor cause in
particular. The power of King Edward was everywhere. Soldiers
guarded crossroads, mailed Tower archers thronged the alleyways,
some thoroughfares had chains pulled across them. Night had
truly fallen but the city, in all its different forms, was watchful.
Bray was relieved when he reached The Devil's Cellar. He
pounded on the door until minehost, garbed in a soiled nightshirt
with a bonnet pulled down over his scrawny hair, threw open the
door, a mallet in one hand and a dagger in the other. Behind
the taverner clustered a coven of kitchen boys, scullions and
servants. The spit-boy next to his master raised the lanternhorn
which was almost as big as him.

'Heaven forfend!' Minehost blustered. 'Master Reginald Bray.
You are welcome but sir, the hour?'

'Hush my friend.' Bray extended his hand so the taverner could
both clasp it and the thick silver piece Bray was offering. The
coin promptly disappeared into the taverner's purse.

'Come in, come in my friend.' Minehost dismissed his retinue
and led his visitor into the musty taproom. He offered a tankard
and a platter of refreshment. Bray just shook his head and walked
towards the great serving board and the shallow box nailed on
the wall next to it containing keys to each chamber. He studied
this then walked back and asked a few questions drawn up by
Urswicke about Robert Vavasour and his stay at the tavern.
Minehost answered them.

'Strange business,' he mused.

'What do you mean?' Bray demanded.

'Well, the sheriff's men came and, as you can imagine, they
were full of questions which I couldn't answer. But, do you know,

on that same day the Guildhall despatched a carpenter and his apprentice, the boy swept that chamber and the carpenter repaired the door. A short while later, a locksmith arrived. The bolts, clasps and lock were replaced, almost as if the murder had not happened. All signs of it, the ruptured door, the broken locks, all cleared away. I did ask why and I was told that it was a mark of respect to the city dung-collectors as they use this tavern as their guildhall. As for the truth of all that.' He pulled a face. 'If you want, you can see the repairs for yourself.' Bray glanced up at the smoke-blackened beams and smiled. 'Master Reginald? Do you want to see the chamber?'

'No, no, sir, I have seen enough, I have learnt enough. It's time I was gone.'

Bray left the tavern, he hurried through the streets determined on the path he must follow. The countess and Urswicke were now deep in the wilds of Essex. There was little point in following them: the greatest danger they faced were those Flemish carracks. Bray was also intrigued. He realised he was being kept under close watch but, as he paused and stared back the way he'd come, he could detect nothing amiss. Bray continued on down towards the river, following the cleaner, broader thoroughfare towards the great cobbled expanse which stretched in front of London's stateliest mansions. Once there, he slipped into the shadows until he reached the steps sweeping up to the magnificent door of the countess's elegant townhouse. Bray was halfway up when he heard the rasp of steel behind him. He spun round and crouched so low the crossbow bolt whirled clear above his head to smash into the polished oaken door behind him. He raised sword and dagger, carefully moving up the steps, waiting for the three assassins, hooded and masked, who had appeared out of the darkness, weapons at the ready. Bray forced himself to remain composed even as he was swept by a mixture of dread and despair at this constant threat. He realised he would have to stand and fight so he waited for his assailants to draw close. The one in the centre reached the bottom step; he was about to edge up when the door to the countess's mansion was flung open. Fleetfoot and a host of servants burst out, armed with whatever weapons they'd found as well as knives, mallets and hooks from the scullery and kitchen. The abrupt and sudden appearance of such saviours, thronging on the top step shouting 'Beaufort' and waving their weapons, proved too much for the assassins, who turned and fled into the darkness. Bray, sweat-soaked, slumped down on the steps. Fleetfoot and the chamberlain ordered the servants back into the house, praising them for their courage and the assistance they'd given to Master Bray. The courier, wrapped in a woollen night-robe, sat down beside Bray. They clasped hands and exchanged the kiss of peace, Bray murmuring his thanks.

'How did you know?' he demanded.

'Oh, we keep close watch on all approaches to this house now the countess has left. Our spit-boys have the keenest sight. They'd glimpsed three men lurking in the shadows. One of the lads went out as if on an errand. He passed all three and noticed they were well-armed, their faces visored.'

'Of course, of course,' Bray retorted. 'They gave up following me in the streets. Our enemies know I am in London and they were simply waiting for me to return here. Master Fleetfoot, you have my grateful thanks but I need one further favour.' Bray turned and grinned at the courier. 'You are a master of disguise. I will enter this house as Reginald Bray, the Countess Margaret's steward. I want to leave it, or rather steal out, as John Sturmy – mercenary, mariner and a man totally dedicated to mischief.'

PART FOUR

'Nature's Struck And Earth Is Quaking'

Christopher Urswicke made himself as comfortable as possible on the small stool in the narrow, cobwebbed, dirty chamber on the first gallery of the ancient royal manor of Thorpe, only a short distance from Walton cove. He was certain that even from where he sat he could hear the dull roar of the sea as it swept into the land. The sanctuary men and all their escort had reached Thorpe yesterday after five days of hard travelling: within two more they would board *The Galicia*. The Breton ship would sail in as close as it could to the Essex coast, lower its ship's boat, collect the ten sanctuary men and take them to the nearest port which, in their case, would be La Rochelle, *The Galicia*'s one and only landfall. Christopher glanced out of the corner of his eye at the countess, bundled in furs, hands extended towards the meagre fire in the shattered hearth.

'I wish it was better, mistress,' he murmured. 'We have this and two other chambers which are nothing more than narrow, filthy closets.'

'Hush now, Christopher. We have to set our faces like flint. Think of those poor sanctuary men, each locked in a narrow cell below. This is an ancient royal manor, fortified and moated, built for war rather than pleasure.'

'My father, Sir Thomas, our worthy Recorder, has made himself as comfortable as possible. The warmest rooms, the choicest rugs . . .'

'We must bear the insults and wait for better times, Christopher. We must keep our temper, restrain our tongue and watch. But I agree, this truly is a winter season.'

Urswicke caught the deep bitterness in the countess's voice. Fleetfoot had arrived earlier that day, carrying Bray's letter written in cipher, hidden within secret symbols. Urswicke had read the dire contents: the attacks on Bray, Zeigler's escape, the murderous assault on Pembroke's kinswomen, Joachim's confinement in that alehouse pit and what Bray had discovered at The Devil's Cellar. There was little in the letter which could provide any comfort, and its contents only deepened the countess's despair, not to mention his own. They had discussed their suspicions, speculated on the different possibilities but they had neither the time nor the power to do anything about them. They were as much Sir Thomas's prisoners as the men chained below.

'What can be done?' Margaret whispered. 'We are invited this evening to sup with your father. He is so keen to act the great lord. He sent retainers ahead of us to prepare this ghastly manor. And now we are supposed to sit and feast while Sir Thomas smiles falsely and prepares to act the Judas. Some of Tudor's most faithful retainers lie chained below. We know they are marked down for death yet if they escape, if we arrange that, they will be hunted down like coneys in a hay field.'

'We are trapped,' Christopher whispered. 'If we allow them to board that Breton cog, they will undoubtedly perish and, whatever happens, Zeigler will be free to prowl and hunt. And what can we do? How can we warn Lord Jasper? It's too late to send messengers. We are not sure how safe that would be and, even if they reach La Rochelle, it might well be too late. Zeigler will be there long before them to wreak whatever damage he can.'

'I agree,' Margaret replied sombrely. 'Both Lord Edmund and my son live constantly under the shadow of the axe, the dagger, the garrotte and the poisoned chalice, only this time the shadow grows deeper and closer.' She crossed herself. 'Christopher, I agree with you. We must not inform Pembroke about the slaughter of his kinswomen.' She paused. 'Not here, not now,' she murmured, 'we dare not reveal to anyone what we know and how we learnt it. Christopher, I have at least set a trap. I have positioned the lure and all we can do is wait on events and put our trust in Master Bray. We have a traitor in our midst, Christopher. We have our suspicions but only time will show us the truth. Now, before we sup with the devil, let me lie down. Send Edith to me.' Margaret abruptly stretched out, seized

Christopher's left hand and grasped it in a surprisingly strong grip. 'Here we are in this benighted, ghost-haunted place. Night is about to fall over this hall of dancing shadows. But God is good. Your wits are sharp. Let us think, Christopher. Let us plot our way out of this loathsome labyrinth.'

'We have already began that, mistress; you have set the trap and primed the lure?'

'I have.' The countess sighed. 'But what I have done is put one of those sanctuary men in mortal peril of his life.' She smiled through her tears. 'And yet they are Welsh. They have taken the blood oath and they regard with hate anyone of their company who would breach such a solemn vow. I might be wrong but, there again, what other way is there? We have both reflected on the intelligence sent by Master Bray. If our enemies have their way, all those sanctuary men will die and many others with them. So yes, Christopher, we are committed.' She leaned over and gently touched this young man whom she loved as dearly as any son. 'The greatest danger is that one of my company has been named as a possible carrier of the Dragon Cipher. So, for God's sake, be vigilant.'

Margaret paused and opened her belt wallet. Urswicke watched curiously. Earlier in the day he had seen his mistress move amongst the sanctuary men, speaking to them individually, sharing out coins. Urswicke thought it was an attempt to comfort the prisoners, he hadn't given it a second thought. Now the countess handed him a pilgrim's badge, a cheap circle of metal embossed with a picture of St Swithun standing by his well, a popular shrine on the Welsh march.

'Christopher,' she murmured, 'I have my suspicions but study that badge and, if anything happens, remember it.'

Once Urswicke had ensured the countess was settled with the ever-shy Edith in attendance, Urswicke returned to his own narrow garret. He sat for a while, half listening to the sounds of the ancient manor house, the constant creaking of weathered timbers, the slamming of doors which did not fit properly, the cries of servants as they prepared for the night. Urswicke curbed his anger. His father really acted to the full his role as the powerful Recorder of London, a true master of the Guildhall, a great Lord of the Soil. Sir Thomas had led the cavalcade along the Mile

End Road through Epping, towards the coast. The Recorder gave
the impression that he really enjoyed the bitter, cold weather
which, at least, made the lanes and trackways passable. Sir
Thomas, swathed in furs, riding a magnificent destrier, escorted
by his entourage of mailed clerks and retainers, openly basked
in his power and responsibility. Christopher truly believed his
father regarded all this as a yuletide mummery, a Christmas
masque in which he was the Master of Revels acting on behalf
of his Yorkist King.

'Well, well,' Christopher murmured to himself, 'let us see how
the game proceeds.' He cleared the small chancery desk, took a
large vellum sheet from his satchel along with quills, inkpot and
pumice stone. He pulled the two-branched candelabra closer so
as to create a pool of light over the parchment as he slowly began
to list his thoughts. Item: undoubtedly a murderous traitor lurks
close to the countess and her household. Zeigler, however, despite
a fog of uncertainty about him, could also play a major part in
proceedings, though Zeigler's threat was aimed more for the
future than these present troubles. Zeigler had been imprisoned
in Newgate when Cromart and the Vavasours were killed. There
wasn't a shred of evidence that this blood-drinking mercenary
had a hand in their deaths or the murderous assaults upon himself
and Bray. Zeigler would only become dangerous if he reached
La Rochelle and was allowed to assume his new identity. Item:
Cromart's murder. The church had been locked and bolted from
within and without, yet that mailed clerk had been murdered and
his belt stolen. Why? The countess had openly speculated about
whether the assassin had been searching for the Dragon Cipher.
Was that the truth? It still didn't explain how Cromart had been
murdered. Urswicke was now certain that St Michael's had no
secret entrances or hidden doorways, whilst its windows were
mere lancets. If the assassin entered and left there could only be
one logical conclusion surely: the assassin must have been
admitted by Cromart but, once that clerk had been murdered,
who locked and bolted the door behind the assassin? Again, the
only logical conclusion was Ratstail. Item: Ratstail had been
murdered in St Michael's, once again the church had been locked
and bolted from within, yet Ratstail had been slain by a crossbow
bolt. Why and how? He and Bray had been there, along with

Pembroke; there was no evidence for anybody else being present. Parson Austin had allegedly seen someone hurrying through God's Acre whilst Urswicke was certain he heard one of the church doors open and close. Members of the parish council claimed to have seen the same. So what had really happened there? Item: the Vavasour brothers. First Guido who had fled from Walton-on-the-Naze and thought he was safe hiding in the cellars of The Hanging Tree. So, who had betrayed him? And when Guido was being led out to execution, was the condemned man, fingers splayed over his face, trying to convey some sort of message to the countess?

'Let me see,' Urswicke whispered. He lifted his right hand, fingers spread to cover his face. He felt a tingle of excitement as he recalled his suspicions and those of the countess. He rose, walked to the door and stared down at the key hanging in the lock; it sparked a memory of that chamber in The Devil's Cellar where Robert Vavasour had been slain. He took the key out but dropped it as the manor bell began to toll the tocsin. Christopher picked up the key and listened intently. The manor had fallen silent except for that incessant pealing. Urswicke hurried out of his chamber. He knocked on the countess's door. This was opened by Edith, her head and face almost hidden by a cowl. Urswicke stared at the maid, he felt intrigued: something was very wrong with this young woman though, he could not say what, at least not now. He urged the maid to stay with her mistress, keep a sharp eye on her and allow no one to enter the chamber until he returned. Edith, her face turned away, mumbled she would and Urswicke, nursing fresh suspicions, hurried down the stairs into the main hallway where his father, Parson Austin and others had gathered. They were listening intently to the captain of the guard who kept pointing to the far wall and the open trapdoor leading to the cellars below.

'Father?' Christopher pushed his way through. Sir Thomas, face all concerned, clutching Parson Austin's wrist as if to reassure himself, simply shook his head.

'I have been down, Christopher. One of the sanctuary men has been foully murdered, Rhys Conwar, a barbed bolt through his forehead. Go, go. See for yourself.' The Recorder flailed his fingers disdainfully.

Christopher sketched a bow and left them to their discussions, which showed little concern for the murdered prisoner and more for Parson Austin's exclamations on behalf of Master Blackthorne. He brushed past the two guards at the entrance to the cellar and went down the steps to the long, freezing-cold passageway hewed through the rock. On either side of it ranged narrow cells, each sealed by a stout, iron-studded door. Cresset torches flared above these. Halfway down the gallery one cell door stood flung open. As he passed others, Christopher heard moans and groans and the occasional raucous shout about what was happening? Christopher reached the open cell and went into the narrow, stinking darkness. Someone had left a lanternhorn which illuminated Conwar sprawled against the wall, his slack face almost hidden by a crusty veil of dried blood caused by the crossbow bolt driven deep into his forehead. Conwar had the glassy-eyed stare of the dead.

Urswicke crouched down, crossed himself and murmured a requiem. He then stared round and swiftly concluded that this narrow stone closet had been sealed with a fortified door locked from outside. There was no secret tunnel or passageway, no door or wall grille, no gap or aperture. Moreover, the crossbow bolt had dug deep so it must have been loosed from very close quarters, a few heartbeats, a click and the barbed bolt released to shatter Conwar's brain. Christopher closed his eyes. He'd seen the tunnel outside, merely a hole carved through rock and these cells were nothing better than fortified stone boxes. So how could the assassin enter and leave so easily?

'So how?' Urswicke murmured. 'How?' he repeated loudly.

'How indeed?' a voice echoed.

Urswicke rose and turned to greet his father, accompanied by Parson Austin and the captain of the guard. Urswicke beckoned his son out of the cell.

'It's so cold here,' the Recorder exclaimed. 'Christopher, what can be done about this?'

'Esteemed father, I must have, on behalf of my mistress the countess, the most urgent words with Pembroke, the leading sanctuary man. I need to ask him,' Christopher shrugged, 'if he saw or heard anything untoward.' Urswicke abruptly recalled the murder of Cromart and Vavasour. He went back to the corpse and pulled up the blood-soaked jerkin, noting how Conwar's hands and ankles were still secured by stout gyves, steel bracelets connected by a chain, though loose enough for the prisoner to walk and eat.

Urswicke inspected the corpse, moving it gently, and concluded, as with Cromart and Vavasour, that Conwar's belt had been taken. Urswicke was about to turn away when he caught a glint of something in the dead man's right hand. He pulled back the cold, hard fingers and plucked out the round medal, a pilgrim's badge, very similar to the one the countess had given him, a medallion which celebrated St Swithun's well. Urswicke inspected this and drew from his own purse the one that the countess had given him; the two were almost identical. He glanced over his shoulder. Thankfully Sir Thomas and his two companions had moved away from the doorway, loudly discussing how they would report this to Archdeacon Blackthorne. Urswicke smiled grimly. This was all a pretence. By the time any messenger reached London, *The Galicia* and all it contained would be destroyed, and what could the archdeacon do then? Urswicke glanced at the corpse, hurriedly repeated the requiem, crossed himself and joined his father in the passageway, flinching at the icy draught which pierced that dark, sombre tunnel.

'How could this happen?' Sir Thomas leaned closer, his face only a few inches from his son's. The Recorder pointed down the tunnel. 'Guards at one end, guards at the other, a most secure place. The lords of this manor used to sit on commissions of Oyer et Terminer. These cells were specially constructed to hold prisoners from all over Essex. Nothing more than chambers hewed out of rock.'

Christopher agreed. He glanced at Parson Austin standing silent and impassive as any statue. Christopher fought to repress a shiver of fear. He could acutely feel a deep unease here in this murky prison: these men may not be his enemies, but they were certainly not his friends. He would receive little comfort or assistance from them. His father couldn't care a whit about Conwar. Secretly the Recorder would be only too pleased that the countess had lost another faithful retainer. Sir Thomas's only worry was that Archdeacon Blackthorne might blame him for Conwar's death, yet there wasn't a shred of evidence to substantiate such a claim. The Recorder would blithely proclaim his

innocence and have Parson Austin as his witness that he'd done
no wrong.

'The prisoner's belt was taken, wasn't it?' Sir Thomas half
smiled and Christopher felt his father was now baiting him. 'I
do wonder why?'

'I must notify the countess about this death,' Christopher
retorted, holding his father's stare. 'She must be informed. But,
as I said, I need to have words with Pembroke.'

The Recorder pulled a face, shrugged then turned to the captain
of the guard, the man's bearded face almost hidden behind the
broad nose-guard of his conical helmet. 'Take him,' the Recorder
grated. 'Let him see the prisoner. One last time, eh? Tomorrow,
God willing, *The Galicia* will be standing off the coast and then
they'll all be gone.'

Urswicke caught the vague contempt in his father's voice. He
stared at the Recorder whose smooth, oiled face creased into a
smile which never reached his eyes.

'Shall we go, sir?' The captain of the guard gestured further
along the passageway. Christopher nodded and followed him
down to one of the doors.

'Before you open that,' Christopher stealthily slipped a silver
coin into the captain's hand which the man swiftly pocketed, 'I
will need the lantern.' The captain went and took one from a
ledge. 'And,' Urswicke pointed at the keyring that the soldier
held, 'one key fits the locks on all these cells?'

'Yes sir, fashioned by the same smith. Crude devices yet strong
enough.'

'And you hold the only key?'

'I certainly do, sir.' The soldier hitched his cloak closer against
the wet dampness. 'This keyring never left my possession. We
saw no one enter or leave. Sir Thomas has given me the rough
edge of his tongue but, as the angels are my witness, I cannot
say how that man was murdered. Sir,' the captain became more
heated, 'look at this passageway, stone above, beside and below.
A strong guard at either entrance.' The captain's voice faltered.
'This is a lonely, haunted place. I will be glad when we are gone.'

Christopher glanced back up the passageway, his father and
Parson Austin had left. 'When are you gone?' He turned back
to the captain.

'Sir, as soon as we reach the coast. Ship or no ship, Sir Thomas has decreed that we turn and ride back to London. He wants to be free of this business.'

'I am sure he does. Very well, open the door.'

The captain did so. Urswicke entered and found Pembroke crouched in the corner. He had pushed away the dirt-caked palliasse as unfit for use. The sanctuary man raised his head as Urswicke entered holding the lantern.

'Good to see you, Christopher,' he whispered, 'how do you go?'

Urswicke caught the lilting tongue of the Welsh valleys. He crouched close to the prisoner. He quietly prayed that he would make no slip, no reference to this man's kin being murdered in a London convent, merciless deaths, brutal slayings, a hideous sacrilege carried out on holy ground. This man's family had been slaughtered and Pembroke, like the other sanctuary men, was probably marked down for death over the next few days. Sir Thomas cared for no one. Urswicke steeled both heart and will. He, the countess and all her household, in this kingdom and beyond, were locked in a ferocious struggle to the death with the House of York. Men, women and children would die in this conflict, but what choice was there? The events of the last few weeks proved the sheer ruthlessness of their opponents in this *lutte à l'outrance* – a fight to the death, as furious and merciless as any clash on the battlefield.

'The darkness is deepening, isn't it?' Pembroke seemed to have caught Urswicke's mood. 'Our flame is fading. Something has happened, hasn't it?'

'Conwar has been murdered.' Urswicke edged nearer so he could whisper. 'How, why and by whom, I cannot say. A bolt to his head, his belt has been taken.'

'Lord save us!' Pembroke hissed. Urswicke stared at that masked face. He found it eerie, as if a man who hid his face also hid his soul.

'I had to come and see you,' Christopher declared. 'The countess regards you as leader amongst the sanctuary men.' He edged even closer so he could inspect the gyves on the man's wrists and ankles. Pembroke seemed as confined as Conwar. 'To cut to the quick,' Christopher continued, 'do you know how Conwar died? Did you hear anything?'

'Nothing at all until the guard came marching along the passageway outside. He banged on each door until the prisoner within shouted back. I heard him banging on one door time and time again, I sensed something was wrong.' Pembroke shrugged. 'The rest you know. Give the countess my regards as well as my prayers that we get safely out of here. We go tomorrow, yes?'

'That is correct and, from what I gather, my father Sir Thomas will take you to the coast then leave.'

'What, to swim or to perish?'

'Keep your courage,' Urswicke murmured as the captain of the guard banged on the door. 'I am sure the darkness will thin and our flame burn more fiercely. Trust me.'

Urswicke sat by the countess and waited for her to compose herself. He had told her what had happened to Conwar. He had shown her the pilgrimage badge and his mistress dissolved into tears, one of the few occasions Christopher had seen her so distressed. She'd just sat and quietly sobbed, the tears rolling down her face as she stared at the medal. Christopher prayed for the strength to keep his own agitation under control. He sensed the countess knew more than she'd revealed. She was deeply saddened at Conwar's death but her grief was more than that. She had whispered about treason and betrayal, about the Judas kiss and the lack of trust which ate like a canker into her soul. Now and then she would lapse into Welsh, talking quickly and quietly to herself.

'Mistress,' he spoke up, 'I understand your grief.'

'Another good man,' she replied. 'Christopher, I have cancelled supper with your father.' She raised her head, her pallid face all tear-soaked. 'My friend,' she continued, 'I cannot sit there and sup with such a man, so seemingly fair yet so foul and false. A true Judas. He rejoices in all this. I know he does. Christopher, what are we to do in these dire circumstances? How do we defend ourselves against the dagger pressed against our hearts?'

Urswicke drew a deep breath. He was certain that he had stumbled on the truth yet he needed more time to reflect and to plan. He also wanted to reassure the countess of his support but he had to wait for the right time for any confrontation with the devil within.

'Christopher?'

'Mistress, I know you are surrounded by traitors but I am true to you and so is Master Bray. We are not Judas men but your most loyal retainers in peace and war, body and soul to the very death. I realise you and kinsman Jasper have as your motto "trust no one", but you must trust us. So first, the Dragon Cipher? Does it really exist? Was it – is it – carried by one or more of these sanctuary men? I must know the truth.'

'Very well,' the countess replied softly. 'The Dragon Cipher is, as I've told you, a most detailed document, written in secret symbols, describing the power and influence of the House of Lancaster and of Tudor in particular throughout Wales and elsewhere. The cipher lists families who are loyal to us, which lords would support us, where weapons are stored, the passability of rivers and streams, possible landing places for an invasion, the nature of tides, the movements of ships, and so on. Now kinsman Jasper and I hold this securely. Please, please,' she held up a hand, 'accept our assurance on that. When appropriate, I will tell you where the cipher truly resides, but not now.' She whispered as if talking to herself. 'Anyway, to distract York and their legion of spies, Jasper and I gave out that the cipher was held by members of the Red Dragon Battle Group, or rather those who survived the slaughter at Tewkesbury. We wanted to distract York from ourselves to create confusion, to send them scurrying hither and thither. The diversion worked. Edward of York detests our battle group. We let him believe that the same adherents of Tudor carried a cipher which York could use to destroy our power in Wales.' The countess paused, as if measuring her words. 'All we inferred,' she continued, 'is that one of our battle group held such a document. Of course we paid a price for our deception, a high price, these loyal retainers, the survivors of the battle group, being hunted high and low.'

'Which is why they eventually all sought sanctuary?'

'Yes, at my advice. I secretly mourned what was happening to them but it diverted York from kinsman Jasper and Henry in Brittany, it afforded them some protection. The members of the battle group, Pembroke included, did not know which of our comrades carried our secret. They were harried mercilessly so, eventually, at my secret insistence, they broke cover and left their hiding places to seek sanctuary in London churches where they could be afforded some protection.' She paused, staring fiercely at Christopher. 'Only then,' she continued hoarsely, 'only then did we realise the extent of the damage inflicted upon us. A goodly number of that battle group never emerged from hiding: they had simply disappeared as if they'd never existed. My only logical conclusion is that they had been betrayed and silently killed.'

'Who would know where they are?'

'Oh,' she replied, 'before this present business such knowledge was common amongst the group. True, some had fallen silent, but we thought that was just the way it should be. Anyway, the survivors emerged and sought sanctuary. I then negotiated with Master Blackthorne that they be allowed safe passage out of the kingdom. He agreed. The Church is always eager to emphasise its authority at the expense of the Crown, especially when Holy Mother Church believes the Crown should be checked. He was only too willing to agree to my suggestion. At the same time, Blackthorne was offering a sop to Edward and his brothers, if these members of the battle group were given sanctuary, they would eventually have to leave the kingdom. Of course, Master Blackthorne surmised correctly: Edward and his council were only too pleased to rid the realm of those they considered lower than vermin.'

'And of course if these survivors were brought together, it provided an excellent opportunity for murderous mischief for the likes of my father and other Yorkist minions.'

'Christopher, that was a risk we had to take. However, at the time, I truly believed my retainers would be protected by the laws and rights of sanctuary, so zealously guarded by Holy Mother Church and so,' she sighed, 'we come to the worm at the very heart of our affairs. Oh, I know traitors abound like flies on a turd, but Jasper and I learnt, to our horror, that we housed a traitor, a member of the Red Dragon Battle Group, a traitor within rather than without. And so powerful is this enemy within that I am now truly fearful that the survivors of the battle group will never see Brittany. They too are marked down for death.' She paused. 'We thought, Lord Jasper and myself, that we could control the game. Now in my arrogance,' she beat my breast, 'I realise how wrong I was. York is slaughtering us and he has twisted my proposal in order to brush the survivors out to sea so others can finish the murderous task.' Margaret clutched her goblet and drank noisily from it. 'I have my suspicions,' she glanced sideways, 'I suspect you have the same. But Christopher, what can we do? We cannot break the journey! To turn off the appointed path would be disastrous, yet we know that even more pressing danger awaits my retainers at sea. So Christopher, what are we to do?'

'As yet, mistress, I don't know. At the moment I put my trust in Master Bray. However, there is one other matter.'

'Christopher?'

'On this, mistress, I beg you not to be so coy. Lady Anne Neville?' He leaned across and clutched her hand, forcing the countess to look at him. 'Lady Anne Neville?' He repeated. 'You had to leave Bray in London ostensibly to search for her. You know that was a waste of time. All the power of the English Crown has been deployed in that search but York has discovered nothing and you know the reason why. Look,' he let go of her hand, 'shall we call your maid Edith?'

'How did you guess?'

'I studied Edith. Master Fleetfoot, your messenger, is a master of disguise. Edith is Lady Anne Neville. You made a few mistakes but, there again, you'd have to be very close to notice them. Edith appeared as if out of nowhere, she is clearly not suited to service, clumsy and inept in her manner. Anne Neville is, I understand, slim with eye-catching golden hair. Now Edith's hair is black though, on careful inspection, it has too much of that colour of the night. I detected artifice rather than nature. Edith's face also provoked my suspicions. On closer scrutiny it appears as if rubbed with some white powder. As for her build and gait, undoubtedly beneath her gown lies bulky clothing to hide her figure, her size and the way she walks. Mistress, time is passing and I fear greatly for what you might do.' Urswicke lapsed into silence though he sensed he had spoken the truth and struck at the very heart of the matter.

'Time is passing.' The countess turned to face Urswicke squarely. 'Anne Neville is my friend. Oh, she is like a little mouse, but little mice can slip in where the cat fears to tread.

She overhears conversations in her sister's household. She informs me how Clarence yearns to destroy me and mine. However, Lady Anne also fears that Clarence intends to do great mischief to her, so she secretly petitioned for my help. True, she has a liking for Richard of Gloucester. In time, he may protect her but, as of now, she has a mortal fear of Clarence and his creature Mauclerc.'

'Perceptive woman!'

'Quite. Anne sent me messages and I replied. Fleetfoot was most skilled in this. Eventually we made our decision and, on an agreed date, Anne left her sister's house and slipped into mine. Only myself and Fleetfoot knew what was happening. Fleetfoot created her disguise whilst I let it be known that Edith was the daughter of a member of my household from our manor at Woking, that she was unused to service, hence her clumsy ways. Edith settled in very easily. She acted the simple country mouse and was accepted as such.'

'So what do you intend?' The countess sat, face in her hands. 'Mistress?'

She took her hands away and stared at him. Christopher kept his face impassive, trying to calm the panic seething within him. 'I will be honest. I shall tell you what I plotted.' She drew a deep breath and took a set of ave beads from her belt wallet, fingering the small crucifix. 'I intended to flee to Brittany and take the Lady Anne with me. No, no,' she rubbed the cross even more vigorously, 'I was not going to desert you. In my plan you and Bray would have come with me . . .'

'In God's name, mistress!'

'No, Christopher, if I took Anne with me, I could have betrothed her to my son Henry. She is a wealthy heiress. We could have set up a court in exile. We would be protected. I would be safe and, above all, I would be with my darling son.' She paused. 'Christopher, I am sorry if it appears that I do not fully trust you and Reginald but I felt attacked on every side. I once talked to a woman who attempted to take her own life. She really intended to die but a friend saved her. When I asked her why she even contemplated such a serious sin, she replied: "Nothingness." Christopher, I asked her what that meant? She declared that she felt alone, that there was nothing or no one, either on earth or in heaven, who could help her, and the prospect of oblivion was the most attractive.'

'And you feel that, mistress? In God's name you have others such as myself who are prepared to die for you.'

'York has been very clever,' Margaret held up the rosary beads, 'sly and cunning. Both Lord Jasper and myself have been fed slowly but remorselessly that we have a traitor deep in our household; such a suspicion corrodes our very souls.'

'And you suspect me, Reginald?'

'Christopher, I suspected everybody, even myself! That's what is so clever about your father, he creates illusions. He is a shadow-shifter, he toys with people's emotions and humours. In Brittany I would at least be safe, I would be able to reflect, to plot my own way out of the nightmare.'

'I can see the logic behind what you say. We would reach the coast. We would all board that Breton ship and its farewell to London. You would publicly proclaim that you were only visiting your son and that you'd extended your protection to the Lady Anne Neville. Bray and I would join you on board *The Galicia*. We would reach La Rochelle and plot anew. But that cannot happen now.' Christopher stretched out and touched the countess gently on the shoulder. She grasped his hand and pressed it hard.

'Let us wait and see, Christopher. Let us wait and see what the redoubtable Bray will do. Listening carefully to the information he sent you, I have a strong suspicion that the Flemish carrack *The Sea Hawk* will have one passenger its master did not expect and, on that roll of Fortune's dice, we pin our hopes.'

Urswicke left the chamber. He met Edith outside and smiled at her but she glanced shyly away. Once back in his own narrow closet, Urswicke sat wondering about the possibilities. He fell into a fitful sleep and woke long before dawn. He swiftly washed, changed, put on his warbelt and cloak and went down to the hall. The servants had cleared all the remains of the grand supper held the night before and were laying out whatever food remained. Sir Thomas was there, swathed in his cloak, eager to be gone. He clasped Christopher's hand and wished him good morrow. He declared that he'd sent out three of his retinue, 'Men with keen sight,' as he grandly described them. They were to ride the short

distance to the Naze above Walton cove to seek out *The Galicia*.
Urswicke nodded, forcing himself to smile before eating some
bread and drinking a stoup of morning ale. Afterwards he went
out to check on the countess's carriage as well as his own horse.
Everything was in order, the three carters, members of the countess's household, assured him all was well. Satisfied, Christopher
walked around the manor and through its overgrown, derelict
garden. The morning was bitterly cold, one of those hard
November days with a clear sky, thanks to the constant winds
which swept the heavens clean.

'A good day for sailing,' Urswicke murmured. 'God help us
and . . .' He broke off at the sound of horsemen thundering into
the nearby courtyard. He returned to the hall where Sir Thomas
was jubilantly listening to his outriders. He glimpsed Christopher
and raised his arms in celebration.

'*The Galicia* has been sighted. Soon it will make a landfall at
Walton cove.'

'And you, dearest father?'

'I am, we are finished here, are we not, Parson Austin?' He
turned to the priest who also seemed pleased at the news.

'Yes, Sir Thomas. Perhaps an escort for the short distance to
the beach so I can inform Archdeacon Blackthorne that we have
faithfully executed our task?'

'Two horsemen only,' the Recorder snapped, his good humour
fading fast. 'Two horsemen, but once they reach the sand hills,
they must turn back and join us in our swift return to London.'
The Recorder clapped his gauntleted hands. 'Let us assemble
everyone and share the good news.'

The prisoners, now freed of their chains and swathed in tattered,
dirty robes with whatever footwear had been available, were
brought up and herded into the hall, a gaggle of dirty, unkempt
men desperate to get this ordeal over. The murder of Conwar
was now common knowledge and this made the prisoners only
more subdued as they were pushed and shoved by Sir Thomas's
guard into a corner of the hall. The countess, escorted by Edith,
her head and face almost concealed by the veil and wimple she
wore, also came down and sat on a chair just within the doorway.
Sir Thomas stood on the dais whilst his captain of guard bellowed
for silence. The Recorder spoke in clipped tones. He proclaimed

how *The Galicia* was now fast approaching Walton. The sanctuary men would make the brief walk down to the beach and wait for the ship's bum-boat to be despatched.

'You will go down to the beach,' Sir Thomas announced. 'You will not leave the procession.' The Recorder jabbed a finger in the direction of the sanctuary men. 'Try to flee, try to stay, and you will be regarded as "utlegati" – outlaws beyond the King's peace, wolfsheads to be killed on sight and nothing or no one can save you. Yes, Parson Austin?' The priest who'd joined him on the dais nodded his agreement. 'I will despatch two of my men with you so be ready to leave. This kingdom will soon be rid of you. I bid you a fond farewell.' The Recorder stepped off the dais. He bowed perfunctorily at the countess and, snapping his fingers, swept out of the hall followed by Parson Austin and the rest of his entourage. The room fell silent. Urswicke stared around, a truly pathetic sight: the sanctuary men stripped of virtually everything except for the rags they wore, and the countess, all cloaked and veiled, with her maid standing deep in the shadows. Urswicke tightened his warbelt and adjusted his cloak.

'My Lady?' He walked towards the countess. 'The die is cast and we must go.'

The sorry procession left Thorpe Manor. The Recorder's two horsemen led the way, followed by the prisoners who stumbled and faltered, unused to walking after their cramped confinement. The countess's carriage brought up the rear with Urswicke riding alongside it. He peered in and caught Edith's stare. She smiled knowingly. Urswicke bowed then pulled back his horse so he could keep the procession in full view. He quietly took comfort from what the countess had told him about Lady Anne Neville. He could just imagine what was happening in London. Richard of Gloucester's men, together with Clarence's horde of ruffians, would be scouring the city for her. They would interfere with each other and yet neither would have any success. The animosity between the two brothers would deepen and all for the good. The countess's plan had been cunning. She'd hid Lady Anne in full sight. Maids and scullions were dismissed without a second glance by the powerful, the Lords and Ladies of the Soil, the great ones of the court. To them Edith was just a plump, black-haired, rather incompetent maid, not worth even a second glance.

Urswicke vowed that he would profit from such a lesson, even the lowliest might not be what they pretended to be. Urswicke also wondered about the sanctuary men and realised he and Bray had made a mistake: they had truly believed the Recorder would have his own spies amongst those released from sanctuary. But, so far, there was no evidence for this.

The scream of a gull flying low above them roused Urswicke from his reverie. He glanced up. The sun was now rising in a cloudless sky to thin the sea mist which had curled in. The weather was bracingly cold yet the strong winter sun provided some comfort as they made their way along the rutted trackway which cut through the sea of tough gorse, wild grass, thorny bushes and copses of stunted trees. They passed the occasional cottage or farmstead and caught the smell of wood smoke and the reek of byre, piggery or hog pen. They met the occasional tinker or chapman plodding through the empty countryside to some lonely village or hamlet. These were followed by a few fishermen, their haul sealed in barrels, eager to reach the isolated markets with their fresh catch of the day. The air reeked of brine and the salty tang of the sea. The cold breeze grew stronger. At last they reached the steep sand hills which overlooked the curving beach of Walton cove. The sanctuary men cheered. The Recorder's two horsemen immediately turned and, without a by-your-leave, cantered back the way they'd come. Urswicke watched them go. He fully understood their haste and that of his father. The Recorder did not want to be anywhere near this lonely beach when those two Flemish carracks closed in. Urswicke closed his eyes and prayed. He then crossed himself, told the countess to stay in her carriage and urged his mount up the highest rise and stared out across the coastline.

The tide was turning, the waves racing in over the pebbled beach. The mist had broken up, shifting and thinning under the strengthening sun. Gulls and other seabirds circled against the light-blue sky, shattering the silence with their strident cawing. A desolate, deserted place, Urswicke reflected, a haunt of lost souls and, unless God or Master Bray intervened, the execution ground for those sanctuary men gathering helplessly on the sand hills beside him. Urswicke stood high in his stirrups and stared out to the sea. He strained his eyes and caught a glimpse of the

Breton cog with its high stern and soaring mast, its square sail bulging under the wind as it tacked closer and closer to the shore. Urswicke continued to search the horizon, yet he could detect nothing else. The clerk fought against his darkening mood. The weather was perfect for the Breton cog, whilst the ferrying of the sanctuary men out to it would pose little problem. Nevertheless, this brilliant, clear day was also ideal for the Flemish carracks sailing in for the kill like wolves sloping through the dark. Urswicke dug in his spurs and returned to the countess. She and Edith were now sheltering deep in the covered cart. Urswicke peered in and this time Edith smiled fulsomely back.

'She knows, Christopher,' the countess whispered, 'she is happy. Do what you can for the other poor souls.'

The countess's carriage moved to a dell, the surrounding trees and bushes afforded some protection against the salty, bitterly cold wind. The countess's three retainers, the carters, swiftly provided canvas cloths so the sanctuary men could gather near the carriage, grouped around the fire Urswicke started with his flint and a little charcoal from the countess's supplies. Once the flames caught, Urswicke poured on a little oil and a heap of dried bracken. The sanctuary men were still subdued. They had now broken into two distinct groups. The survivors of the Red Dragon Battle Group clustered around Pembroke, the others were just relieved to be so close to escape, moaning and muttering against the cold. The countess's men distributed the little food they had brought with them: bread, cheese, dried bacon and a skin of surprisingly good wine. Urswicke ate a little; he then had words with the countess, mounted his horse and rode back to his watching post. He sat slouched in the saddle staring out at the fast-approaching Breton merchantman. A crow cawed. Urswicke glanced up, watching the bird soar out to sea. His heart skipped a beat as he glimpsed two dark smudges against the far horizon, the Flemish carracks! It must be. Even as he stared the blotches became more distinct. The wolves had arrived! Urswicke grasped the reins of his horse, closed his eyes and prayed that Reginald Bray was aboard one of those vessels and he would act to avert the deadly threat.

PART FIVE

'Wondrous Sound the Trumpets Ringeth!'

C hristopher Urswicke would have hardly recognised his comrade-in-arms, Reginald Bray. The skilful ministrations of Fleetfoot had transformed the dour-faced, soberly garbed household steward into a foul-mouthed freebooter, a mercenary harnessed for war and all the mayhem, mischief and murder it provided. Fleetfoot had shorn Bray of all hair so his head was bald as a goose egg and his face all marked and bruised from the edge of a rough razor. Bray was now dressed in the garish motley garb of a true mercenary: loose trousers, good sturdy boots and a mailed jerkin, with one warbelt strapped across his chest and a broad, heavier one clasped around his waist. Bray's teeth had been blackened, his breath stank of ale and he had a patch across his left eye. Bray had served in the Middle Sea where he sold his sword to the hospitallers who organised a fleet of galleys and carracks to protect Christians and Christian ships as they carried cargo to Outremer and even beyond. Bray had frequented most of the ports, be they in North Africa, Greece or the kingdom of the two Sicilys. He had lived, slept, fed and fought with the men he was now imitating. He had even adopted the rolling walk of the professional seafarer, that swagger and slight sway, a warrior who didn't give a fig for God or man.

Once Fleetfoot had finished his ministrations, as well as providing him with the most recent news from the countess and Urswicke, Bray had packed a battered pannier and made his way down to Queenhithe quayside where *The Sea Hawk* and *The Gryphon* lay berthed and ready for sea. Bray strolled along, deeply relieved that the master of *The Sea Hawk* Johann Keysler was still recruiting. Bray approached. Keysler and his henchmen called him over. Bray introduced himself as John Sturmy, seaman and soldier. Keysler asked a few questions about Bray's previous experience and the ships he had served on. Bray, in a harsh guttural accent, answered all the questions easily enough and, when Keysler insisted, Bray drew both dagger and sword, skilfully twirling them in swift arcs of light in the true fashion of the born street fighter. Keysler nodded his approval. Bray sheathed his weapons and the ship's clerk, a veritable mouse of a man, opened the book of indentures resting on a nearby barrel. He copied Bray's false name and Bray made his mark beside it. Keysler then thrust a coin into his hand and slapped him hard on the shoulder.

'John Sturmy,' he declared, 'or whatever your real name is, welcome aboard *The Sea Hawk*. You will regard me as God almighty and, aboard this ship, that's what I am. If you refuse an order, or act the coward, we will cut your throat and toss you overboard with the rest of the slops. You do understand?'

'And my rewards?'

'I take a quarter of everything, my henchmen receive the same and the rest is fairly shared out amongst the crew. Do you accept that?'

'I have made my mark.'

'Good, then welcome aboard.'

The Sea Hawk sailed on the evening tide followed closely by *The Gryphon*. Both these powerful carracks, copied from the ships of the Middle Sea, had a raised castellated stern and jutting bowsprit. The deck was even-planked and smoothed. The stern housed a master cabin beneath it; everything else was stored in the cavernous hold below decks. *The Sea Hawk* was a powerful fighting ship, with three masts, foremost, main and lateen; it could, with the right wind, run down any cog, hulke or fishing smack. The carrack was certainly well-armed not only with a fighting crew, it also possessed culverin, cannon, bombard and even hand-held hackbuts; these – along with the barrels of precious black fire powder and crates of shots – were stored beneath deck. *The Sea Hawk* boasted gun ports in prow and stern. However, as was common with this type of warship, such armament was raised and used on deck because of the danger of fire, the carrack's one great weakness. Bray made careful note of this. He had seen the most powerful carracks sweep down on their opponent; one good shot from a cannon could rip the cog apart. He had also seen how a skilful, sly enemy would use on-board catapults to loose bundles of fire at a carrack. All it would take would be for one of these to reach some of the black powder and the carrack would simply cease to exist.

Bray studied the ship and its escort closely as both carracks made good sailing down the Thames before turning east, keeping as close to the coast as possible. They passed into the Narrow Seas and tacked further out where they were hit by a furious winter storm. The gales swept in, threatening mast, bowsprit and sail. Cords were snapped, ropes pulled loose. Bray worked along with the rest, clearing bilges and ensuring the hold remained sealed against the water and pebble-drenched seaweed which washed over the deck. The gales were so ferocious that Keysler brought down the lookouts from their falcon nests on the mast-heads. Bray took great care as the deck turned slippery and treacherous. Two men were swept overboard, they weren't given a second thought or even the briefest of prayers. Someone shouted that the sky above them was black with demons who winged around the ship waiting to drag them down to Hell. Another seaman retorted that they were in Hell already, so why worry? At last the storm faded, the air remaining freezing cold, though sea and sky were now clear and calm. Once the winds subsided, both carracks slipped out into open sea. Bray, reckoning the days, realised both vessels were simply waiting, anticipating the arrival of the Breton cog and, until then, the carracks would withdraw, watch the sea lanes and plot their course.

Bray was relieved: he'd soon found his sea legs, whilst the different duties he was assigned were light enough; adjusting sails, clearing rubbish and carrying out minor repairs. The crew were all veteran seamen, former soldiers who fought for a share of the profits. A few were English but the rest were Flemings, Hainaulters, some French and a group of surly Easterlings. Bray kept to himself, though when possible he closely scrutinised Zeigler, who had now changed his earth-coloured Franciscan robe for the leggings, boots and mailed jerkin of a fighting man. Listening carefully to the gossip amongst the crew, Bray learnt that Zeigler was more of a guest than a member of the ship's company. Keysler and his henchmen paid him considerable atten-tion, whilst Zeigler was included in all the discussions which took place at the foot of the great mast or in the master's cabin.

Keysler did his best to placate Zeigler when they first cast off
from Queenhithe. Zeigler, in a thick, growling accent, loudly
demanded that they wait for 'his good friend Joachim'. Keysler,
however, was insistent that they didn't know where Joachim was
or when he might return. Meanwhile, the master pointed at Bray
standing nearby, they had a good replacement. Zeigler turned
and glared hard at Bray who held the man's stare. Zeigler was
a truly ugly man with his shiny bald head, fleshy jowls, piggy
eyes and thick slobbering lips. Heavy in build with a short,
bulging neck, Zeigler reminded Bray of a bull preparing to charge.
Bray, mouth dry, took a step forward, hand extended for Zeigler
to clasp: his opponent simply looked at him from head to toe
and promptly walked away. 'I shall certainly remember that,'
Bray whispered to himself. After that he kept his distance from
a man he was determined to kill.

Bray tried to discover as much as he could about what was
being planned in the days ahead. He'd already learnt how both
carracks would take up position off the Essex coast, though he
was intrigued to discover that, after what happened there, both
carracks were to return to Queenhithe. For the rest, Bray busied
himself winning the approval of the crew when he went fishing
with a small net and caught a number of bright-sided, thick,
slippery fish, the only real source of fresh food the crew could
eat. Bray cheerfully shared this with the ship's company and
helped the ship's cook set up a grill close to the taffrail. Once
the cog hoved to, the cook roasted the filleted red fish over trays
of glowing charcoal. During the feast which followed, a wineskin
being shared, Bray made his plan. If the carracks tried to attack
The Galicia, he would strike fast and ferocious. *The Sea Hawk*
was a formidable fighting ship but, as Bray had already discerned,
it had one great weakness, its armaments. Bray had already been
down to the hold and glimpsed the barrels of black powder heaped
in one corner. He had also found a coil of fine rope, cut a portion
off, and kept this secreted beneath his jerkin along with the sharp
tinder he always carried with him. The carrack was a floating
fortress yet Bray knew only too well that the capture and fall of
many a castle, fortress or tower was usually achieved by the
enemy within. The same applied to *The Sea Hawk*: its crew were
united, as close as any wolf pack, they regarded themselves as

hunters of the sea and would never dream that their lair housed a trap to catch them all.

Bray reckoned the days carefully and on the morning of the feast of Saints Simon and Jude he woke early on his rough, sack-covered palliasse under the shelter of the forecastle. Bray washed his hands and face in a bucket of seawater and crossed to where the ship's cook had brewed hot broth which soaked the hard bread it contained. Bray was given a bowl of this pottage, a stoup of ale and ordered to join the watchers along the taffrail. Darkness still hung as thick and heavy as an arras. Nevertheless, the sliver of moon was beginning to fade and the stars now dulled under the strengthening glow from the east as the sun began to rise. The ship was roused. Fresh lookouts despatched up the rigging to the falcon nests on the mastheads. The deck was prepared for battle: fighting platforms laid out, sand shaken against the slippery surface and barrels of water prepared lest the enemy possessed a catapult to loose fiery bundles. The weapon chests were opened, though most of the crew had their own harness and armaments at the ready. *The Sea Hawk* thrust on, cutting through the swelling of the waves, shuddering and creaking as the ship tacked to catch the strong southerly breeze which bulged all its sails. Keysler the master, along with his henchmen, took up position on the stern deck close to the rudder crew. The carrack was now a surging ship of war. Keysler kept shouting at the lookouts, Bray watched and listened intently and his heart lurched as one of the lookouts bellowed that he could glimpse the top of a sail due west. Keysler ordered the ship cleared for battle. A drum began to beat, a dull, hollow sound though full of threat and menace. The carrack cut through the waves, catching the force of the tide now sweeping backwards and forwards towards the land. The lookout kept up his chant.

'Nothing to the north, nothing to the south, nothing to the east but a sail due west.'

Only then did Keysler order the culverins and cannon to be brought up along with barrels of black powder. The crew hurried to obey. Boxes of shot were placed on the deck and Keysler himself took possession of a hand-held hackbut. The crew now waited and raised a cheer as *The Galicia* came into full view, tacking towards the coastline which was becoming more distinct and clear as the early morning sun burnt through the mist. Bray, climbing up on to the taffrail, stared to the left and right trying to discover if *The Galicia* had lowered its ship's boat. He heaved a sigh of relief, it hadn't, so the Breton cog was free to try and escape the trap about to close. Bray realised the situation was truly desperate. The two carracks now swept towards the Breton, blocking any escape back to sea. *The Galicia* would be left with little choice but to stand and fight a battle it would certainly lose. The alternative was equally bleak: the Breton ship could keep sailing towards the coast to beach in shallow waters, but this would leave it vulnerable to attack by the carracks, which would pour in hotshot followed by a direct assault from both ships. Bray climbed down from his perch. *The Sea Hawk* was shuddering and shaking in a chorus of creaking wood, flapping sails and the clatter of cords. Bray stared around, it was time. Zeigler and Keysler were shouting at each other, the master ordering the burly assassin to shelter in the cabin beneath the stern.

'So Zeigler is valuable?' Bray whispered to himself. 'Well, of course, he has a task to perform in Brittany.'

Eventually the master had his way and Zeigler, like some chastened scholar, slouched across to the cabin and went in, slamming the door behind him. Nobody gave this a second glance; the crew were now watching *The Galicia*, eager to bring it to battle.

'Cometh the hour,' Bray murmured, 'cometh the judgement.' He drew his dagger and crossed the slippery deck, grasping the sail ropes and other rigging to steady himself. No one was watching, all eyes on the sea and their intended prey. Bray opened the cabin door and closed it behind him. Zeigler was standing with his back to him. Gulping noisily from a tankard. He turned, lips all slobbery, and glared at Bray.

'What do you want, you one-eyed bastard?'

'The countess sent me. I bring greetings from her.'

Zeigler, mouth gaping, lowered the tankard. 'Who?' he spluttered. 'What greetings?'

'This,' Bray retorted. He darted forward, thrust his dagger deep into Zeigler's belly, then sliced to the left. His opponent, face all shocked, dropped the tankard as he slumped to his knees. Bray moved closer. He withdrew his dagger and thrust again, opening a deep wound across his opponent's throat. Zeigler, blood gushing out like wine from a cracked jug, collapsed on to his face. Bray leaned over as the dying man gargled something about a cage floating on water, shuddered and lay still. Bray left the cabin and hurried back to his post. The carrack was now closing the distance between itself and the merchantman, its sister ship likewise. Cannon and culverins were being primed, those skilled in such armament preparing to loose a shower of fire. Bray moved to the open hatch and, muttering about searching for something, slipped down the ladder into the inky darkness. For a few heartbeats he simply stood steadying himself, letting his eyes become used to the shifting light. He stared around. The bulwark was protected by thick canvas cloth nailed to the planking on all sides. Bray relaxed as the soft, eerie darkness enveloped him, the sounds of the ship echoing dully, though the turbulent pitch and rise of *The Sea Hawk* made him stumble. Nevertheless, he knew exactly where the barrels were. He staggered across, grasping the canvas cloths to steady himself as he crouched, pulling a barrel forward. He carefully broke the seals on this and laid out the piece of fuse. He placed one end in the barrel, positioning it carefully. Bray then unravelled the rest. He took his tinder and struck a flame to light the other end. He carefully cupped the flickering tongue of fire with his hands until he was convinced it was strong enough, then he left.

Bray reckoned the explosion would take place mid-ship, so he went up into the poop, clinging to the tangle of ropes around the bowsprit as if fascinated by the way *The Sea Hawk* was lancing through the seas. He stared to his left, *The Gryphon* was also closing fast, the Breton now turning to confront this dreadful threat. Bray closed his eyes and murmured a prayer. He just hoped he would damage *The Sea Hawk* and remove it from the fight. He'd hardly finished when the roar from below erupted like a clap of thunder. *The Sea Hawk* shuddered from poop to stern, part of the deck – and those crew clustered there – simply disappeared as further roars ripped through the vessel and orange tongues of flame leapt up like a horde of deadly dancers. *The Sea Hawk* immediately began to list and the water pouring in did little to lessen the force of the fire below. Panic set in. Some of the crew immediately jumped into the sea, others tried to lower the ship's two bum-boats. Thick black smoke seeped across the deck like a shroud being pulled up over a corpse. The smoke obscured view, stung eyes and deepened the confusion. Bray, still standing high in the poop, glanced across at the other carrack and, despite the danger, he exulted with joy. *The Gryphon* now ignored its Breton quarry, turning against the wind to go to the assistance of its sister ship. Shading his eyes, Bray watched intently. He sensed that *The Gryphon*'s master was not as experienced and skilled as Keysler or Savereaux, captain of *The Galicia*.

Bray had seen similar battles in the Middle Sea and witnessed the confusion which could so easily spread. Ships became damaged, sails and rudders destroyed so they drifted. Other vessels closed in only to become entangled. Savereaux, the Breton captain and a veteran of battles in the Narrow Seas, saw the possibilities to turn the tables. One carrack was burning and the other more intent on reaching it than anything else. The hunted became the hunter, the prey the predator. The Breton ship was now shadowing *The Gryphon*. If the latter turned to flee or fight, the sailors on board would have to abandon their comrades whilst the Breton could block their passage. A more seasoned captain would simply try to break free, but *The Gryphon* chose to ignore the real danger of entanglement and drew in even closer to its sister ship. In fact there was little that could be done. *The Sea Hawk* was now doomed, fire and smoke billowed backwards and forwards. Bray glanced across at the stern; one of the rudder men was still trying to direct the ship, another had cut the cords so the sails could flap freely and not be so quickly engulfed by the leaping flames. Bray made his decision. He left the poop and hurried across the deck, keeping to the taffrail where it still existed, avoiding the men stumbling around the gaping rents in the deck. He climbed the ladder on to the stern and hurried towards the solitary rudder man.

'Save yourself,' Bray screamed, 'there is nothing more to be done.' The sailor needed no second bidding. He staggered off into a cloud of smoke. Bray waited until this had cleared. *The Gryphon* was now very close. *The Sea Hawk* lurched sickeningly. Bray grasped the rudder and pushed with all his strength to starboard. The carrack, damaged as it was, responded, putting it on a direct collision with *The Gryphon*. Bray readied himself. Battles at sea were particularly fickle. Fortune's Wheel could spin rather than slowly turn and the Flemish pirates would soon realise this. *The Sea Hawk* lurched on. *The Gryphon* tried to tack to port. Its sails were already lowered, its rudder men, clustered on the stern, were frantically trying to turn it but the sea decided the battle. The swift running waters pushed both ships closer. *The Gryphon* struck *The Sea Hawk*, its prow cutting into its bowsprit, a veritable tangle of ropes which meshed with those of its sister ship. Again *The Gryphon* turned, only to crash into the side of *The Sea Hawk*. The flames from the burning ship seemed to leap like deadly dancers, running up the ropes and coursing along the slats of wood. *The Gryphon* was now on fire: its crew were frenetically trying to throw barrels of black powder overboard but another dull explosion sealed the fate of both carracks. Bray readied to leave. He stared through the murk and glimpsed *The Galicia*, the hunter was closing in. The law of the sea was vicious. The Bretons would show no mercy. Prisoners would not be taken so he had no choice but to trust himself to the sea. Bray shouldered his way through the panic-stricken sailors trying to escape the disaster which had so swiftly engulfed them, as if some demon had emerged to set fire to their ships and claw them all down to destruction. Bray reached the damaged taffrail. He gazed around and glimpsed a pallet used to store rope. Bray drew his dagger and cut some of the rope, using it to create grips, a hold which would make the pallet into a make-shift raft. He knocked aside those milling about him, dragged the pallet up and threw it down into the waves where it bobbed and turned. Bray drew a deep breath, crossed himself, climbed over the rail and dropped into the sea.

On the headland above Walton cove Christopher Urswicke could only stare and marvel at what was happening out at sea. On either side of him clustered the sanctuary men and the countess sitting deep in her canopied carriage. Everyone watched the ferocious battle being played out below them. *The Galicia* had made no attempt to lower its bum-boat. The abrupt arrival of the two Flemish carracks had put an end to such a plan. At first sight, *The Galicia* simply wanted to turn and escape, then the real drama began. Urswicke witnessed the sudden explosion of fire and smoke on one carrack and immediately suspected that this must be the work of Bray. He had then watched the deadly dance which ensued. *The Sea Hawk* had been transformed into a floating, flaring fire full of threats. Naturally its sister ship had also tacked and turned to provide assistance. It was drawing as close as it safely could but then *The Sea Hawk* abruptly veered and collided with *The Gryphon*, both ships becoming closely entangled. The battle had turned. The Breton ship was now the aggressor, eager to deal out death and destruction; no quarter would be given, no mercy shown. The crews of both carracks were pirates who had openly sailed under the red and black banners of anarchy, a real and deadly threat to any other vessel they encountered. Along this coast and in the Narrow Seas the Flemings were especially feared. They would run down the smallest fishing smack as well as pillage craft of any kind sailing under any flag. They had played the part so now they would pay the price. *The Galicia* stood off, its master Savereaux and its crew mere spectators to the fiery destruction of their opponents. At last the Breton ship intervened. Bum-boats were lowered, all of them thronged with armed men. The rowers moved their craft amongst those still floundering in the sea. Even from where he stood, Urswicke caught the flash of steel as the boat crews dealt out death. One of the Breton bum-boats cut its way through to beach on the waterline. Its crew hastily disembarked and pulled the boat up across the pebble-strewn sand.

'Bray!' Urswicke exclaimed. He stretched out and grasped the edge of the canopy of the countess's carriage. 'We must look out for Bray.' He declared. 'The Bretons are going to wait for any Fleming who staggers ashore. They will kill them out of hand. Bray will survive, I know he will . . .'

Margaret now pushed aside the fur-trimmed rugs and covers, nodded in agreement. 'You have my seal?'

'I certainly have.' Urswicke mounted his horse and skilfully guided it down the sand hills on to the beach. He rode leisurely, not wishing to alarm the Bretons gathered around their boat. Once he was close, Urswicke reined in and raised a hand shouting '*Pax et bonum.*' One of the sailors beckoned him closer. Christopher rode on. The Bretons gathered about him. Christopher noticed how they were splattered with blood, he tried not to look at the corpses now shifting on the surge of the incoming tide. He glanced down as one of the sailors seized the reins of his horse. Urswicke pulled back his hood and handed him a copy of the countess's seal, explaining in French who he was and what he wanted. The man glanced up and smiled.

'I speak English. We shall look for the man you describe.' The Breton squinted against the light. 'Rest assured my friend,' he continued, 'as soon as that carrack caught fire, we realised there was an enemy within. As for *The Gryphon*,' the man turned away and spat, 'its master made the most dire mistake. Mind you, I've seen the same before.'

'Where?' Christopher demanded, his curiosity pricked.

'Oh, not so much the black powder, but the galleys the Turks use in the Middle Sea. They are rowed by slaves. God help the crew if those slaves break free during any battle or storm. Anyway, rest assured, Master Reginald Bray will be regarded as our saviour.' He let go of the reins. Urswicke turned his horse, quietly praying that Reginald Bray would stumble ashore.

He turned and rode further up the beach where he could watch the dire drama unfold. The sea continued to wash up bodies and the Bretons carefully scrutinised each one. Survivors stumbled ashore to be immediately despatched by sword or dagger thrust. No mercy was shown, no quarter provided, no survivors to babble tales and invoke the blood feud. The destruction of two Flemish carracks would be greeted with utter disbelief but the weeks would pass and the truth would emerge and vengeful Flemish captains would go hunting. However, if Savereaux had his way, there would be no one left to describe this gruesome masque off Walton cove. Urswicke wondered if his father had left some spy or lookout but, there again, what had happened was so unexpected. Urswicke smiled grimly, it would come as a total surprise! He glanced up at the sky, daylight was strengthening. Out at sea the two carracks were smouldering, smoke-shrouded wrecks, their burnt timbers pounded and tossed by the waves. Now and again a crack would echo across the water as wood split and toppled.

Urswicke grasped the reins of his horse as he heard shouting. The Bretons had surrounded a survivor who was freeing himself from ropes attached to a pallet. Urswicke shouted his delight and spurred his horse to canter back along the beach. Bray! He was sure that most remarkable man had survived.

By midday the killing had ended. Bray and Urswicke sat closeted with the countess in some ancient ruins surrounded by a copse of stunted trees, a short walk from the beach. A fire had been lit, some food and wine distributed. Bray was relieved to be ashore: he cheerfully accepted the teasing over his appearance by Urswicke and the countess. Bray had also delivered a pithy description of what had happened since they parted. Urswicke already knew some of this but he listened carefully as Bray described the different incidents: his visit to Newgate, the murder of the two women at the Minoresses', the attacks on him and, above all, what he'd learnt from the city, finishing his account with a description of his good fortune on board *The Sea Hawk*. The countess heard him out then informed him about the true identity of her maid Edith and what she planned to do about it on her return to London. Bray chuckled, rubbing his hands and praising his mistress's cunning at hiding Lady Anne in full view. He and Urswicke also agreed on how the countess had decided to return the young woman to the bosom of those who cared for her, or at least for her rich estates.

'I was always kind to Lady Anne,' the countess declared, 'and I do admire her. She acts like a little mouse and, of course, people regard her as such. However little mice have the courage to stand at doors or beneath windows and hear all sorts of conversations.'

'Mistress?'

'Well, as we suspected, our present troubles do not originate from Clarence and certainly not Richard of Gloucester. Your father, the noble Recorder, is the fount and source of all this present mischief. However, Anne warned me against Clarence and Mauclerc. The only restraint on the murderous duke is that the King has made it very clear that I am not to be physically harmed. Nonetheless, I suspect our Yorkist King wouldn't really weep if Lord Jasper, my son and, of course, myself simply disappeared like smoke on the breeze.'

'And of course you will not,' Urswicke declared, getting to his feet. 'But mistress, Master Reginald, please wait for a while.'

Urswicke then left to give instructions to Savereaux, who had now come ashore, about the transporting of the sanctuary men. These now sheltered further up the beach in a makeshift, tattered bothy constructed out of pieces of wood and other flotsam brought in by the tide or found amongst the gorse along the fringes of the sand hills. The Breton agreed to furnish the sanctuary men with a little wine and whatever victuals they could. Urswicke pronounced himself satisfied, pointing back to where the countess had taken shelter, reminding Savereaux that any decision about leaving must be agreed by her.

Urswicke then rode back to his mistress. Bray had made their encampment more comfortable. The three carters sheltered behind the carriage whilst Edith was warm enough inside with blankets and a finger-warmer, a small chaffing dish crammed with scraps of glowing charcoal. Urswicke, Bray and the countess crouched before the fire as Urswicke, pleading with them to be silent, described the conclusions he'd reached during his journey from London which, he toasted Bray with his cup, had only been corroborated and supplemented by what he'd been told. Urswicke had prepared his bill of indictment, as he called it, and delivered it as skilfully as any lawyer would before King's Bench at Westminster. Once he had finished, both the countess and Bray questioned him closely but then accepted that both the indictment and the conclusions Urswicke had listed were logical and based on reasonable evidence. The assassin, the traitor had lurked in full view, yet he was, in all logic and truth, the one common factor in all that had occurred.

'I believe you, Christopher,' the countess murmured. 'As you know I nursed my own suspicions. I beg pardon if I seemed to lack trust in you but, of course, Christopher, that's what your father worked so hard to achieve. The Tudor tree grows strong and supple and your father has tried to slash its roots. However, in all truth, what you say echoes with what I now suspect.'

'But are you sure, certain, because sentence must follow swiftly?' Bray declared.

Urswicke was repeating his arguments when one of the carters shouted for him. Urswicke rose, walked out of the shelter, and raised a hand in greeting at the Breton sailor who had first accosted him on the beach.

'Monsieur Christopher,' the man pushed his way carefully through the gorse, 'monsieur, our master says we must go. It is time. The news about what happened here will spread. We need to lose ourselves out at sea.' He grinned. 'Monsieur Savereaux believes the sun will create a thick mist and we shall be most grateful for that. Monsieur Christopher, please inform the countess we have now finished all our business and fair stands the wind . . .'

Urswicke beckoned him closer and spoke pointedly about what the countess wanted. The Breton looked surprised but he pulled a face, shrugged and said they would do what was asked.

'Nevertheless, monsieur,' he added, 'we must go. You must bring your lady down to the beach as soon as possible.'

Within the hour, Urswicke and Bray, both carrying an arbalest already primed, with a quiver of bolts attached to their warbelts, escorted the countess down to the water's edge where the ship's boats stood ready. Once she had left the sand hills, the countess paused and stared back along the beach. She glimpsed the gallows, turned and walked slowly towards it. She stood, whispering the Jesus prayer as she stared at the soaring three-branched scaffold standing gauntly on a hillock, a sinister shadow against the light-blue sky.

'Is that the gibbet?' she asked over her shoulder. 'Is that where the corpses of my two poor retainers were hanged?'

'Yes, my Lady, but don't distress yourself with such memories, or what you see now.'

'So ghastly, so ghastly,' the countess breathed.

'Mistress, do not concern yourself,' Urswicke repeated, standing behind the countess. He glanced around. The signs of the recent conflict had been cleared from the beach. Only blackened spars and splinters from the carracks floated on the incoming tide. The corpses of those pirates who'd reached the shore had been stripped and dragged across to the gibbet, now decorated with at least a dozen cadavers, ropes lashed about their necks, their dirty-white flesh exhibiting the death wounds inflicted. A macabre, chilling sight. The dead men just hung, swaying slightly. Nothing more than hunks of flesh, bereft of all dignity.

'Truly a place of violent death,' Margaret declared. 'In this lonely place, ghosts must ride the winds, carried back and forth on the tide until reparation is made. Reginald, Christopher,' she beckoned both henchmen closer, 'when this is finished and we return to London, despatch a cohort of men to take these corpses down. Bury them honourably in the poor man's plot of the nearest church. Give the priest a purse of coins to cover the cost of the death pit, as well as to sing requiem masses for the repose of the souls of all those killed here. Yes?'

'It will be done,' Bray replied.

'My Lady!' a voice shouted.

Margaret lifted her head, smiled and hastened to greet Savereaux, the captain of *The Galicia*, who went down on one knee, kissed her beringed fingers and rose, his bearded face wreathed in a smile. For a while they exchanged pleasantries, discussing what had happened. The Breton master clasped hands with both Bray and Urswicke, thanking them for all they had done. He turned back to the countess. 'My Lady, we must be gone. I assure you,' he declared, 'as long as I have breath and a ship, I will be at your disposal and take you safely wherever you want. You have my word on that. But first I have a prisoner for you, you might find him interesting.' Savereaux stumbled over the English. 'Come, come, my Lady.' He led them across to the bum-boat, now riding on the strengthening tide at the water's edge. He rattled out orders to the two seamen on guard. These went round the bum-boat and dragged out a red-haired prisoner, thin and white as a willow wand, with blinking green eyes and a pock-marked face. He was brought to kneel before Savereaux, who promptly slapped him on the face and poked him in the chest.

'Tell the countess,' Savereaux leaned down, 'tell the lady what you told my henchmen when the sea tossed you ashore and you begged for your life. We recognised you were English so we gave you a hearing. So come, come, I haven't time to waste. Speak the truth or I will cut your throat.'

'My name is Norreys,' the prisoner gabbled, 'a seaman who hails from Hunstanton in Norfolk. I know this coastline like the back of my hand. I drifted into London some weeks ago where Keysler, master of *The Sea Hawk* recruited me.'

Bray, now intrigued, crouched down to face the prisoner. 'So you claim not to be a pirate?' he taunted.

'I am a navigator,' Norreys retorted, 'hired because of my knowledge of this kingdom's eastern coast. I am being honest. I brought in *The Sea Hawk* against *The Glory of Lancaster*. It was easy to track. That cog escaped but not due to me. I did the same today when we closed on *The Galicia*. Sir, I do what I am paid to do, nothing more.'

Bray stared hard at Norreys as he wracked his memory and recalled Keysler and the others clustered at the foot of the great mast. 'Yes, yes,' Bray murmured. 'I saw you with the rest gathered by Keysler to plan your journey. Your fiery-red hair caught my eye.' Bray grinned. 'Indeed, it may secure your life. What do you have to tell the countess?'

'Sir Thomas Urswicke hired the Flemings.'

'We know that.'

'He is set,' Norreys squinted up, 'he is set on your total destruction.'

'We also know that,' Urswicke snapped, crouching beside Bray. Norreys peered at Christopher, smiled and pointed a finger.

'You are young Urswicke, yes?'

'Yes.'

'He said, Keysler did, that you were really your father's minion, his spy on the countess and, in the end, you would strike at her as he would. Keysler claimed to have heard this direct from Sir Thomas's mouth.'

'I am sure he did,' Christopher retorted, hiding his unease at Bray's sharp intake of breath. Urswicke tapped the pommel of his dagger, wondering what his father really knew. Christopher played the game of being a professional spy who would sell anyone and anything for the right price. He fed his father juicy morsels but nothing significant. Did his father genuinely believe that his son would one day join him, or was he trying to force a deadly breach between himself and the countess?

'That's what he said,' Norreys exclaimed.

'Peace, peace,' the countess murmured. 'Norreys,' she continued, 'why should Keysler tell you this?'

'We gathered for discussion. Keysler's henchmen were very wary about entering English waters and attacking a Breton ship.'

'Of course, they would be,' the countess replied. 'If Keysler sank a Breton vessel, a host of troubles would descend. Duke

Francis would not take it kindly, especially the loss of a cog like *The Galicia* along with its most experienced captain.'

'There's more,' Norreys stammered. 'Keysler informed us that once this business was finished, we would return to London to collect certain individuals, then go through the Narrow Seas and stand off the coast of Wales. This was to be a new task. We were to land assassins there, but that's all I know. Keysler described it as a great enterprise supported by Sir Thomas Urswicke,' Norreys looked meaningfully at Christopher, 'and his son.'

'And who were these assassins?' Bray demanded.

'Sir, I don't know, but apparently they would do great damage to the Tudor cause in Wales. Keysler was very happy with this. He said the task would take months and we would all be well paid. And that is it. Mistress,' Norreys looked pleadingly at the countess, 'what will happen to me now?'

'We cannot let him go,' Urswicke declared, trying to hide his own disquiet. 'He cannot be allowed . . .'

'I could join the Bretons,' Norreys retorted. 'I am a veteran seaman, a plotter of courses.' He fell silent as the countess raised her hand and turned to Savereaux.

'I am always searching for good mariners, my Lady. We will take him. He is a navigator and he has been of use to you.'

'He certainly has,' Margaret replied, 'and if you take him, he will not be able to tell anyone else what he has witnessed.'

'And if he does,' Savereaux bent down and glared into Norreys's face, 'if he breaks his word or the indenture he is about to seal, God help him because I won't.'

Norreys was bundled away and the countess then moved to clasp hands with the sanctuary men, distributing coins and thanking them for their work. Urswicke watched her as he reflected on what Norreys had told them. He was sure that both the countess and Bray trusted him fully but, there again, there was always that deep unease when it came to his father. He and the Recorder were locked in a deadly shadow fight and Christopher put his hopes in his father's one profound miscalculation: Sir Thomas could never really believe or accept that his son was a fervent adherent of the House of Lancaster and Tudor in particular. As long as his father continued in that delusion, Christopher felt he was safe. Nevertheless, he quietly promised himself that he would do all in his power to continue this deception of the honourable Recorder. Meanwhile, he turned to Bray standing beside him.

'Soon,' Urswicke whispered, 'we will strike soon.'

PART SIX

'Lo! the Book Exactly Worded, Wherein All Hath Been Recorded'

Both Urswicke and Bray watched as the countess approached Pembroke, now standing slightly apart from the others. When she reached him, the countess simply stared sadly and beckoned Urswicke and Bray forward. They hastened to obey and, with the help from the Bretons whom Urswicke had advised about this, seized Pembroke in a short, savage scuffle. The masked man screamed his protests and fought back, but at last he was bound fast around the arms and chest. Urswicke and Bray pulled him away whilst the countess spoke to the others saying there were matters which had to be dealt with. She thanked them all for their loyalty and declared that Lord Jasper would reward them further as well as provide comfortable refuge. She nodded at Savereaux, who immediately ordered all the sanctuary men into the waiting boats.

The countess raised a hand in farewell and followed Urswicke and Bray, now helped by the three carters, to drag a still protesting Pembroke up into the sand hills. The countess returned to her carriage; her two henchmen forced their prisoner to mount Urswicke's horse and the small procession made its way along the narrow trackway to a now deserted Thorpe Manor. Thankfully, Sir Thomas had been in such a hurry to leave, the gate to the cobbled yard hung open; they entered then forced a door into the house itself. Urswicke and Bray pulled Pembroke from the saddle and hustled him through the stone-paved kitchen into the small hall, which still reeked of the food cooked the night before. The prisoner was lashed securely to a chair. Urswicke whispered to Bray to kindle a fire in the hearth as well as one in the cleanest bedchamber he could find for the countess and her mysterious maid. Urswicke heatedly insisted that Edith stay in her room until this business was finished. He then informed the countess that he would leave for a short while to ensure *The Galicia* had safely set sail into the Northern Seas.

Urswicke, once satisfied that Pembroke was held fast and that Bray would take care of all matters within, returned cloaked and hooded to the courtyard. The carters were busy unharnessing the horses as well as moving coffers and chests into the manor. Urswicke had a few words with them and mounted his own horse. The day was drawing on, though the weather remained crystal clear, the sky was cloud free whilst the autumn sun provided some meagre warmth. Urswicke rode to the headland and stared out to sea. He heaved a deep sigh of relief. The bumboats had reached the cog, which was now turning to catch the stiff northern breeze, its mainsail billowing and bulging, whilst from the top of the masthead the colours of Duke Francis fluttered bravely. Urswicke glanced to his right and left but he could detect no other vessel. The sea was empty except for the fast-disappearing cog which would soon lose itself in the vastness of the fast-running northern waters.

Urswicke continued to stare as he reflected on what was about to happen and how he had reached the conclusions of his indictment. He fully recognised that the House of York and its minions, his father in particular, had plotted to root up the Tudor tree, both at home and abroad. They'd cast their net wide across sea and land, totally intent on destroying any support for the countess. He suspected that his father would never accept that his son was the countess's man, body and soul, in peace and war. Such a miscalculation was a matter of pride to the Recorder, both as a father and as a minion of York. Nevertheless, Christopher also acknowledged that something had to be done to check his father's constant attacks on the countess. Norreys had confessed how Keysler was to be used to land assassins in Wales and, of course, if Sir Thomas's plot had been successful, these men would have been armed with all the information contained in the Dragon Cipher. They would know which officials were loyal, which parish churches concealed weapons for war, what taverns, religious houses and manors espoused the Tudor cause. Such men could have inflicted considerable damage, be it the assassination of some official or the destruction of armaments and other impedimenta.

Christopher started as a fox yipped shrilly from the gorse beside him. The eerie stillness of the beach was broken, seabirds cawed back, whilst the clamour of the waves grew as the tide swept in. *The Galicia* eventually disappeared, leaving nothing but a lonely beach littered with debris from the carracks, and the occasional corpse swept in on the fast-running waves. Urswicke glanced to his left at the great scaffold with its truly macabre burden. He recalled those two unfortunates, stabbed to death and slung like carrion from those pitch-black beams. Some compassionate soul must have cut the cadavers down and given them a semblance of Christian burial. The souls of those men and others now demanded justice, and Urswicke was determined they would get it. He would not be deterred by his father's malicious mischief. He suspected Bray felt discomfort indeed, he always had, that his closest ally was the son of his greatest enemy. Nevertheless, whatever happened, Christopher knew the countess would stand by him as he would her for all time. He murmured a prayer, crossed himself, turned his horse and rode back to the manor.

Bray had been busy, the fire in the hall's mantled hearth now flamed fiercely. The countess, wary of the carters, had sustained the pretence about Edith the maid. The young woman had dined and returned to her chamber, while the carters were happily clos-eted in the small buttery broaching a casket of ale. Before they had adjourned there, the men had helped Bray tie Pembroke fast to the chair, but had left the prisoner's hands and arms free so he could eat and drink whatever Bray had given him. Urswicke swiftly broke his own fast then he, Bray and the countess sat on chairs facing the prisoner.

'I would like to remove your mask,' the countess began, 'so I can clearly see your face, whatever its wound. Yet, I suppose, that does not really concern me. What strikes me to the heart are the very deep wounds you have inflicted on me and mine. Gareth Morgan, popularly known as Pembroke,' Margaret's voice grew stronger and more vibrant, 'you truly are a Judas man, a dyed-in-the-wool traitor and the most sinister assassin. You cannot be tried before the King's justiciars, for indeed, they have played a part in the malignant conspiracies and foul treasons committed against me and mine. I cannot plead to the Crown or its ministers, men totally bent on my utter destruction. Instead, I invoke the ancient customs of the lords of Pembroke, the very name you adopted. I have, according to its laws, the God-given right of a seigneur to hold court and pass judgement. I do so know.' Pembroke, fastened firmly to the chair, just slumped, head down. 'If you are innocent,' Margaret continued, 'then you can plead with counter-argument. But the case weighs heavily against you. Christopher!'

'I shall begin,' Urswicke declared. 'Gareth Morgan born in Pembroke, you are a Welshman to your very heart. A retainer of the House of Tudor whose livery you wore. You swore the most solemn oath to be loyal to that house even to death. You gave great trust and even greater trust was shown you. You were patronised and favoured by my countess and others of her family. You formed and led the Red Dragon Battle Group at Tewkesbury. After that disastrous defeat, you and others fled to Lord Jasper Tudor and our mistress's son exiled in Brittany. You, like all of your coven, tasted the bitter dregs of defeat; refuge in foreign parts, penury and poverty, not to mention your total exclusion from your own homeland, your kith and kin. In your case, a mother and sister whom, I suspect, you were devoted to . . .'

'Were?' Pembroke abruptly lifted his head. 'You said were?'

'Yes, yes quite.' Urswicke glanced at Bray. They had all agreed that the slayings at the Minoresses' should be kept secret from Pembroke for as long as possible. 'You acted as an emissary,' Urswicke continued, 'as an envoy between Tudor in Brittany and the countess.'

'Very skilled,' Margaret interjected. 'I thought you very reliable and highly trustworthy.'

'Yet the rot had set in, hadn't it? During those secret meetings in London, when you acted the role of the wandering dung collector, be it that or a member of some mummers' troupe. Such disguises could hide and protect you. Anyway,' Urswicke sipped from his goblet, 'during these secret forays into London, you also discovered that Parson Austin Richards, the royal chaplain who so bravely rescued you from Zeigler's cruelty, was now parish priest at the ancient church of St Michael's. Naturally you visited him. At first Parson Austin may not have realised who you were or what you were doing, but eventually his suspicions were aroused. He would come to realise that although the war was over, you were still a fervent adherent of the House of Lancaster. He could make careful search of the lists of those who had sued for a pardon as well as those who had not and were proscribed for that.'

'Your name and title, along with those of other rebels, were posted on the cross at St Paul's,' Bray declared, 'Parson Austin must have seen that proclamation.'

'There was no need,' Pembroke seemed more composed, 'why should I deny it? Parson Austin was my confessor, both within and without the Sacrament.'

'So he knew who you truly were? What you did and where your loyalties lay?'

'Yes, Master Urswicke, he did.'

'And I wager you expressed your true self. You were no longer a warrior from that battle group. You were tired, exhausted, bitter about the exile and the penury, the humiliation, the constant danger! Of being cut off from your country, your kith and kin, still following a cause which, to all intents and purposes, had been utterly destroyed.' Pembroke's eyes, glaring through the slits of his mask, never wavered. 'You confessed your despair. You made yourself vulnerable to other persuasions. Parson Austin may have encouraged you in this. I cannot give you chapter and verse, but eventually the good parson informed a leading Yorkist in this city, a man dedicated to the total destruction of Lancaster.'

'Your father.'

'God forgive him, yes. A man of bounding ambition with the talent to match. He immediately saw the possibilities yes?'

'I confess to nothing. I am simply your prisoner, forced to listen to what you say.'

'Sir Thomas sowed seed on very fertile ground. He realised you were ripe for the plucking. For the first time ever, he had someone close to the countess and he pounced. Through the good parson, Sir Thomas turned your mind, subverted your loyalty and opened a new path for you to follow. No more exile, no more poverty, no persecution, no danger of being caught and suffering the most gruesome death. A royal pardon, yes? And your family, your mother and sister, taken out of Wales where they might suffer grievous harm once your change in allegiance became known.' Urswicke paused. 'And there was something else.'

'Why should I espouse York?' Pembroke touched his mask. 'I wear this as a constant reminder of its enmity.'

'Ah yes, I will come to that. Zeigler! That violent, nasty soul, the villain who threw you into the bear pit. Zeigler the killer, who left the service of York to immerse himself in the turbulent world of London's rifflers. A dreadful mistake because he exposed himself to my devious father. Now . . .' Urswicke paused, he glanced across at his mistress, who'd turned slightly away, as if she could not bear to look directly at their prisoner. Bray sat nursing an arbalest, ready and primed in his lap. He too did not look at Pembroke but stared into the fire, eyes half closed as he listened intently to what was being said.

'I concede,' Urswicke continued, aware of how dreamlike the hall had become, the glowing candles and leaping fire flames keeping back the threatening, creeping darkness, 'I concede,' he repeated, 'that I do not know all the details. However, my dear father offered you one further lure, the best of bribes. You know what I am talking about, the total destruction of Zeigler. He offered you revenge, to personally witness Zeigler's execution, being hanged on the common gibbet above Tyburn stream. He watched Zeigler like a cat would a mouse. Zeigler the riffler took part in an alleged raid on a warehouse where two men were killed. Innocent or guilty, my father would not care. Zeigler was arrested and tried. He was found guilty and the prospect of watching him hang was conveyed to you. My father didn't care for Zeigler, he intended to use him. The riffler's trial and imprisonment were managed carefully so you would be in London when sentence was carried out.' Urswicke picked up the goblet of Bordeaux and took a deep sip. He stared around to reassure himself. All the battered doors out of the manor were firmly locked; the three carters would act as guards whilst the maid Edith, as she still styled herself, was confined to her chamber.

'You will not accuse Parson Austin?' Pembroke exclaimed. 'He did no wrong.'

'Oh yes, Parson Austin,' Urswicke retorted. 'You know that we cannot move against him. He is a priest well favoured by the crown. In fact, I believe the good parson to be a man of integrity and I suspect he was no more than a messenger, an envoy, a conduit for the treachery which flowed between you and my father. Parson Austin may have been aware of the process but not the conclusions. Whatever, you made your decision. You confirmed your choices. Zeigler's condemnation would only have reinforced your determination to plough your own treacherous furrow.

'And our Recorder would have demanded a high price,' Margaret declared. 'The betrayal of your companions, indeed anyone supporting the Tudor cause. And he was successful,' she added bitterly, 'we soon realised there was a traitor in our midst. Both I and kinsman Jasper became deeply concerned. Cromart and others were murdered but some members of the Red Dragon Battle Group have simply disappeared, wiped off the face of the earth as if they never existed. Were they murdered?' She shrugged. 'Have they fled our cause and now shelter in hiding? Have they assumed new names, different trades, moved to different parts of the kingdom? We don't know.'

'You may have had a hand in all of this,' Urswicke accused, 'but then the final and deadliest part of your treachery began with your journey back to England, ostensibly to support the surviving members of the Red Dragon Battle Group. My father must have been delighted. Our countess, fearful of what was happening to her retainers, had advised them to seek sanctuary in London churches and she would arrange the rest. You determined on a totally different course of action, a deadly jab at the heart of our mistress's cause. You left Brittany on board De Vere's ship, it docked at Dordrecht giving you fresh opportunities to advise York about what was happening. *The Glory of Lancaster* then slipped through the straits of Dover, aiming like a well-loosed arrow up along the Essex coast, cutting through the Northern Seas keeping as close as possible to the shoreline. De Vere's ship was in fact being kept under close and constant scrutiny both by land and sea. When it hoved to off Walton, my father and his comitatus would ensure they also reached the agreed location at the agreed time. Our high and mighty Recorder simply had to wait as those two Flemish carracks did.' Urswicke picked up his goblet, gesturing at Bray to continue the indictment.

'Oxford's ship would have been keenly watched in its voyage north. Fishing smacks, herring boats and other such craft would soon take note of a great war cog, it truly was just a matter of waiting.' Bray cleared his throat. 'What was plotted that night was a mortal blow to the House of Tudor. *The Glory of Lancaster* would be attacked and destroyed, a leading supporter of Tudor, the Earl of Oxford, either captured or slain. As for the four members of the Red Dragon Battle Group on board, well, three of these would be killed whilst the fourth, you the traitor, would run free to wreak even more hideous damage to our cause.'

Pembroke just sat shaking his head, whispering beneath his breath. Urswicke realised the traitor would understand he could not escape the guilt of the indictment laid against him. He could not walk away free and unpunished. In fact, Urswicke suspected that their prisoner was desperately searching for a compromise. Something to win protection for at least his kin who, as he would soon discover, were now beyond all such help.

'At the same time,' Urswicke continued, 'my father wanted to weaken the countess even further. He would strike at her two loyal henchmen, myself and Master Bray. He hired assassins to murder my friend, though he gave them instructions not to harm me. I suppose even my father feels some faint moral responsibility. We killed both of them, but one of the assassins, as he lay dying, mumbled something about me not being the intended victim, or words to that effect. We were watched and we were followed. York then tried to delay my friend Bray in London to assist in the fruitless search for Lady Anne Neville.'

'I was alone,' Bray interjected, 'more assassins were despatched to kill me. They also failed.' Bray leaned forward. 'You once told us how you went down amongst the Dead Men, those nightmare figures who prowl London's underworld. You could move easily among such sinners, hiding behind your mask, pretending to be a dung collector, the lowest of the low. Did you, masked and cowled, hire those assassins on behalf of the Recorder? Did he furnish you with gold as he did to pay for your mother and sister's sojourn at the Minoresses'? If he didn't pay, who did? You are a fugitive, or supposed to be, constantly in hiding. You have little treasure. My mistress and Lord Jasper provided some sustenance. However, such lodgings amongst the good nuns are costly. Where did you get the means to hire a chamber there for days, even weeks?'

'I . . .'

'Where did you get such monies?' the countess demanded. 'I doubt if your mother and sister could afford all the costs of a long journey from Wales and a prolonged stay in the city. I never gave you such monies and, strangely, you never asked for any. So, who paid?'

'You do not understand,' Pembroke retorted. 'You could never feel what I did . . .'

'An admission of guilt?' the countess demanded. 'That you, Gareth Morgan, popularly known as Pembroke, my supposedly loyal man is, in fact, a traitor and an assassin?'

'I concede nothing.' Pembroke's voice turned more defiant. 'If I am guilty, then execute me and let's be done with it.'

'No, no,' the countess shook her head, 'that is not my way. You must confess. You must openly admit to your crimes. You killed your comrades for what, profit? Self-advancement for yourself and your kin because you were tired? Oh no, I want to know the reason why and, more importantly, I need you to open a door into the minds and souls of those who persecute us. You must have information about them. Christopher?'

'You murdered,' Urswicke returned to his indictment, 'you killed so as to weaken the Tudor cause, to strike at the very roots of support for our mistress. However, you were also searching for something truly valuable to both her and York, the so-called Dragon Cipher. A document which, behind secret symbols, provided a detailed description of all those who supported our mistress in Wales – be they officials, the gentry, the Church – and the whereabouts of stores and weapons. Once you had that, York would move to root out all those named. The same silent struggle would take place in South Wales as occurred elsewhere. Members of the Red Dragon Battle Group would either disappear or die in the most mysterious circumstances. Those Flemish carracks were to land assassins in Wales once the cipher had been seized and the House of York had the information they needed.'

'I don't know, I don't know.' Pembroke shook his head. 'I admit there was chatter about the cipher.'

'You killed because of it,' the countess declared. 'Now the Dragon Cipher does exist. Lord Jasper and I have mentioned it in messages back and forth. Sometimes we would make open

reference to the cipher, I suppose,' she sighed, 'and it is logical
that those who wanted to seize it believed that it was carried by
a member of the Red Dragon Battle Group, that it was hidden
where couriers often conceal such messages, in a secret pocket
on their warbelt. We fostered such a belief as it suited our own
secret purposes. We wanted to distract York, to mislead our
opponents.' She crossed herself. 'God forgive us, it led to dreadful
betrayal and hideous murder, but we did not intend that. At the
time we did not realise the malevolence of the enemy within.'
The countess tapped the side of her head. 'The cipher was
common knowledge amongst the Red Dragon Battle Group but
none of them had it. The only person who knows it in its entirety
is me, Master Pembroke.' She leaned forward and again touched
the side of her head. 'I have it here in my soul at the very core
of my being. Times, places and people, those who espouse our
cause, not only in Wales but here in London and throughout
the kingdom.' The countess spoke so forcefully there was absolute
silence when she had finished. She then pointed at Pembroke.
'So, despite all your crimes and sins, you were in truth hunting
a will-of-the-wisp, a mere form without substance.'

'You certainly hunted.' Urswicke returned to his indictment.
'You and the three others were on board *The Glory of Lancaster*
as it made its way along the Essex coast. You were put ashore
and immediately my father pounced.' Urswicke shrugged. 'But
you know all this. Two of your comrades were seized and hanged,
their belts taken. They were shown little mercy. My father knew
they would tell little. More importantly, you realised that the
ambuscade on the beach would eventually confirm our deep
suspicions about a traitor in the countess's household. If those
men had been spared, it might have only been a matter of time
before such suspicion fell upon you, who, with Vavasour, managed
to escape. Did those two other men, as they were seized, realise
that something was very wrong? Did they glimpse that deliberate
gap in those milling horsemen for you to escape?'

'As did Guido Vavasour,' Pembroke retorted.

'Precisely,' Urswicke agreed. 'And that explains what happened
in London with poor Guido. Forget all that nonsense about you
not knowing where Vavasour and his brother were hiding. You
knew Guido was sheltering in the cellar of The Hanging Tree

tavern. You also knew Guido would be demanding the same truth as we did. What did happen at Walton? Who did betray their landing? He would also hear, as the entire city did, about Cromart's murder in St Michael's. I can only speculate, but did Vavasour realise that all these disasters began with that landing at Walton? Did Vavasour also detect something amiss during that sea voyage from Brittany?' Urswicke wetted his lips. 'Only you, Pembroke, knew what would happen on that beach. We are talking about a matter of heartbeats. To cut to the quick, you were allowed to escape and Vavasour followed you. Did he later sense that something was very wrong? I admit it is speculation,' Urswicke declared, 'but Vavasour was a highly intelligent man, a skilled courier, a man with sharp mind and nimble wits. He would certainly ask questions. Only God knows what these were, but you had to silence him. Of course, Vavasour was captured and interrogated. Now, the question could be asked, why didn't you murder him as you did the rest? Would that be too close to the bone? Provoke even greater speculation about you and your true allegiance? Or did my father want to interrogate that poor soul in the torture chamber beneath the White Tower? Yes, I am sure the Recorder had his own nefarious purposes; nevertheless Vavasour's arrest and interrogation also protected you. Ostensibly you could not possibly have been involved in Vavasour's seizure as you didn't even know where he was hiding. It would strengthen the suspicion that the traitor must be somebody else.'

Urswicke stared hard at the prisoner. 'Why was Vavasour tortured?' Urswicke continued. 'To reveal secrets about the countess, the whereabouts of the Dragon Cipher? Whatever, Vavasour was brutalised, his tongue torn out lest he speak. You see Pembroke, I only have slender proof for this but I suspect that Vavasour, after he'd been seized, realised that you were the traitor. As I have said, perhaps he noticed something on board that ship, or was it that York closed in so fast? Or was it simply that the only person who knew he was hiding in that cellar at The Hanging Tree was you?'

'Vavasour,' the countess spoke up, 'tried to warn us as he was led out to execution. York wanted me to feast on that disaster, watch a loyal and devoted retainer be cruelly despatched. Was Vavasour taunted with that? That I would be forced to witness such an outrage whilst he could do nothing about it, battered and bruised, his mouth an open wound, his tongue removed? They did not want him to speak, to voice his suspicions,' she crossed herself, '*Jesu miserere*, Guido was so sharp and keen, loyal to the last. God knows how long he languished in that dungeon but, quick-witted as ever, he realised he could do one thing, so he put his hand over his face, fingers splayed.'

'And?'

'He was accusing you,' Urswicke declared heatedly; 'he was, with his fingers, imitating a mask, as well as desperately trying to form words which he could not utter. He was levelling an accusation at a man wearing a mask, that was you.' Urswicke stared into the darkness around him. 'So much I do not know, but poor Guido was accusing you, and the testimony of a dying man is sacred.'

'As for Robert Vavasour.' Bray edged forward in his chair, finger pointing.

'I was with you when Robert revealed where he was hiding, that message was delivered by a street swallow.'

'Nonsense,' Urswicke snapped, 'you knew where Robert Vavasour was staying. Indeed, I wager you advised him to lodge at a tavern patronised by the Guild of Dung Collectors, the very disguise you used to move through this city. You lured Robert there and you killed him.'

'Why should I kill Robert?'

'First, he was a member of the battle group. Secondly, he was a confidant of the countess. Thirdly, he may have also had his suspicions and, most importantly, there was the real danger that Guido had sent messages to his brother, yes? Shared secrets with him? And, finally, there was always the possibility that Robert Vavasour was the one who held the Dragon Cipher. Now whatever you claim,' Urswicke shook his head, 'I am sure you can prime an arbalest as skilled as any man. You are a soldier, a man-at-arms. So, to return to my indictment, Robert went up to that chamber in The Devil's Cellar. He would be frightened, wary, he would lock himself in. I am not too sure whether he knew his brother had been taken up and executed, yet Robert was no fool, Cromart's murder was public knowledge and he would at least worry about where his brother might be. He would wait for you locked in his chamber. You, dressed as a dung collector, wandered in. As I have said, The Devil's Cellar is a hostelry for the Guild of Dung Collectors. You'd know all about the tavern, especially that frame fastened to the taproom wall, close to the buttery, where a second key to Robert's chamber hung along with others. In the confusion and chaos of that day, during which the tavern's jake's pots and cesspits were emptied, you took that key and went up to Robert's room. He let you in. You lifted your arbalest and killed him. You then searched for any documents and took Robert's warbelt in the hope that the Dragon Cipher might be concealed there.'

'And how would I leave that chamber locked and bolted from within?'

'Oh very easy. You drew your dagger and ruptured the bolt and clasp at the top of the door so it truly appeared that both had been forced. Of course, this would be cleverly concealed. First, by the rupture of the wood around the bolt when minehost hammered the door open. Secondly, I recall thick wedges of wood lying around the floor. Now the light was dim, Bray, I and others were milling about. In the confusion it would be easy for you to kick or pick up that thick piece of leather you'd used to jam the door shut so it looked as if it was firmly clasped from within.'

'And the key?'

'Oh, you hung the key Robert carried into the lock, not fully inserted, but balanced just within. You then pulled the door over inserting that leather wedge.' Urswicke made a face. 'I am not too sure if you needed to lock it from outside, perhaps you did, perhaps not. Suffice to say that door appeared shut, locked and clasped from inside. Minehost and ourselves pushed at that door, we were concerned with only one thing, getting into that chamber. Of course we couldn't, so we reached the logical conclusion that it was sealed. It wouldn't open whilst the very act of forcing the door would conceal your devious handiwork.'

'As for the street swallow,' Bray intervened, 'mere mummery! Minehost at The Devil's Cellar clearly informed us, and did so again when I returned after the countess had left for Thorpe Manor, that Robert Vavasour ate and drank in the taproom then adjourned to his chamber. He was cautious, wary, perhaps troubled by his brother and wondering about Cromart's death. He wouldn't want to wander the streets of London or sit too long in the taproom open to scrutiny. According to the taverner, Robert did not go out and he received no visitors. As I have said, I went back to The Devil's Cellar and the taverner repeated all he'd told us before. Apart from food and drink, Robert asked for nothing else, be it ink, quill or parchment. He never wrote any message, nor did he hire a street swallow to deliver it. No such messenger appeared at the tavern that day. Minehost said he'd find it difficult to recall individuals, but a street swallow he would remember, for why should his customers, dung collectors, need to hire one? No, Master Pembroke, you knew where Robert Vavasour was hiding, you wrote that letter as a ploy. You hired that street swallow to deliver the message and then disappear. I did wonder about that.'

'What do you mean?'

'When I hire street swallows,' Bray retorted, 'they love their pennies and are quite patient in waiting for their pay. Now that particular street swallow delivered his message and promptly disappeared. I noticed that when we left the countess's house. On reflection, the reason for his disappearance is obvious: you paid him to deliver the message then go, which he certainly did.'

'Master Bray,' the countess intervened, 'has been very busy. As he said, after my departure for Thorpe, he revisited The Devil's Cellar. Minehost informed him that the door to Robert's chamber had been repaired, the room swept on orders from the Guildhall, ostensibly a sop to the dung-collectors' guild on whom the city so depends.' She paused. 'I doubt it! They were hiding your handiwork and, more importantly, making sure that Robert Vavasour had not hidden the cipher deep in some crevice or crack.'

'They would discover nothing,' Bray declared, 'but they had to make sure. After all, that chamber had been used by Robert Vavasour. When we visited it, you declared, all a-fluster, that we should leave before the sheriff's men arrived. You couldn't search Robert's room and you certainly didn't want us to – we might discover something amiss or, God forbid, find the cipher, so you left that task to the Guildhall.'

'You shrouded Robert Vavasour's murder in mystery so as to

protect yourself and mislead us,' Urswicke continued.
'Nevertheless, you must have become increasingly frustrated.
You took Vavasour's belt but there was nothing there, no secret
cipher, nothing to hand over to your master at the Guildhall. You
were searching for that from the very start. Once you had escaped
from Walton or, rather, been allowed to escape, you went into
London hunting that cipher. First Cromart. Your expectations
must have been high. You believed Cromart, a skilled clerk, would
be carrying the cipher. You soon discovered that he was sheltering
at St Michael's. Garbed in the dirty clothes of a dung collector,
your face all masked, you visited Cromart in sanctuary. According
to Ratstail, Cromart's humours were disturbed, some ailment of
the belly. I did wonder if you gave him something to agitate his
stomach. Whatever, your meeting with Cromart would be easy
to arrange, nor was it difficult to plot his murder.'

Urswicke paused. He wondered if his father might return, then
he reflected on the season and the distance between Thorpe and
London. His father probably believed the mischief he'd concocted
would reach fulfilment whilst he put as much distance between
himself and Walton as possible. Only when he was back at the
Guildhall, sometime over the next few days, would Sir Thomas
hear about the disastrous events off the coast of Essex, two
Flemish carracks blazing from stern to poop and a Breton cog,
the cause of their misfortune, fleeing out to sea. Urswicke took
a deep breath and glanced up. No, he reasoned, he still had time
to lodge his indictment and bring this criminal to the judgement
he so richly deserved.

'You seem to forget,' Pembroke grated, 'Cromart was murdered
in a church locked and sealed from within. Cromart,' his voice
faltered, 'was my comrade.'

'A farrago of lies,' Urswicke retorted. 'And your protests are
false and futile.' Urswicke paused at a ghostly rattling behind him.
The noise disturbed him. He rose, bowed at the countess and
walked into the shadows to secure the shutter. He glanced over
his shoulder, Bray was coaxing the prisoner to drink from a goblet
of wine. The countess sat, head down. She was quietly reciting
the rosary, pausing after every 'Ave' to murmur the requiem.
Urswicke knew the countess did this constantly. She was praying
for her dead kinsmen, the members of the once powerful Beaufort

family, now gravely weakened, she their only survivor, her relatives being summarily sent into eternal night by the axe, sword or loose. Urswicke quietly vowed that today, over the next few hours, he and Bray would strike those who oppressed their mistress. He returned to his chair and sat down, tapping his booted feet against the hard paving stones. Pembroke lifted his head. Urswicke pointed at him.

'I shall return to my indictment. You murdered Cromart by a very simple device. Yes, the church was locked and bolted from within, but Cromart opened the door, probably the one in the sacristy which leads out to the jake's pot. Cromart invited the wolf into the house. As I've said, you visited him earlier that day, slipping into St Michael's, lighting a taper perhaps before the Lady altar or one of the other shrines. Then you'd wander the church, going over to the sanctuary, peering into the enclave. To all appearances a wandering dung collector curious about some fugitive sheltering in the church. Cromart would be only too willing to meet a comrade. A short conversation followed. You would claim that you wanted to help, that you would bring messages from others or the countess. Anyway, you would come back. St Michael's has an hour candle and you'd say at which hour, which red ring, it would be best to return. Cromart would agree then you'd disappear. Cromart had no reason to distrust you. Why should he? You are a comrade fresh from Brittany. You'd braved the sea voyage and escaped the traps of your enemies. So, at the appointed time, Cromart opened that sacristy door and went out. God knows what exactly happened, but you followed him back in and released that killing bolt.'

'Yet the sacristy door was locked and bolted from within?'

'Oh yes, your constant defence. You love that don't you? Such mystery distracts and, of course, we must not forget Archdeacon Blackthorne. The murdered men, even Ratstail, were protected by sanctuary. On no account could any blame be laid at York's door hence all the mystery. Now, the sacristy door was locked and bolted because you arranged that: masked and cowled, hiding deep in the shadows, you threatened Ratstail. You menaced that poor, hapless felon, despite his damaged hands, to lock and bolt the door once you'd gone, otherwise you'd return and kill him. I suspect you also bribed him, tossing your victim a coin. And why should Ratstail refuse? He was a felon but not a fool. A street dweller from his early days, all he wanted was to survive, so he agreed. Ratstail was his own man. You lied when you claimed he was in York's pay, that was just a ploy to muddy the waters.'

'If that's the truth,' Pembroke replied, 'if I threatened and bribed him, if I knew exactly what Ratstail was, why did I need to kill him?'

'So far I haven't said you did.'

'But you are going to?'

'Of course. It was a logical step. You could not risk the sharp-witted Ratstail reflecting, remembering and recalling the events of that dire night. True, you were masked and hooded. You could change your voice, yet Ratstail might have stumbled on to the truth, especially when you yourself took sanctuary in St Michael's.'

'You did so,' Bray declared, 'because you felt safe there. Parson Austin was a comrade and, of course, that's what the Recorder would have ordered. You also wanted to return to St Michael's to search that church for anything Cromart might have hidden. You had murdered him and taken his belt but you'd found nothing that would intrigue you. You began to wonder if Cromart, a cipher clerk, might have hidden it in some crevice in that ancient church. And, of course, there was Ratstail. You had to silence him, close his mouth for good, especially as he was marked down to join us on that slow, arduous pilgrimage to Thorpe Manor. Oh yes, it was best if Ratstail was despatched into the dark.'

'And Parson Austin was my accomplice?'

'No, no, again a suspicion encouraged by you to distract and divert.' Urswicke smiled thinly. 'Clever and devious! Parson Austin is undoubtedly an adherent of York but, basically, he is a good man. He is also a priest and a pastor. Oh, Pastor Austin can be used by his Yorkist masters; he may even entertain his own suspicions about what has happened but nothing more. Indeed, I am certain that he would not be party to murder in his own hallowed sanctuary. York simply used Parson Austin and so did you. After you murdered Cromart, you removed his belt and threatened Ratstail, you went into the bell tower of St Michael's and tolled the tocsin, then you fled. You wanted to deepen the mystery around Cromart's murder. You also needed a witness to what you had done. If you'd simply left, Ratstail would have just cowered in the enclave until Parson Austin or his parish council opened the church for the Jesus mass the following morning. If that happened, the mystery would not be so great. People might not recall what was open and what was shut. Indeed, Ratstail might have panicked and fled elsewhere. He would have certainly been caught and heaven knows what he might blurt out to save his neck from the noose. No, you threatened Ratstail into silent compliance.' Urswicke paused to sip from his goblet. 'I have no doubt,' he continued, 'Cromart and the others were killed on the orders of York, but the murders had to be concealed in a fog of deep mystery, that is certainly true of Ratstail's murder.'

'I had no weapon.'

'Oh shut up!' Urswicke retorted. 'You had a crossbow primed and ready, provided by York, hidden somewhere deep in the shadows of that ancient church, a hand-held arbalest easy to use.'

'But Ratstail suspected someone was lurking in one of the transepts, he glimpsed shifting shadows . . .'

'A blatant lie! Ratstail was bribed by you to say that. Remember, you left us to check on him. You told him to fashion some story about creating a distraction, a diversion to Bray and myself and our constant questioning. Ratstail would love such mischief, especially when he was paid for it. Again, remember, I searched his corpse. I found two coins, good silver pieces on his person. How could a fugitive, no more than a beggar, have such wealth? Indeed, as we have discovered, you seem well-furnished with silver, be it for bribing Ratstail or providing comfortable lodgings for your mother and sister. I suspect both those silver pieces were given by you. First, when you threatened Ratstail about locking and bolting the sacristy door behind you, and on the second occasion when we visited you at St Michael's. In fact, you made a mistake,' Urswicke declared. 'I reached Ratstail's corpse first and found those coins before you could secretly reclaim them.' Pembroke, now resting back in the chair, just glared at Urswicke and strained at the cords around his chest. 'Oh yes, you staged a murderous masque,' Urswicke continued. 'When Bray and I wandered the church, Ratstail stayed where you probably ordered him, sheltering in the enclave, hidden deep in the shadows and screened off by the high altar. You slipped back, picked up the arbalest, wherever it was concealed, and loosed the killing bolt. You then joined in that pretend search, the arbalest beneath your cloak.'

'You did not see one?'

'No. That's because it was small so you could easily and swiftly dispose of it through one of those lancet windows – a mere heartbeat in time. The weapon would be lost in the tangle of gorse and bramble which surrounds that church. You kept myself and Bray under close scrutiny – an easy enough task. St Michael's is like a hollow shell and every sound carries. This helped deepen our suspicions about someone hiding in the church, an impression you strengthened by swiftly opening and shutting a door in one of the transepts; that was heard by me as well as glimpsed by one of the parson's watchers in the cemetery. You successfully created the illusion that an assassin had stolen into the church, locked and bolted as it was, killed Ratstail and left just as mysteriously.' Urswicke pulled a face. 'Another murder shrouded in the fog of speculation yet, in the end, who cared for Ratstail alive or dead? No one. He wasn't a spy for York or anybody else, just a poor wretch caught up in the bloody turmoil between the great ones of the land. You, Pembroke, killed Ratstail to protect yourself and so sustain the mystery surrounding Cromart's death. Now Ratstail should have been your last victim but then we decided to trap you, yes mistress?'

'When Master Bray eventually came ashore,' Margaret smiled at her steward, 'I had close counsel with him and Urswicke. I informed Master Reginald that Christopher had already reached his own conclusions about you Pembroke. During our journey from London along the Mile End Road, Christopher had assessed everything he had learnt. He constructed an indictment based on logic and whatever other evidence he had managed to collect and he shared this with me. In the end we decided to set a trap, a truly deadly one.' She crossed herself. 'Poor Conwar was your next victim though, to a certain extent, we are all responsible for his death.'

'What do you mean?' Pembroke lurched forward, straining at the cords which bound him.

'You hail from Wales,' Margaret continued remorselessly. 'I

am a Beaufort but once I was the beloved wife of Edmund Tudor. He liked nothing more than to share with me the history and customs of his people. Now one of the things he told me was that among the Welsh tribes there is the blood bond, a chain of deep affection and loyalty founded on kinship, family and oaths of loyalty. This chain binds communities together in life and in death. You should know all about that, Pembroke, even if it now means very little to you. You shattered these chains. You cut yourself off and, in doing so, became a deadly threat to those who trusted and depended on you.' Margaret sipped from her goblet. Urswicke noticed how her hand trembled slightly. Margaret put the goblet down. 'I prayed, I reflected then I approached Conwar. I informed him about my suspicions founded on the conclusions Master Urswicke had reached about you. I could do this easily enough, moving amongst the sanctuary men dispensing charity, be it a scrap of food or a coin and, of course, I made sure you could not eavesdrop.'

'Yes, yes I saw you,' Pembroke muttered. Urswicke wondered if their prisoner was truly listening. Had the shock of this confrontation proved too much for his wits?

'Anyway,' Margaret continued, 'Conwar listened carefully and, to my surprise, he took very little convincing. He too had reached the logical conclusion that a traitor within was responsible for all the deaths amongst the Red Dragon Battle Group since you had landed at Walton-on-the-Naze. He also confirmed what Master Christopher suspected – that you, Pembroke, were a common factor in all these deaths: the two unfortunates who came ashore with you and were hanged; Guido Vavasour, who accompanied you, was captured, tortured and executed, even though his hiding place was known to no one, or supposedly so. Robert Vavasour was in communication with you before he was mysteriously murdered. Cromart was in sanctuary in the days following your arrival in England. Ratstail was sheltering in the same church as yourself. True,' Margaret shrugged, 'this is not evidence enough to hang a man but it certainly made me reflect and wonder. Oh yes, Conwar had watched events unfold and formed his own suspicions, though he'd kept these to himself. I argued how I needed to unmask the traitor and he courageously consented to my suggestion. I shared my suspicions with him that the secret assassin was probably searching for the Dragon Cipher, supposedly concealed on the warbelt of one of the Red Dragon Battle Group. Conwar agreed. What other reason could there be for all these deaths, one after the other? I then informed him that I was going to let slip to you, Pembroke, that Conwar carried the Dragon Cipher.'

The countess's voice trembled with emotion. 'Conwar, as you know, was the oldest of the group, a henchman of my late husband, a soul I truly trusted. God save us all. Conwar never gave my suggestion a second thought. He whispered that all this mysterious, murderous nonsense must be brought to an end once and for all. He added that if his death could achieve this then, like any warrior, he would gladly give up his life for me and mine. Once I knew he fully agreed, I gave him a medal, a pilgrim badge from the shrine of St Swithun's. I warned him that if you were the traitor, you'd act swiftly and ruthlessly. I advised Conwar that he would only be given a few heartbeats. God rest him, Conwar still agreed to what I asked. If you emerged as the traitor, he was to grasp that medallion tightly in his right hand. If not, he was to hold it in his left. As simple as that. The confrontation, when it took place, would certainly be in the dark, so you would scarcely notice him moving something from one hand to another. After all, you didn't really care for Conwar. All you wanted was his life and, once dead, the Dragon Cipher, allegedly hidden away in the lining of Conwar's warbelt.'

'No, no.' Pembroke protested, though his voice betrayed his deepening desperation. 'Your father, Sir Thomas, led the cortege. He was keen to ensure that all the sanctuary men safely reached the coast. He had the power to seize and search any belt. He did not want one of those in his custody to be killed. Archdeacon Blackthorne and Parson Austin were clear in their warnings.' Pembroke rocked himself backwards and forwards in the chair. Urswicke felt a touch of pity. Pembroke knew he was going to die and he was simply trying to delay the final confrontation for as long as possible in the hope that something might happen, a futile hope! Sir Thomas would be riding back to London and, even if by chance he heard about the sinking of the Flemish carracks, it would be fruitless for him to return. By then Pembroke would be dead, buried deep in his grave, and who else could betray them? Edith the maid had her own reason to remain silent whilst the carters were not only the countess's liege men but also deeply involved in the capture and interrogation of this prisoner. 'Sir Thomas,' Pembroke's voice was almost a wail, 'did not want any of the sanctuary men killed.'

'A farrago of lies,' Urswicke retorted. 'Sir Thomas had no power to search any of these sanctuary men. Canon law is strict on this issue. The bodies and possessions of sanctuary seekers cannot be violated. Archdeacon Blackthorne and Parson Austin would certainly enforce these regulations. True, my father would be most reluctant to order such a slaying, but once he learnt what you did about Conwar, he would give you every support, that would be easy enough. When we arrived here, it was dark and cold, people milling about in the courtyard. My father pushing his way through, then a brief conversation with you in the shadows and the matter was settled. He would give you every assistance. He wanted that cipher before the sanctuary men were bundled aboard *The Galicia* on their short voyage to destruction. He did what he could. You and the others were placed in cells below the manor house, a row of narrow closets locked by the same key. My father, very much the lord of this manor, gave you a second key.'

'My hands were chained! I was manacled, a prisoner . . .'

'No you were not,' Bray snapped. 'Oh, you had gyves fastened around the wrists and ankles but they were simply clasped, not locked. Once that passageway was deserted, you took off your manacles and grasped the arbalest Sir Thomas had hidden away. Using that common key, you slipped into Conwar's cell; the tunnel below is dark and cold. Oh yes there were guards at both ends but Sir Thomas was cunning. He'd tell them for comfort's sake they could stand outside, and soldiers of course make themselves as comfortable as possible. You however, became busy enough. You slipped silently into Conwar's cell. He would immediately realise the truth of the situation. My Lady the countess was correct. Conwar grasped that pilgrim badge in his right hand even as you loosed the killing bolt. You then took his belt and left, locking the door behind you. You re-entered your own narrow closet, locked the door and hid the arbalest beneath the dirt piled there. God knows there was enough to hide a chest of weapons.'

'And the belt?'

'Oh you probably strapped that around your own waist whilst you waited for an opportunity to hand it over.'

'Naturally,' Countess Margaret spoke up, 'Sir Thomas would have been truly mystified. After all, I had allegedly informed Pembroke who was carrying the cipher. Conwar's belt was searched but nothing was found. However, time was short, the pilgrimage was drawing to an end. Our good Recorder would have loved to seize that cipher but he also knew what was planned. The sanctuary men were to be led to the coast, embark on *The Galicia* and perish with everybody else when those Flemish carracks swept in. Perhaps the captains of both vessels were given strict instructions to search the corpses of everyone aboard *The Galicia*, the countess smiled thinly, 'and that would include yours. You were also marked down for death, wasn't he Christopher?'

'Oh yes!' Urswicke replied. 'Believe me, Pembroke, when you made an agreement and entered into an alliance with my father, you truly sat down to sup with demons. According to your understanding, you would join the other sanctuary men and eventually reach Brittany, where you would continue your treacherous ways until you and my father had done what could be done, and then what? A return to England? A royal pardon? Your thirty pieces of silver? A small manor house with lands where you, your mother and sister could live serenely and securely? Ah well,' Urswicke rubbed his hands together, 'as I said, when you sup with demons, you must be prudent and bring a very long spoon to the table. Our noble Recorder had studied you, Pembroke, and offered one further inducement, a great favour to entice you to play the Judas man to the very full.'

'What do you mean?'

'Zeigler Pembroke. As I said at the beginning of my indictment, my father promised you that the man who had blighted your life would be captured and you could watch him slowly strangle on that great gibbet over Tyburn stream. If the hangman was paid correctly, that could take a very long time. You and your loved ones could watch him die. This was a bait you could not refuse.' Urswicke spread his hands. 'You know what happened. Zeigler was captured, imprisoned, tried and condemned to death.

You even saw him hoisted on to the execution cart but then Zeigler escaped. You may have been suspicious, but my father would reassure you that the malefactor would soon be recaptured, detained and hanged. Now that was a lie and, believe me, Pembroke, just the beginning of what was being plotted in this deepest, darkest nightmare. You see, we know Sir Thomas organised Zeigler's escape.' Urswicke ignored Pembroke's sharp intake of breath. 'Oh yes, the execution cart should have been more closely guarded. Those rifflers, the Sangliers appeared, flaunting their scarlet livery led by Joachim, Zeigler's henchman. They freed the criminal and my father protected him. Now Zeigler loved to dress as a Franciscan friar. I glimpsed both Zeigler and Joachim in their brown robes sheltering on board the Flemish carrack *The Sea Hawk*, berthed at Queenhithe. Bray suspected both *The Sea Hawk* and its sister ship *The Gryphon* had been undoubtedly hired to stand off Walton and destroy *The Galicia* and kill everyone on board, including you.'

'And Zeigler?'

'Zeigler was a former Yorkist mercenary, a man who hated the Welsh and the Red Dragon Battle Group in particular. Zeigler was a born killer but he had sharp wits, he needed these to survive as a man constantly in battle harness. Zeigler was proficient in the Breton tongue: he was to be taken to Brittany where he would inveigle himself into the household of our mistress's one and only beloved son.'

'Impossible!' Pembroke shouted.

'Who would gainsay him?' Urswicke demanded. 'Who could contradict? Our mistress? If Sir Thomas's plot had achieved success, the Countess Margaret Beaufort would have few envoys or trusted messengers to send to Rennes in Brittany. It might take weeks for her to learn and recover from the disaster which was supposed to take place off Walton. By then, Zeigler may have carried out his murderous mischief. And, as I've asked you, who could gainsay him? Master Pembroke, you and all the other members of the Red Dragon Battle Group, together with the crew of *The Galicia*, would have been wiped off the face of the earth. The Flemish carracks should have been victorious, the pirates would have pillaged the corpses, taking their belts along with any letters or documents. These would be seized and later used in Sir Thomas's planned deception. We learnt that the Flemish carracks, once they had achieved their task, would sail back to Queenhithe where their captains would undoubtedly secretly account to Sir Thomas Urswicke. Zeigler would be prepared, armed with letters and whatever else he needed. Zeigler would then be despatched to Brittany to present himself as the only fortunate survivor of the murderous mayhem perpetrated off Walton-on-the-Naze.'

'Zeigler would not be believed.'

'Oh yes he would,' the countess retorted. She sighed deeply. 'I am certain that Sir Thomas would secretly advise and prepare him. Zeigler would be convincing enough and all he had to do was wait for the moment to strike.'

'My father did not,' Urswicke resumed his indictment, 'care for you or yours. Sir Thomas is as cunning as Reynard. You now realise that, don't you Pembroke? You might have entertained suspicions about Zeigler's escape but, only when you were on board *The Galicia*, with those two Flemish carracks closing in, would you have realised you had been deceived, trapped and condemned.' Urswicke gestured at Bray. 'Tell him now.'

'I killed Zeigler.' Bray leaned closer, staring intently at the prisoner. 'I boarded *The Sea Hawk* and I killed Zeigler as I did his accomplice. Both men were fit for Hell as any I have met, but listen.' Bray took a deep breath. 'Zeigler discovered that your mother and sister were lodged at the Minoresses'. Perhaps someone at the Guildhall let slip to him where they were. Perhaps my father, he doesn't give a fig for anyone. There again, Zeigler may have surmised it himself as he glared down at you and your womenfolk from that execution cart.' Bray ignored Pembroke's heart-chilling moan, as if he realised what was coming. 'Zeigler and his accomplice Joachim were received by the good Minoresses who accepted them for what they appeared to be, Franciscan friars bearing important news. This is nothing out of the ordinary, the good brothers are often used as trusted messengers. Zeigler was allowed to go alone to the chamber where your mother and sister were lodged. He killed both of them, swift and deadly, with the crossbow he'd concealed. Rest assured . . .'

Bray broke off at the hideous cry which seemed to come from the very marrow of Pembroke's soul, a heart-rending shriek which trailed away to a mixture of curses and muttered prayers. Pembroke rocked himself backwards and forwards, then abruptly tore the mask from his face, hands free, he unloosed the buckles, undid the clasps and let the mask fall to the ground. In the dancing light of the fire, Urswicke could only stare in horror at the mangled face beneath. Pembroke's right cheek was wholesome but the entire left side of his face was simply a hardened, blood-red scar darkened by the years. A most gruesome wound which stretched from the corner of his eye down to just above his chin. Pembroke raised his hands, lips moving soundlessly, tears streaming down his wounded face. Urswicke stared pitifully at him then he recalled the prisoner's treachery, the murders he had committed, the devastating damage he had caused. Pembroke had chosen the Judas path, he had sown the tempest and now he was reaping the whirlwind.

'Master Pembroke,' the countess's voice was sharp, 'Master Pembroke, I weep for you but I also weep and mourn for your victims, good men loyal and true.'

The prisoner simply pointed to the mask on the floor. 'I have lived with that,' he whispered hoarsely, 'so I shall die with it, please.'

Bray glanced at the countess, who nodded. The steward rose, picked up the mask, handed it to the prisoner and helped him buckle the straps and secure the clasps. Once finished, Bray returned to his chair while Pembroke, bound tight by the cords around his chest and the back of the chair, simply slouched, head down, staring at the floor.

'Master Bray,' he murmured, 'was it swift? My mother . . .'

'God rest them, it was very swift. I doubt if they realised what was truly happening.'

'All finished,' Pembroke murmured. 'All dark. What can I do? What can I say? Master Urswicke, your indictment is true, it's lawful, and I recognise my guilt. Oh, you have the detail wrong on some of your accusations, but what does it matter now? My Lady, I confess my perjury and my betrayal. I have no defence. I simply became tired of being hunted, of living in constant fear of being arrested, tortured and suffering the most excruciating death. I was separated from my beloved family. I wanted to be with them. I had enough turmoil. I wanted peace and Parson

Austin showed me a path I might follow. I took that path. Let me say Parson Austin was only the conduit, a messenger, an envoy, nothing more, nothing less. Oh, I am sure he nourished his own suspicions but that's the good parson. He does what he's told and, provided it sits easy with his conscience, he will not demur. Your father, Christopher, was the true architect of my misfortune. Naturally, when Zeigler escaped, I wondered. Only when I saw those Flemish carracks sweep in, did I realise the full depth of Sir Thomas's treachery.'

'How did you meet?' Urswicke demanded.

'Oh, before I took sanctuary. It was easy enough, flitting like a shadow around London, this place, that place. The same is true of our journey to Thorpe. Ah well.' Pembroke stretched out a hand towards the countess, 'Mistress, I never intended to hurt you and yours, not really. I was just tired, exhausted.'

'But you did hurt, most grievously.'

'Sir Thomas Urswicke,' Pembroke continued defiantly, 'is determined on your total destruction. He sees this as his great prize to offer the House of York. He set his mind and soul on annihilating the Red Dragon Battle Group completely. You too, Master Bray, were marked down for destruction, though he gave orders that his son,' Pembroke spat the words out, 'should be separated from the countess through stealth and treachery.'

Urswicke, thoughts racing, held up his hand to silence. 'Oh yes,' he whispered, 'I see how the dice was meant to finally fall in this hellish game of hazard. *The Galicia*, a cog which offered great assistance to our mistress, is utterly destroyed, as are the last remnants of that battle group, and there is more. Zeigler the assassin, on the loose like a hunting wolf in the court of Brittany, watching, waiting ready to pounce. If he was successful, the Tudor cause beyond the seas would have been completely annihilated. In England, the countess is bereft of husband and child, her loyal steward and henchman cut down in some stinking alleyway or dingy taproom. And, as for me? Oh yes, suspicions sprouting as thick and rich as weeds amongst the remnants of the countess's adherents. They would point out that I am Sir Thomas's son, that there was no attack on me. Oh yes,' Urswicke rose to his feet, 'that's why my dear father has been, at least publicly, so benevolent towards me: that purse of silver and the robe despatched for me, there'd be a record kept of that and other such gifts.' He glanced at the countess and held her stare. 'Heaven help us, mistress but, if all that happened, you could scarcely be blamed for beginning to wonder about my true allegiance.'

'There's more,' Pembroke grated. 'Much more. I do confess the indictment laid against me is true. I killed Cromart as you said. I visited him earlier in the day pretending to be a dung collector busy about the jake's pot outside the sacristy door. I informed Cromart that I would return at a certain hour and wait for him to open that door. Cromart was ill and disconcerted, some humour of the belly, but that had nothing to do with me. Cromart was, like myself, exhausted.'

'But still loyal,' the countess interjected. 'A good, true soul.'

'I returned that night.' Pembroke seemed hardly aware of what the countess had said. 'I returned at the hour we agreed. I followed him back into the sacristy.' Pembroke shrugged, 'The rest you know. Ratstail had to be silenced. He was a coward, easy to frighten, but I did not trust him. I knew it was only a matter of time, so I killed him. An easy enough task. The Recorder's men hid an arbalest for me deep in the shadows of that church. Once I had finished, they collected it from beneath the lancet window I slipped it through. I did open that door to create a false impression of someone fleeing. Parson Austin's watchers glimpsed figures moving through God's Acre – they were the Recorder's men. You see, once I had dropped the arbalest through the agreed window, it was a sign for everything else to happen—'

'All an illusion,' Urswicke interrupted. 'You created an illusion of an assassin loose in the church and then fleeing. And Conwar's murder?'

'As you described it. I did wonder about a possible trap. Conwar seemed so hostile, as soon as I entered his cell, he began to challenge me. I killed him immediately and took his belt. Oh, it was simply done. The Recorder had given me a key and I knew there was no one in the passageway outside. Robert Vavasour also had to be silenced and I achieved that the way you described.'

'You said there was more?' Urswicke demanded.

'Guido Vavasour,' Pembroke breathed out noisily, 'he truly believed there was a traitor, a spy in the countess's household.

Now I became very wary of him. When we landed on the beach at Walton, Sir Thomas's comitatus appeared out of the dark. They circled us but Sir Thomas allowed a gap for me to slip through. Vavasour followed. I grew extremely worried that, on reflection, he might regard my escape as truly suspicious. Now during our flight from Walton, Guido was obsessed with this notion of a traitor in our midst. I had to divert him. I, I . . .' Pembroke turned his head away. 'I had to do this.' Pembroke's voice had fallen to almost a whisper. 'True, your father offered me enticing bribes but he also threatened dire consequences for my mother and sister if I did not cooperate with him.'

'What did he do?' the countess demanded.

'Until his capture, Vavasour truly believed that you, Christopher Urswicke, were the spy, the traitor in the Tudor camp. I encouraged him in that belief. He told me that if I was ever taken up, he would confess the same, so your father would realise that you had been unmasked. Guido also vowed that if he safely returned to Brittany, he would advise Lord Jasper to warn the countess. I supported him in this, providing what scraps of evidence I could. I also informed your father of the same when I told him that Vavasour was hiding in the cellars of The Hanging Tree.'

'But how can this be?' the countess demanded. 'When poor Guido was dragged from the dungeons of the White Tower to be hanged on that scaffold, he approached me. He splayed his fingers to cover his face. We later realised he was imitating a mask. Master Christopher, Reginald, you argued the same?'

'Something happened during Guido's interrogation,' Pembroke replied, 'but the only person that knows the truth about that will be Sir Thomas and those who tortured Vavasour, yet what does it matter now? You will discover soon enough. Your father is truly treacherous, Urswicke. I believe he tortured Vavasour. Guido persisted in his belief that you were the traitor then your father whispered in his ear that it was in fact me. He would enjoy that. He also ensured that Vavasour, even in the few hours left to him, would never be able to tell that truth to anyone else.' Pembroke's voice was now weary, a man who knew that he was condemned and death was imminent. 'Countess, my Lady,' he touched the mask on his face, 'for what it is worth I am truly sorry. Promise

me again that you will light candles and have requiem masses
sung by a chantry priest for the good of my soul and those of
my kin.'

'I promise.' The countess's voice was harsh.

'And one last favour.' Pembroke strained against the ropes. 'I
have a powder secreted on me.' Again he touched the mask on
his face. 'When the pain comes, the potion eases the hurt. Too
little is useless, too much would send me into an eternal sleep.
If I confess even more, will you allow me that?' The countess
glanced at Bray and Urswicke and both her henchmen nodded
in agreement. 'As God is my witness,' Pembroke breathed. 'Be
on your guard, mistress, against the Recorder. He hates you for
who you are and what you do. He passionately resents the control
you seem to have over his son. I am sure,' Pembroke continued
hoarsely, 'that in the very near future, before Yuletide comes and
goes, Sir Thomas will proclaim "The last and true confession of
Guido Vavasour, traitor". He will have this published in some
broadsheet by a London bookseller, probably the one who trades
under the sign of The Red Keg close to St Paul's. Copies of this
proclamation will be posted on the Cross in the graveyard there,
as well as in Cheapside.'

'And?' Christopher fought off a shiver of ice-cold fear; he
almost sensed what Pembroke was about to say.

'Everything,' Pembroke retorted, 'everything I have done will
be ascribed to you, Master Christopher.'

'In what way?'

'In your indictment, you claimed that I was the common factor
in all these deaths. However, you were at Walton-on-the-Naze
and so was your father. You were in London when Cromart was
murdered, when Guido was taken up and his brother captured in
that tavern cellar. This final confession will argue that you were
at Thorpe Manor when Conwar died and so on and so on.'
Pembroke cleared his throat. 'Copies of this alleged confession
would be despatched to Duke Francis and Lord Jasper in Brittany.
You, Master Urswicke, will be depicted as the traitor in the
countess's household and who can gainsay it? The Vavasours
are dead and, if Sir Thomas had his way, everyone else who
boarded *The Galicia*.'

'My father,' Christopher snarled, 'may tarnish my name. He

has done so before in the hope of driving a real wedge between myself and the countess.'

'Ah, but have you been accused of being the countess's lover?' Pembroke paused, twisting in the chair. Urswicke just gaped in surprise. The countess whispered a prayer and turned to Bray who simply shrugged.

'This true confession despatched to Brittany and Lord Jasper.' Pembroke continued remorselessly and Urswicke suspected the prisoner took some pleasure in this revelation. 'The true confession,' Pembroke repeated, 'would describe a countess who is obsessed, who dotes on her young clerk so much so that she will never believe that you, Master Urswicke, caress her with one hand and betray her with the other. A woman who is truly witless when it comes to you. A countess who wouldn't even accept the warnings of her other henchman, Reginald Bray.'

'God forgive the blasphemy,' Bray interjected. He clutched the arbalest even tighter. 'In my early days I did warn the countess. I did advise her to be prudent but Christopher has proved his loyalty more than enough. I trust him as I do myself.'

'But of course,' the countess declared, 'who can refute such an outrageous claim? If Sir Thomas had his way, Bray would now be dead, his mouth silenced and his murder placed at Christopher's door!'

'Sir Thomas is capable of anything. He is known for his cunning and, as for his son,' Urswicke caught the hatred in Pembroke's voice, 'well, people will argue that the apple always falls close to the tree.'

'Enough!' the countess, her pale face mottled with anger, sprang to her feet. 'Enough!' She clutched her stomach, heaved a great sigh and sat down again. She put her face in her hands, whispering a prayer, then glanced up. 'Is there anything else?' she murmured, pointing at Pembroke. 'I adjure you. Is there anything else you could, you should in all justice confess to me?'

'My Lady, I am sorry.'

'On that,' she replied, 'we both agree. I have promised and I will keep my pledge. Masses will be offered for the repose of your soul and those of your family.'

'My Lady, thank you. I beg you to make it swift.'

Urswicke recalled Vavasour, mouth all bloodied, being dragged

from the torture chambers to strangle on that high gibbet. He
was about to remind the countess about that when Bray rose to
his feet and walked over to confront the prisoner.

'Swift?' he demanded.

'As swift as you can.' Pembroke stared up at Bray.

'Then God speed you.'

Bray stepped back, raised the arbalest and, before Urswicke
or the countess could intervene, released the catch so the barbed
bolt sped out to take Pembroke deep in the left side of his chest,
a killing blow to the heart. The prisoner rocked backwards and
forwards in his chair then lurched forward, vomiting blood, which
gushed like a fountain out of his nose and mouth. Pembroke
gargled for a while before he slumped forward, head down.

'We could have let him take the powder,' Urswicke protested.

'Aye, and we could also continue to listen to him spout his
wickedness.'

'Not truly his,' the countess retorted, 'but, God forgive him,
your father's.'

'Justice has been done,' Bray declared, putting the arbalest
down. He crossed and examined Pembroke's corpse. He pressed
a hand against his victim's throat. 'I feel no life beat,' he muttered.
'Pembroke is dead and gone to judgement. Christopher, help me.'
They searched the corpse carefully but found nothing untoward,
except a pouch of white powder which Bray threw into the fire.
'I wonder,' Bray whispered, staring down at the corpse which
they had laid out on the floor, 'I wonder if Pembroke ever realised
we suspected him?'

'He may have done,' Urswicke replied. 'Perhaps he hid this?
Perhaps he trusted my father's plan for him, until those Flemish
carracks appeared, and what could he do then? If he tried to
escape, I could have ridden him down, not to mention the two
guards my father left. They would know nothing except a sanctuary man had escaped, trying to flee, so he could be killed out
of hand.'

'Yes, yes. Pembroke must have been as surprised as anyone
at what truly unfolded.'

'Remove him.' The countess turned her back to the corpse and
walked further down the hall. 'Take him away.' Urswicke caught
the sob in her voice. 'Take him,' the countess repeated, 'place

him outside. Tomorrow morning bury him. Place a cross above the grave, he will certainly need all its power.'

Bray and Urswicke removed the corpse, placing the blood-soaked cadaver on the floor of the shabby scullery. Bray pulled a roll of sacking over the corpse, tightening it carefully against the vermin which scurried across the cracked, mildewed paving stones. Urswicke fashioned a crude cross and placed it at the foot of the gruesome bundle. He then murmured a requiem which Bray echoed, and they returned to the solar where the countess had rearranged the chairs before the hearth and refilled the goblets.

'I feel my hands are bloodied,' she declared. 'There are times when the dead seem to throng around me, following me, desperate to speak. Am I responsible for their deaths? Never mind, never mind.' She shook her head. 'Let us recite the ancient hymn for the departed.'

All three stood and recited the 'De Profundis', followed by the verses from the 'Dies Irae', the sombre words echoing around that ghostly hall. Once they'd finished, the countess, sitting between her two henchmen, quietly cried. Urswicke found it all the more piteous by his mistress's silence as she leaned forward, staring into the fire, the tears rolling down her cheeks.

'We killed a man,' she exclaimed.

'No, we executed a criminal and a traitor,' Bray replied, 'a true Judas who would have cheerfully despatched Urswicke and myself to the gallows to suffer an excruciating death, being torn apart by the hangman whilst you, mistress, would be exiled to a convent deep in the bleakest wilds of this kingdom.'

'And now what?' Urswicke insisted. 'What can we say? What can we do to counter what Pembroke has revealed?'

'Let us be blunt and honest.' The countess lifted her wine goblet and silently toasted Urswicke. 'Everyone,' she declared, 'or at least those in our world, recognise that you, Christopher Urswicke, lurk in the shadowlands of politic and power. Only we three know the truth but others ask if you are really mine, body and soul, or do you work for your father, or do you work for us both? An ambitious young clerk who pursues nothing but his own advancement as he quietly slips from one group to another? A man dedicated to nothing except his own self-promotion?'

'But, you know the truth about that, my Lady.'

'Of course I do, Christopher, and I couldn't really give a fig about what other people think. Indeed, the world can go hang, for such confusion greatly aids our cause and protects you as well as ourselves. However, your father's present plotting is truly dangerous. These fresh allegations twist matters in a very sinister fashion. The minions of York will whisper to Jasper Tudor, Duke Francis, De Vere of Oxford and others that you, Christopher, truly are a traitor to the core. They will point to the present mayhem and destruction of the Tudor cause. These same minions will argue that I am blinded by love and lust for you. So obsessed, I cannot distinguish day from night. I cannot accept that you will betray me so I ignore all warnings and advice.' The countess paused. 'Even more dangerous,' she continued, 'will be the whispered malice about our treatment of my poor husband, Sir Henry. I shall be depicted as an unfaithful wife, a hussy,' her voice broke, 'an adulterous whore who plays the two-backed beast with her chancery clerk. How I do this, lecherous and as hot as a spring sparrow, even as my husband, grievously wounded in the service of the King, lies mortally ill at our manor of Woking. You can only imagine how the powerful Staffords will regard such treatment of their dear kinsman. Yet all this is a lie, a damnable, demon-inspired lie.' Bray went to speak, Urswicke too. 'No, no,' she continued. 'When all this was done, I would be left isolated. No son, no kin, no loyal henchmen, no cause. No support in Wales or elsewhere. God be my judge, but your father, Christopher, must pay for all of this.'

Urswicke was about to reply when Bray abruptly rose to his feet and walked to the hall door.

'Can't you hear it?' he declared. 'There is a horseman in the yard outside, I am sure.'

Urswicke and Bray hastily collected their warbelts, strapped them on and hurried down the ice-cold passageway leading into the square, cobbled yard. Bray took a sconce torch from its crevice in the wall, opened the door and went out. The man crouching down to hobble his horse, rose to his feet and turned.

'Master Bray, Master Urswicke.'

'Fleetfoot!' Urswicke replied.

'I bring urgent messages for the countess.'

They led the courier back into the house and into the hall. The countess deliberately sat in the shadows to hide the grief on her face. Fleetfoot, however, squatted on a stool, stretching his hands out towards the fire before gratefully accepting the wine goblet thrust into his hands.

'I rode as fast as I could, mistress,' he began. 'You are well, mistress?'

'Your message?' the countess replied. 'Why now, in the dead of night?'

'My Lady, both Richard of Gloucester's men as well as Clarence's bully-boys, led by Mauclerc, have visited your mansion. They demand to speak to you, they want to know the whereabouts of Master Bray. They are furious,' Fleetfoot smiled, 'that they cannot detect him in the city and they wonder what progress, if any, you and yours have made in searching for Lady Anne Neville.'

'Oh, I am sure they do. Very well, very well.' The countess rose to her feet. 'It's time we returned to London. Let us enter that nest of vipers.'

PART SEVEN
'Then Shall Judgement Be Awarded'

F ive days later, Margaret Countess of Beaufort rested in the luxurious solar of her riverside mansion in London. She sat enthroned in a sturdy, intricately carved chair, flanked by her two henchmen, Urswicke to her right, Bray to the left. A fire roared in the hearth, exuding warmth and light, whilst the table, which separated the countess from her two guests, gleamed in the light of the candelabra placed there. Margaret raised her goblet in toast to Richard Duke of Gloucester and his constant shadow, Francis Viscount Lovel.

'Your Grace, my Lord, you are most welcome. What news of the King and court? Is the Queen *enceinte*, is she expecting a child? I pray that she does.' The countess held Gloucester's gaze, for she knew from rumour and gossip that this young prince hated the Queen and all her Woodville faction.

Gloucester replied tactfully and Urswicke studied both visitors as they sipped at goblets of Rhenish and took the occasional sweetmeat from the silver platter before them. Both the duke and his henchman had removed their diamond-studded bonnets and thick military cloaks, unfastening the clasps of the costly leather jerkins beneath. Gloucester had explained how there had been shooting at the butts on Tower Green when they'd received an invitation, delivered by Fleetfoot, to visit the countess on a matter of the deepest importance. They knew full well what that was, yet both men hid their impatience behind courtly curtseys and tactful niceties. The countess had deliberately delayed this meeting until she had recovered from that 'deep night of the soul', as she described her feelings at what had happened at Thorpe Manor. Now composed, resolutely determined to push matters ahead, she sat as serenely as any high-born court lady, though she deliberately dressed like a nun in a dark-blue kirtle, a veil of the same colour on her head with a white, starched wimple framing her smooth, pale face. She had discussed in great detail this meeting with Bray and Urswicke and both had agreed that it was the best course of action. Urswicke stiffened as Gloucester abruptly leaned forward, slamming his goblet down on the table and tossing the remains of the sweetmeat he had been eating back on to the platter.

'My Lady,' Gloucester now dropped all pretence, 'you invited us, well, I would say summoned us here.' He flicked his fingers at Bray. 'We have been searching for him and we could not find him so, let us move to the arrow point. Have you discovered the whereabouts of the Lady Anne Neville?'

'Your Grace,' the countess retorted heatedly, 'earlier this year you gave me assurances about the safety of my beloved son exiled,' she coughed, 'I mean sheltering in Duke Francis's court in Rennes.'

'And I have not violated such promises?'

'And the latest farrago of nonsense? Your Grace, you know full well how the sanctuary men were taken to Walton and what happened in that cove. You are the King's brother, aren't you? You do know, don't you?' The countess's barbed questions surprised even Urswicke, who glanced at his mistress, sitting so rigidly in her chair, ave beads wrapped like a weapon chain around her right hand.

'My Lady, I had no part in that.'

'Your brothers?'

'The Lord Edward is King and can do what he wants, whilst Clarence will always do what he wants.'

'And there are others?'

'Such as?'

'Sir Thomas Urswicke, Recorder of London, father of my dear and beloved clerk Master Christopher.'

Gloucester leaned forward, his thin, pale face now tense, eyes ever shifting as he glared at the countess and her two henchmen. 'My Lady, I will be as blunt as you. My brother the King is furious at that debacle off the Essex coast. A Breton ship attacked and two Flemish carracks destroyed, along with their crews. I will not,' Gloucester gave a lopsided grin, 'pretend otherwise, though,' he leaned back in his chair, fingers tapping the hilt of his dagger, 'I am not too sure about what really happened out there, whilst my brother is equally mystified. Oh, we know the ways of the court, don't we Francis?' Lovel just nodded. 'Yes, yes we do,' Gloucester continued, 'we all know that the King of England hires Flemish carracks to do his will, but what's the use of wondering about that now?'

'The Lord works in mysterious ways.'

'He certainly does, madame!' Gloucester snapped. 'And so now, the Lady Neville?'

'Your Grace,' the countess replied, 'what about Sir Thomas Urswicke?'

'Let his son,' Lovel jibed, 'take care of that.'

'My good and loyal steward,' the countess continued, tapping Bray on the shoulder and ignoring Lovel's insult, 'Master Reginald, has worked very hard on your behalf. We have found the Lady Anne.'

'Where?' Gloucester almost shouted at Bray.

'On pilgrimage, your Grace, though she asked me to keep that secret.'

'Pilgrimage?'

'Yes, your Grace, but I am sworn to secrecy, and the Lady Anne, too, has taken a vow. She will tell no one, other than that she sheltered in an anchorite's cell to pray.'

'For what?'

'For you and herself, your Grace, and more than that I cannot say.'

'How did you find her?' Gloucester demanded.

'A matter of logic, your Grace. Where can a noble lady safely hide? My mistress, the countess, has just accompanied sanctuary men to the coast . . .?'

'Of course, of course,' Gloucester was now relaxed and smiling, 'pilgrims are equally protected by Holy Mother Church. They look after each other, they journey peaceably and lodge in comfortable taverns. Very clever, Master Bray. Is that why you changed your appearance, so you could slip out of the city and search for her?'

'Your Grace is as perceptive as ever. My lords, I have sworn to the Lady Anne that I will not reveal where she went or who helped her. Suffice to say, she is now safe and looking forward to meeting you before this day is out.'

Gloucester picked up his goblet and sat back, smiling at the countess.

'We have further business.' Bray's voice was now harsh. 'Sir Thomas Urswicke, our noble Recorder, holds certain information about my Lady which is due to be published in a broadsheet. This is a quiver of malicious lies about her personal life, highly detrimental to our countess. You know, your Grace, as does this entire city, indeed the kingdom, that Countess Margaret Beaufort is a woman of the utmost integrity. This broadsheet is to be drawn up at the sign of The Red Keg, near St Paul's.' Gloucester just nodded.

'Your Grace,' the countess declared, 'what Master Bray said is true, but it's only the flower not the root. I need, and I will say this in the presence of Sir Thomas's son, I need a rest, a respite, protection from the Recorder's constant malice.'

'He certainly achieved little success in that venture off Walton,' Lovel drawled. The viscount fell silent as Gloucester turned and glared at him before turning back to the countess.

'My Lady,' Duke Richard declared, 'I will watch, wait and see. On that, you have my word. But the Lady Anne . . .'

'I know you are a man of your word.' The countess kissed the crucifix hanging on her ave beads. 'Rest assured,' she continued, 'you will meet the Lady Anne shortly. Let darkness fall and, once the vesper bell has tolled, return here, my Lords, and the Lady Anne will be waiting. I must impress upon you what Lady Anne has told me. She will not be questioned about her disappearance, which she describes as a pilgrimage. She was safe there. We know such groups,' the countess smiled, 'as the great poet Chaucer attests, are orderly and devout. My Lords, I thought I should tell you that.'

Gloucester and Lovel both thanked her and the meeting ended in a flurry of hand kissing and assurances of goodwill. Gloucester seemed as delighted as a man on his wedding day, smiling to himself, constantly tapping the front of his brocaded jerkin, eager to be gone as he said, to prepare himself for meeting the delightful Lady Anne. The duke and Lovel made their farewells and, once the countess was sure they had left, she invited Urswicke and Bray to sit close.

'So it is done,' she declared. 'Fleetfoot is now busy transforming my maid Edith back into the Lady Anne. She will be ready by this evening. Now,' she turned to Bray, 'what Gloucester described as the debacle of Walton is common knowledge throughout the city. No one knows the full truth except us three, and we will leave it at that. However, I have learnt from my own enquiries that the King is furious. Your father, Christopher, even more so. Has he asked to see you?'

'Not yet, mistress, but I am sure he will. Can we trust Gloucester?'

'As much as we can anyone. So, my friends,' the countess rose to her feet, 'once again we wait on our noble Recorder . . .'

On the Monday following Gloucester's visit to the countess, Urswicke received an urgent invitation from his father to visit him in his chambers at the Guildhall. Urswicke prepared himself well. He dressed in his costliest cotehardie over a crisp, white shirt of cambric linen, pure wool leggings and high-heeled boots of Moroccan leather. He shaved himself close and dressed his hair in the clerkly fashion. Strapping on his warbelt, he picked up his cloak and left the countess's mansion. He made his way through the maze of foul-smelling streets into the busy heart of Cheapside. Despite the intense cold, the markets were busy, with many of the citizens buying and selling in preparation for the celebration of Advent and the great feast of Christmas. Yuletide poles had been set up, festooned with garlands and wreaths and four great tallow candles to mark the weeks of Advent. On the top of the pole perched the largest candle of them all; this would be lit early on Christmas Eve. Beneath one of these poles, a dark-skinned chanteur proclaimed how he had lately come from Bethlehem. He described to the citizens what it was like to kneel and pray on the very spot Christ was born.

Urswicke walked on, pushing his way through the crowd, one hand on his sword hilt, the other on his money wallet. Despite the vivid, colourful scenes around him, Urswicke was distracted, though pleased with the way matters were proceeding. Gloucester had kept his word, or at least part of it. Bray's street swallows had reported how the parchment maker, the producer of broadsheets drawn up in his shop under the sign of The Red Keg, had been visited by Gloucester's bully-boys, all wearing the livery of the White Boar. They had pushed their way into the shop, cowed those inside, and left with sheaves of parchment which they tossed on to a nearby bonfire, lit by some kind soul for the benefit of the poor and homeless during this freezing season. Gloucester's retainers had stood laughing and talking, sharing out a wineskin, not leaving until every scrap of parchment had turned to ash.

Gloucester, as arranged, had met the Lady Anne. According to the countess, he had ecstatically embraced the young lady and solemnly promised that he would not enquire where she had been but would only rejoice in her return. Urswicke smiled to himself as he made his way around the stalls selling all kinds of produce; be it jewel-encrusted leather from Cordova or the finest linen from the Baltic towns. Everyone seemed busy. The air was riven by a myriad of different smells, as well as the constant shouting of traders: this was echoed by their apprentices who scurried as nimble as squirrels through the crowds, trying to entice customers to their stalls. Beggars swarmed around, a phalanx of needy yet aggressive men, jostling the good citizens for alms until beadles broke them up and moved them on.

The place of punishment, near the Tun in Cheapside, was thronged with Guildhall officials; these were busy around the stocks, thews and lashing posts, where felons found guilty of petty crimes would receive punishment before the Angelus bell. The cries, screams and shouts of the victims were chilling and noisome, and Urswicke sighed with relief as he entered the majestic gatehouse leading into the Guildhall yard. Two bailiffs stopped him, demanding to see his warrants. As soon as they glimpsed Sir Thomas's seal, both officials became fawning, ushering Christopher up to his father's gloomy chamber on the second floor of the main Guildhall building, its windows overlooking the heart of Cheapside. Sir Thomas, swathed in gilt-edged robes, rose from behind his chancery desk to greet 'his dear son'. They exchanged the kiss of peace, then Sir Thomas ushered Christopher to a comfortable chair on the other side of the table before returning to his own. The Recorder offered refreshment; Christopher refused, watching his father intently, for Sir Thomas did not seem a happy man.

'You are well, my son?'

'Thank God I am sir, and yourself?'

'A little disturbed.' Sir Thomas leaned across the desk. 'In God's name, Christopher, what happened off Walton?'

'Esteemed father, you should have waited.'

'I had to leave, what happened?'

'Esteemed father, you left and we took the sanctuary men as close to the shoreline as possible. We waited and we watched. *The Galicia* hove into sight followed by those two Flemish carracks. One of these caught fire and became entangled with the other.' Christopher shrugged. 'Father, you know how common it is for black powder to catch fire and explode. Ships can be obliterated. They also become entangled. Savereaux, the master of *The Galicia*, has a reputation of being the best in Brittany. Father, I watched him do it! He cunningly forced one Flemish vessel to collide with the other. Again, Father, such entanglement is common enough.'

'But the fire which started it?'

'An accident . . . Such incidents are common enough but,' Christopher drew himself up in the chair; he was thoroughly enjoying himself, though increasingly curious about his father's apparent unease.

'And the malefactor known as Pembroke?'

'Esteemed father, he went with the rest on board *The Galicia*. I am sure he will reach his final destination.'

'Yes, yes quite.' The Recorder played with an inkpot on his chancery tray, opening and shutting the lid. He abruptly glanced up, his face wreathed in the falsest of smiles. 'And the Lady Countess?'

'Safely returned to London, though she is busy enough with matters at her manor of Woking. However she will, or rather the Staffords on her behalf, petition the Crown regarding the growing lawlessness in the city.' The smile on the Recorder's face immediately disappeared. 'Oh no, Father, this is no criticism of you,' Christopher was now truly enjoying himself, 'more the officials who work for you. I mean, one of her late husband's most loyal retainers was murdered whilst in sanctuary in a London church. Now that man may have been a rebel but he also had his rights. Another sanctuary man, allegedly under this city's protection, was foully slain at Thorpe Manor.' Christopher spread his hands. 'And, there again, there are the murderous attacks on her loyal steward Master Bray. We hear of a condemned felon, Zeigler, escaping from an execution cart, whilst rumours abound about two innocent women murdered in their chamber at the Minoresses'. She must also bring to the King's attention how Flemish pirates were bold enough to attack an innocent Breton ship deep in English waters. Where was the protection such a ship should enjoy? Duke Francis will not be pleased . . .'

Urswicke's voice petered out. All breathless, he finished his litany of complaints: his father, who seemed to be only half listening, glanced up.

'Christopher, my son, whom do you really work for?'

'Esteemed father, you have asked me that before and I have replied. Myself.'

'But you could provide me with more intelligence than you have. I mean, how did the countess discover the whereabouts of the Lady Anne Neville?'

'Esteemed father, I do not know. You really should ask Master Bray. Remember, he was the one ordered to stay in London to search for her.'

'Yes, yes, quite. Ah well,' the Recorder put his face in his hands and let them fall away, 'Christopher my son. Yesterday I was invited to court. The King has decided that I will lead an embassy to treat on certain matters in Rome. I am to be his envoy to his Holiness the Pope. I shall be leaving shortly after the Epiphany and, God knows, I will be out of the city for many a month.' He waved a hand. Christopher kept his face impassive, 'I am to be joined by Parson Austin. He will be our chaplain. And his Grace the King, well . . .'

'Well what, Father?'

'I did ask if you could accompany us. I was surprised at his response. The King was resolutely opposed to this. He said you were to stay in England where he would keep close watch over you. What does he mean by that?'

'Esteemed father, I don't know. However, when you leave, you will never be far from my thoughts. I will look after your interests and, where possible, I will use the countess's influence to resolve any problem.' Christopher was now finding it difficult to hide his sheer enjoyment at this item of news, which would delight the countess. 'Is there anything else, Father?'

'No, no, no.'

Sir Thomas got to his feet and came round the desk, Christopher rose to greet him. They clasped hands and exchanged the kiss of peace. Sir Thomas hugged his son close before letting him go. 'Of course, we will meet before I leave.'

'Of course.' Christopher bowed and walked to the door.

'Dearest son?'

Christopher turned. 'Esteemed father?'

'You will always stay with me, won't you?'

'Esteemed father, rest assured, to the very end.'

AUTHOR'S NOTE

D*ark Queen Waiting* is of course a work of fiction but it is firmly based on a range of historical facts. The disappearance of Lady Anne Neville did occur as described, although there's no proper explanation for it. Some commentators allege she was kidnapped by Clarence and made to work as a scullion in some tavern or alehouse in the city. Others speculate that she may have simply fled to escape the growing tension between the two royal brothers over her rich inheritance. However, in the end, Lady Anne did return to court life, married Richard Duke of Gloucester and became his Queen when he usurped the throne in 1483.

In the Middle Ages, the power of the Church was most evident. Becket's murder in his own cathedral had won the Church certain rights, especially over clerks who had received minor orders as well as the question of sanctuary. Both of these privileges were jealously guarded by the Church and God help anyone who tried to infringe them. For example, in 1305, the city zealously pursued Richard Puddlicot who had committed treason and robbery by plundering the royal jewels which, at the time, were kept in the crypt of Westminster Abbey. Puddlicot was an openly avowed traitor and thief who, hunted by the Crown, took sanctuary in a London church. Certain city bailiffs invaded that church, seized Puddlicot and hauled him off to the Tower. Nevertheless, despite his heinous crimes, Puddlicot was a sanctuary man and the bailiffs responsible for his abduction were solemnly excommunicated.

The printing press still had to make its impact, but the appearance of anonymous pamphlets in Medieval London was a fairly common occurrence. The use of propaganda is not an invention of the modern age. During the short reign of Richard III, a famous doggerel appeared in London attacking Richard of Gloucester and his principal ministers, Viscount Lovel, Catesby and Ratcliffe. It ran as follows: 'The rat, the cat and Lovel the dog rule all

England under the hog.' The author of this, a gentleman called Collingbourne, suffered the full horrors of the law for treason, being hanged, drawn and quartered. Again, on the eve of Bosworth, John Howard, Duke of Norfolk and Richard III's commander, allegedly had the following warning pinned to his tent: 'Jockey of Norfolk ride not so bold for Dickon your master is both bought and sold.' Psychological warfare and 'the weaponising of words' is, I suppose, as old as human conflict itself.

I chose Walton-on-the-Naze as one location for my story because that stretch of the Essex coastline was often used by invaders of England, be it marauding Danish armies or the successful landing of Queen Isabella and her lover Roger Mortimer in 1326. The battle at sea between *The Galicia* and the two Flemish carracks is a fair reflection of such clashes. The introduction of cannon and culverin on board ship was revolutionary yet fraught with a veritable multitude of dangers. If we study the original manuscripts, the miniature pictures, etched to reflect battles at sea, constantly depict ships tangled with those of their opponents. Sails and rigging became tightly meshed. Of course, if fire broke out, it would sweep both vessels with devastating effect. The Flemish pirates described in my novel were a real and present threat to shipping, especially in the Narrow Seas. Indeed, the merciless nature of warfare at sea is captured by the poet Chaucer's depiction of the seaman in the Prologue to his *Canterbury Tales*. Chaucer describes the mariner as a sailor who truly believed, 'Dead men tell no tales!'

Finally, the situation in England following the great battles of Tewkesbury and Barnet is as I have described it. The House of York was triumphant and King Edward swept into London to enforce his peace and to enjoy its fruits. However, the seeds of destruction were already sown. The tensions between George Duke of Clarence and his brother Richard were never resolved, whilst the enmity between Gloucester and the Woodville faction resulted in the collapse of the House of York, the disappearance of the two princes in the Tower and the successful invasion by Henry Tudor. I have always believed that during the period 1471 to 1485 some dark nemesis stalked the House of York. I suspect this nemesis was the innocent-looking yet very shrewd Margaret Beaufort, Countess of Richmond. Margaret was a truly brilliant strategist and a 'master of politic': a woman assisted by her two clerks, Reginald Bray and Christopher Urswicke, who themselves matched their mistress's talents. Indeed, some historians hale Urswicke as the founder of the British Secret Service, an accolade I would certainly agree with.